KSENIYA MELNIK was born in Magadan, in the north-east of Russia, and moved to Alaska in 1998, at the age of fifteen. She earned an MFA from the New York University. Her work has appeared in *The Brooklyn Rail*, *Epoch*, *Esquire* (Russia), *Prospect* and *Virginia Quarterly Review* and was selected for *Granta*'s New Voices series.

Praise for *Snow in May*:

'An accomplished debut collection … *Snow in May* takes us deep into the complex fabric of Magadan, an isolated fishing and mining town in the northern reaches of Russia that once served as a transit center for prisoners dispatched to Stalin's labour camps. With this rich setting as backdrop, Melnik's characters – young and old, male and female – live quiet lives burdened by the constant weight of conflict'

MOLLY ANTOPOL, *New York Times Book Review*

'Melnik is very talented, and this is an unerringly assured and dextrous first book. It's a big compliment when I say it merits comparison to Jennifer Egan's wonderful *A Visit from the Goon Squad* – the way perspectives prismatically glide from character to character and era to era, showing the simultaneously redemptive and remorseless work of time in lucid and elaborate cross-section. Needless to say, though each story works on its own, they build beautifully together. The writing itself is achieved, finished, and gleams with unexpected imagery, gorgeous idiomatic reconfigurations of clichés and me… N BARRETT, *Young Skins*

'Funny and sad, tender and tough, Melnik's stories reveal a writer who is wise and insightful beyond her years. Melnik's grasp of the realities of the twentieth-century Russian Far East is startlingly accurate, but these stories are not anthropological studies – the characters transcend the setting, and they will break your heart'
ANYA ULINICH,
author of *Petropolis*

'The stories take place throughout the second half of the twentieth century: in 1958, a girl marries a military officer in order to escape the mundaneness of her life; in 1993, a young boy sees visions of war when he plays Tchaikovsky. Together, the stories convey a varied portrait of Russian life and the dark history of the author's hometown'
ANDREA DENHOED, *New Yorker*

'The best story collection you'll read this year'
DARIN STRAUSS, author of
Chang and Eng, *More Than It Hurts You* and *Half a Life*

'It may be a collection of nine stories, but Kseniya Melnik's debut, *Snow in May*, has the thematic breadth and cohesion of a novel … It's an impressive thing, the way Melnik is able to evoke so much from a landscape of frozen tundra'
Grantland

'Achingly beautiful, this collection signals a writer to watch'
Kirkus Reviews, starred review

'In her first book, Melnik's nine tender, linked stories comprise a stark mural painted against the backdrop of political change in late-twentieth-century Russia and the Soviet Union, images only a Russian could craft … It's difficult to pick a favourite among Melnik's striking tales'

Booklist, starred review

'Melnik tackles tragic subject matter while dramatizing daily struggles, giving equal weight to both. With dry humour and detailed description, Melnik creates a historically enlightening time capsule of an unfamiliar world'   *Publishers Weekly*

'Fabulous … In beautifully narrated story after story, we get an art boutique version of something we might call "Real Housewives of Siberia" before Glasnost and after. Along with keenly composed stories, Melnik gives us beautiful images [such as] when a woman named Tonya recalls how as a young girl she sat on the bank of the Volga River and lifted up her eyes in time to see the last sunray strike a little fire on the golden cupola of a country church on the opposite bank. Although her future seemed vague, it's every mysterious facet glimmered with light and possibility. As does the literary career of wonderful new story writer, Kseniya Melnik'

ALAN CHEUSE, NPR *All Things Considered*

'Touching … These stories might be inspired by a place most of us have never heard of, but they come straight from the heart'   *Seattle Times*

'A powerful achievement … [Melnik] writes evocatively of the textures, smells and bone-chilling temperatures of this exotic land in prose that is burnished and precise'

San Francisco Chronicle

'Exceptional … magical … By recollecting the past, [Melnik] has discovered a deep mine of beauty and sadness'

Minneapolis Star Tribune

'These stories sparkle with the brilliance and charm of Chekhov – while possessing a modern grace and rare intimacy that are unique to the literary talent of Kseniya Melnik'

SIMON VAN BOOY, author of
Love Begins in Winter and *The Illusion of Separateness*

'Kseniya Melnik's beautiful *Snow in May* is an education in how history is routed, refracted, and reconciled inside the human heart. In sonorous, evocative prose, the triumphs and tragedies of Magadan are vividly brought to life. In 1890, Chekhov traveled to the Russian Far East – had he made the journey a century later, and gone a little farther north, these stories may well have been the result'   ANTHONY MARRA,
author of *A Constellation of Vital Phenomena*

'Melnik's stories have a ruminating, relentlessly unhappy tone … She is able to reveal human deficiency, even monstrosity, and connect it to the conditions under which her characters grew up'   THERESA MUNOZ, *Sunday Herald Life*

'Kseniya Melnik's breathtaking debut, *Snow in May*, is extraordinarily perceptive about how landscape shapes us – and continues to shape us long after we have left it. Though the stories revolve around haunted, wintry Magadan, they are anything but cold. Alight with wry humor and compassion and complex truths about the conditions of the soul, Melnik's tales burn with life' LAURA VAN DEN BERG, author of *The Isle of Youth*

'Like some improbable magician of the mundane, Kseniya Melnik waves her literary wand over drab Soviet cities and their unsmiling denizens and the world cracks into colour. A mouldering Khrushchyovka, an endless line for an ill-fitting dress, a dance studio in disrepair all form a key to mysterious interior landscapes teaming with hope, heartbreak, and the ever-tantalizing prospect of salvation. *Snow in May* is like that fabled snow globe of your dreams – to open it is to be transfixed' ALINA SIMONE, author of *You Must Go and Win* and *Note to Self*

'Kseniya Melnik's stories are full and expansive in the way of Alice Munro's; the reader is pulled under, willingly, into seedy and sensual worlds, like 70s Moscow and a Russian military base. Melnik's characters long for happiness and stability and face morally complex lives, the threat of menace and failure just around the corner. To read her striking, original work is to be enchanted and utterly transported' MEGAN MAYHEW BERGMAN, author of *Birds of a Lesser Paradise*

SNOW
IN
MAY

Stories

~

Kseniya Melnik

MIX
Paper from
responsible sources

FSC

FSC C007454

FSC™ is a non-profit international organization established to promote the responsible management of the world's forests. Products carrying the FSC label are independently certified to assure consumers that they come from forests that are managed to meet the social, economic and ecological needs of present and future generations, and other controlled sources.

Find out more about HarperCollins and the environment at

FOURTH ESTATE • *London*

Fourth Estate
An imprint of HarperCollins Publishers
1 London Bridge Street, London SE1 9GF
www.4thestate.co.uk

First published in Great Britain by Fourth Estate in 2014
This paperback edition first published by Fourth Estate in 2015

1

Some of the stories in this collection have appeared elsewhere, in slightly different
form: 'The Witch' in *Granta*'s New Voices series on Granta.com, 2010; 'Rumba'
in *Epoch* magazine, 2012 series, Volume 61, Number 3; 'Love, Italian Style' as
'In the queue' in *Prospect* magazine, May 2011; and 'Closed Fracture' in the
Virginia Quarterly Review, fall 2011. Lines from 'But could you?' by Vladimir
Mayakovsky, translated by Dorian Rottenberg; lines from 'То не ветер' ('Kruchina'),
music by A. Varlamov, lyrics by S. Stromilov; lines from 'When Youth Leaves',
music by V. Sorokin, lyrics by A. Fatianov.

A catalogue record for this book is available from the British Library

ISBN 978-0-00-754872-9

Page design by Meryl Sussman Levavi

Printed and bound in Great Britain by Clays Ltd, St Ives plc

In loving memory of my grandmothers, Olga and Irina,

and my friend Allison Powell

Contents

~

SNOW
IN
MAY

Love, Italian Style,
or in Line for Bananas

1975

~

"**G**razhdanka, it's forbidden to sit here. Follow me."

Tanya looked up from her shopping list. The stewardess's curt demeanor was so incongruous with her childlike face, Tanya felt a swell of pity. Here was someone already kicked around by life, her defenses permanently raised.

Moments earlier, Tanya had sat in one of the open seats directly behind a group of men in identical blue T-shirts and track pants. On an otherwise full airplane, they were buffered both in front and behind by an empty row. Preoccupied with planning the most efficient shopping itinerary for Moscow, Tanya hadn't given this much thought.

Now she wrestled her frayed carry-on from the overhead compartment and followed the stewardess. The empty rows were puzzling indeed. When she looked back, the blue-T-shirted men grinned at her over the tops of their seats. There was something glossy in their appearance, something one didn't see in everyday people. With their smooth faces, shiny hair, and lime-white teeth, they looked freshly washed and wrung free of life's problems.

Tanya's assigned seat was in the last row, beside a middle-aged couple.

The husband turned to Tanya. "The Italian soccer team," he said with enthusiasm. "They're trying to keep us away from them. International security measures, you see. But if seriously, what secrets do they think we could give them? That the country's short on soap and rope?" He snickered. "Soap and rope, yes."

"Who thinks? The Italians?" Tanya said. She'd never seen a foreigner before, not even someone from the Eastern bloc—the so-called Soviet camp—although she'd heard they were easily spotted in the bigger cities. But these were real foreigners, real Westerners. There were separate hotels for them, and shops and restaurants. Separate seats at the Bolshoi Theatre. She felt embarrassed for having sat down behind them now.

"*Them*. The—"

"Sasha, quiet," his wife said, glaring at him as though the plane was bugged by the KGB. And who knew? Maybe it was.

The plane taxied for takeoff from Leningrad, where Tanya had spent five days slumped in a seminar room at the Hermitage. She curated the arts wing of the Regional Museum in her hometown in the northeast and every five years attended these educational programs, required and paid for by the countrywide arts board. During the day, she half listened to lectures on "the portrayal of socialist reality through painting and sculpture." In the evenings, she strolled down the Neva embankment, its austere neoclassical buildings the color of cucumber flesh, omelet batter, sour-creamed borsch. What a shame it was that she had to travel so far to see real beauty.

She closed her eyes and thought of all the things she needed to get in Moscow to take back home to Magadan, where the grocery stores weren't empty but also had no variety. Leningrad, with its theaters and museums, was Russia's starving artist; the capital was the rich merchant, the pride of the country—a requisite stop for everyone on the way back to the provinces. She and Anton had saved all year for this shopping trip. Baby Pavlik needed a winter coat, and Borya needed a backpack, notebooks, and all the bright school accessories to get him excited about first grade.

Fruits and good vegetables. Avitominosis was common during spring in Magadan. Tanya loved cabbage for its excellent transportability. She'd have to get three or four heads. Juicy southern tomatoes, too, if she could find a sturdy box. Apples, oranges, pears. And maybe something exotic and a little magical to jolt their life, if only for a moment, out of its bread-and-potatoes doldrums. Pineapples or bananas if she was lucky, though even in Moscow they were a rarity. Anton had asked for color film and photo paper, preferably East German. He loved taking pictures on his geological expeditions. She wished she had time for the shopping bus tour that went to all the foreign import stores: Warsaw, Dresden, Budapest, and, of course, Belgrade.

Tanya pulled out *Eugene Onegin* and opened at the bookmark.

"Ehhhhh. *Ciao, bellissima.*"

She looked up. It was one of the Italian soccer men. His right arm was propped on his hip; the other inched toward her with a piece of paper. He was mockingly handsome—his features oversized, his full lips shiny as though dabbed with olive oil. He stared at her with intensity, the way the blue-cloaked Zephyr looks at Venus in her favorite Botticelli.

A pang of sweet fear seared her stomach.

"Ehhhhh. Would like rendezvous," the Italian said.

His arms were tan and muscular, and not at all hairy, as she had expected of Italians. People were turning back to watch. Some even stood up to get a better view.

"*Bellissima. Sono Luciano. Per favore,* Hotel Rossiya. Eight." The Italian thrust his note at her. She took it, if only to divert the spotlight from herself. He held on to her hand and kissed it wetly. "Luciano."

He kissed her hand again and sauntered back to his seat. It wasn't only his arms that were muscular, she noticed.

Tanya's neighbors looked at her as though she were a chicken who had suddenly learned to fly. She turned back to *Onegin,* her face flushed. Not once in her thirty-three years had she been paid such a compliment by a stranger. And from Italy—the birthplace of art and beauty. It was a miracle.

"What did he want?" asked Tanya's neighbor, the wife. She hadn't dared look up from her knitting.

"He invited me to meet him at his hotel, I think."

"You will go? It's not illegal, but—"

Tanya caught the accusation in the woman's tone. "You must be joking," Tanya said.

"It is discouraged. Yes, it is strongly discouraged," the husband whispered. "You will be put on a list for observation, if they even let you into that hotel."

"I have two children, seven years old and one and a half," Tanya said. "A good husband. Nondrinker."

Anton was much more than a nondrinker, of course. Had he been a bachelor, he would have made a perfect personal ad: thirty-five, ethnic Russian, tall, nonsmoker, employed. And he'd never raised a hand to her. Tanya loved him for his decency, for being a good father to her sons. Yet, he'd never looked at her as she thought the Italian had, as if she were a newly discovered Michelangelo painting. Anton told her that she was getting a bit plump and to please bring him his coffee and a piece of cheese, for which she had to stand in line for an hour.

Italians, on the other hand . . . Don't make me laugh, please, Tanya thought not without pleasure. She knew all about them from films: *Marriage, Italian Style* and *Divorce, Italian Style*. They didn't have divorce in Italy, and the only way out of marriage was to catch your spouse cheating and then kill him or her to protect your honor. And the lover, too, while you're at it. The sentence was more lenient for a crime of passion. She tried to remember whether Luciano wore a wedding band.

"Luciano Moretti, Hotel Rossiya, 8," the note said in loopy, Rubenesque letters. She peeped out. Luciano was looking at her over his headrest. But thinking rationally: What did a sportsman of international caliber, rich and free, see in a tired, ground-down Soviet woman? She went back to her reading.

�

An hour later the plane landed in Moscow. The Italians were let off first, followed by the running-of-the-bulls-style disembarkation of everyone else. Tanya got punched in the ribs and her feet were stepped on several times. To her surprise and mortification, the entire soccer team greeted her with cheers and whistles at the arrivals terminal. Luciano, blocked by the large bosom of a peroxide-blond interpreter, sent her a battery of air kisses. Must be weariness from the all-male company, she thought. It won't be long now, given the women in the Intourist welcoming delegation.

Studying herself in the mirror of the airport bathroom, she felt dismayed by her own credulousness. Her face was red, her mascara had flaked under her boring pale-blue eyes. Her blondish hair, badly in need of a root touch-up, was frizzy in the back, while in the front her bangs were glued to her forehead with sweat. The neckline of her old traveling blouse was hopelessly stretched. Luciano must be blind.

Outside, the spring morning was in full bloom, and Tanya found herself wishing she'd worn a short-sleeved dress to let her skin breathe. To her right stretched an endless taxi line. To her left, a bus was about to depart for central Moscow. Just off the curb, the Italian soccer team was boarding the Intourist van. Luciano waved and cried out, "*Otto! Otto, per favore!*"

What a peculiar man, Tanya thought. Italians . . . This was

a real cliché. She tried to keep from smiling. She stole one last look at Luciano and ran for the bus, her heavy carry-on banging against her legs. It was almost nine hours until *otto*, plenty of time to forget about the way he'd looked at her.

※

Exhausted by the multitransport trip from the airport, Tanya rang the doorbell of Auntie Roza's fifth-floor *kommunalka*. They kissed hello. Auntie Roza smelled like Tanya's late mother, of sugary sweat and fresh-baked bread, scents that calmed Tanya no matter how stressed she was. She noticed that while she'd been in Leningrad, her aunt had given herself a makeover: she'd tweezed her eyebrows down to threads and dyed her graying hair the color of peeled carrot.

"Look at you, Auntie. Ten years younger! For the May Day party at work?"

"Trying to keep up with you."

"Me?" Flattery was in the air today.

Tanya changed into a pair of house slippers and followed Auntie Roza through the darkened hallway, which branched off into rooms where different families lived. All the doors were closed. Every few steps Tanya bumped into something— boxes, metal-edged trunks, wood boards, a bicycle, a baby stroller, and God knows what else.

Halfway down the hallway they almost collided with Sergeich, who was carrying a bowl of eggs and a packet of sausages to the kitchen.

"Good afternoon, Roza Vasilievna. You look wonderful as always. Ah, I see Tanechka is back."

"Good afternoon, Mikhal Sergeich. Thank you for the compliment."

He pressed his barrel-shaped body against the wall to let them pass.

"Are you hungry?" Auntie Roza said when they reached her room.

"I want to take a shower, wash off that airplane grime."

"Why shower? You'll be running around dirty Moscow all day. Besides, Ivanova has the bathroom for the next two hours."

"When's your turn?"

"In the evening, Tanya, in the evening. Weekends are busy, you see, everyone's home. You rest now while I warm up borsch and cutlets." Auntie Roza opened her fridge and pulled out two pots.

"I'll help. Want to tell you something, you won't believe."

On their way to the kitchen they ran into a tall, heavyset woman with a column of sooty hair piled on top of her head. Letting her pass, Tanya tripped over the bicycle, and it crashed to the floor with a ring. Fierce yapping started up at the other end of the hallway.

"I'm sorry," Tanya said.

"To the devil!" the woman yelled, gesticulating with a pot of pea soup in front of her heaving bust. "That bicycle was new. If it's broken, you'll be standing in line for a new one yourself, Roza Vasilievna."

"Broken!" Auntie Roza came to an instant boil. "You should see your sons ride it down the stairs. First bicycle, then their necks, I'll say. Broken—*tfoo*."

"That's none of your business. You better tell your niece here that she turned on our lightbulb when she splashed in the washroom for a whole hour last week, and we now have to pay for that electricity," Pea Soup said. "Do I look like a millionaire to you? She's the one from Magadan here."

"And who's going to pay when your boys steal my—"

"Sergeich!" Pea Soup hollered. "How many times do I have to tell you that pets are not allowed in the common areas?"

The communal kitchen contained five ovens, five tables, several standing and hanging cupboards, most of them with locks on their doors, and a sea of kitchenware occupying every available surface and wall. The entire space was segmented by bedsheets, towels, and various other laundry articles hanging to dry from a network of ropes. An invisible radio babbled the news. The smells of fried onions, pea soup, and fish fought for airspace. A beautiful young woman with curlers in her bleached hair flew into the kitchen, chirped hello to Auntie Roza, and carried away a whistling kettle.

Auntie Roza turned on the gas and struck a match. "Now tell me what happened, Tanechka."

In a half whisper Tanya told her about Luciano.

"I'd go," Auntie Roza said.

"But you . . ." Her aunt's husband had left her many years ago, when their children were still in grade school, and she'd never remarried. "How will I look Anton in the eye? It'd be so stupid for me to run there like some prostitute. They already have their own, from Intourist, KGB-trained."

"Not like a prostitute, Tanya. Like a woman. When will

you have a chance to enjoy such an exotic man again? Italians, they've got a temper. Anton is a good man, I'm not arguing. But . . . he's Anton. He'll be there on that couch for all eternity. Go, enjoy. Could be your last chance. I met, once, in Bulgaria, a certain engineer . . . Bulgarians love Russians, you know." Auntie Roza pressed her ringed hand to her chest, which was rosy and laced with delicate spiderwebs of wrinkles. It struck Tanya as incredibly beautiful—and this, too, reminded her of her mother. She was overcome by a desire to rest her head on Auntie Roza's soft shoulder—to forget about Luciano and her obligations to her family.

"He was tall, very good-looking. Such beautiful black eyebrows," Auntie Roza continued. "I didn't go, I was a good wife. To this day I bite my elbows in regret."

The bedsheets next to them moved.

"What, Sergeich? Spying on us?" Auntie Roza said.

Sergeich emerged from behind his cover. Balding, with a stained undershirt stretched over his paunch and a grouchy expression, he seemed to have stepped out of the dictionary entry for "*kommunalka* neighbor, male."

"Err . . . Roza Vasilievna, would you be so kind as to spare a pinch of salt. I'm all out." His bite-sized white poodle twirled around his feet.

"Oh, you should have listened," Auntie Roza said, holding out her salt dish.

Sergeich blushed. "You"—he addressed both of them, his tone philosophical—"you womenfolk are odd. I want to say . . ." He dove under the sheets to his oven, then reappeared and returned the salt. "First you complain . . ." He looked at the floor and said through his teeth, "One simply cannot understand women, and it's your own fault." He pouted his thin, lilac lips.

"My dear Mikhal Sergeich. Don't get so upset. Like all normal people, women just want a little corner of happiness." Auntie Roza smiled coquettishly and threw the poodle a piece of her cutlet.

"If it were me, I'd be careful with the foreigners." Sergeich looked in Tanya's direction. "There's a reason why the State wants to keep us regular citizens away. It's for our own protection. I've never met any real foreigners myself, but I've heard such stories—*ogogo*!"

"What stories?" Tanya asked.

"Well, I heard from a friend of a friend who knows someone who's friends with one of the Party kids. You know, they all travel to the West like it's Crimea. So, that particular comrade lived in America for a year and he said that they have special pornography schools there." Sergeich made a sour face at Auntie Roza. "They teach . . . technique and some kind of philosophy of love there, as if it could be taught." He hit his chest. "It's amoral and it's expensive. They don't have free education there, so not everyone can attend. Those who do, you know, they have to bring a partner. They don't have to be married, and—can you imagine?—it doesn't even have to be a woman for a man. You know what I mean? They study special books and have homework assignments, also class demonstrations. As if it was some woodworking class!"

Pea Soup barged into the kitchen, tore through the bedsheets, and yelled out of the window: "Kolya! Grisha! Lunch is ready. March home on the double!" The poodle began to yap again. Pea Soup squatted down and clapped her big hands right by the dog's flappy ears.

"Don't you dare do that again, *grazhdanka*!" Sergeich yelled after Pea Soup. "*Tak*, where was I? These so-called students learn to hold—well, you know what I'm talking about—for a whole hour and sometimes more. And during the, the . . . during this, they see God. Yes, God. It is insulting to me even as a nonbeliever. But this is in America, I don't know about Italy. Or Bulgaria." Tanya thought she saw Sergeich wink at Auntie Roza.

"Are you sure it's not the yogis in India?" Tanya said.

"An orgasm for an hour? That would finish Comrade Brezhnev right off." Auntie Roza laughed, a beautiful, throaty trill. Sergeich's face was completely purple now. "Those Americans must have a lot of free time. Italians, on the other hand, they don't need any special schools. They have passion in their blood."

"Now is not *Yezhovshchina*, of course, but it never hurts to be careful," Sergeich whispered, then in full voice: "Remember that the State disapproves of intermingling with foreigners. It's for our own protection, Tanya."

"But what could happen?"

Sergeich stared at her with incredulity.

Tanya envisioned Luciano's shapely olive arms. Her skin prickled.

"Every room in the hotel is bugged by the KGB. You may get accused of spying, that's what. Arrested," Sergeich said. "Or you could get recruited to spy on the Italians."

"Mikhal Sergeich, my darling, what are you talking about? First of all, this is a onetime thing. Second, she's not going there to talk." Auntie Roza finally gave him the smile he'd been waiting for.

"Spying . . . I don't have time for a second career," Tanya said, a little exhilarated just thinking of the idea.

The women picked up their pans of food and went to eat in Auntie Roza's room.

"Don't listen to him, Tanechka. Listen to me," Auntie Roza said, meeting Tanya's eyes over the perfect nostalgic borsch.

❧

The giant Children's World department store stood across the square from Lubyanka, the KGB headquarters. Entering the first floor, with its marble columns, a sparkling double-decker carousel, and endless rows of toys still gave Tanya the same thrills she'd felt here as a child on her family's transits through Moscow. Practical things first, Tanya said to herself, and marched up to a line that started at the base of the stairs. She took her spot at the tail and tapped the woman in front of her on the shoulder.

"What are we standing for?" Tanya asked.

"Finnish snowsuits."

"God help us. What number?"

The woman showed Tanya her palm with "238" written on it in pen. Tanya pulled a pen out of her purse and wrote on her own palm: "239."

The woman's cheekbones were beautifully pronounced,

convex like the bowls of soupspoons. "And where are you from?" she asked Tanya in a soft, friendly voice.

Too nice for a Muscovite.

"From Vladivostok," Tanya lied.

Magadan was famous for having been the entry point to the cruelest of Stalin's network of camps. People might think her parents had sat there; and if they were arrested, then there must've been a reason. Now people were paid good money to live in the northeast. It wasn't a good idea to advertise either.

"And you?"

"Odessa. I'm buying the snowsuit for my relatives in Arkhangelsk."

While they chatted about children and tricks for procuring this or that *defitsit* item, the line crawled up the stairs. The woman's name was Zina. Tanya also made friends with a man behind her, Denis from Sverdlovsk, and asked him to hold her place. In the shoe department on the third floor, she was lucky to happen upon some Yugoslavian winter boots. She got two pairs, two sizes too big for the boys to grow into. For now, she'd sew a little pouch of wool inside the toe.

The line for Finnish snowsuits climbed to the second landing. Denis gave Tanya a nod of cooperation, and she dashed to the fourth floor, where she stood in two lines for a pencil box, a stack of notebooks, and a yellow backpack with cars printed on the flap. Others held Tanya's place in the toy line on the ground level, while she held places for Zina and Denis in the snowsuits. The store was stuffy; in the thick of the lines it reeked of sweat and cologne. She ran downstairs and prized out a microscope for Borya, lettered blocks for Pavlik, and a box of toy soldiers for her friend's son.

Tanya returned to the snowsuits line, which had finally scaled the second floor, and waited for another hour. She could already see the big brown box out of which fluttered the puffy aquamarine snowsuits. After a few more minutes of waiting she heard screams at the front of the line. A wave of people threw her back, and immediately she knew: They'd run out. They'd run out of Finnish snowsuits!

At first Tanya bobbed in the whirlpool of other anguished shoppers—elbows out, bags in—all hoping for a miracle. Her throat prickled with tears, and eventually she gave up. She knew that the clerks had stashed away extra pairs, but they would distribute them through their network of relatives and friends. There was no use begging.

She staggered out to the street. She didn't have time to waste, yet she couldn't bear leaving the store. She still had so much to find. When she returned home, Anton wouldn't go out of his way to praise her exertions. There was nothing heroic or special about these shopping expeditions, a common burden shared by hundreds of millions of her fellow *grazh-danki*. It seemed unbelievable that just a few hours before, Luciano had invited her to a hotel. What was he doing now? Training on a soccer field or sightseeing the best, cleanest, approved-for-foreigners parts of Moscow with the voluptuous Intourist spies?

Tfoo, princessa. Her mother and Auntie Roza had lived through the famine and war, and here she was—too good for lines. She looked at the Lubyanka building, where so many of Magadan's prisoners had started their journeys.

A babushka, her face yellow and wrinkled like a spoiled apple, pulled Tanya down the street and around the corner. From prior shopping adventures, Tanya knew that the pensioners who lived close to the big stores often got up early to stockpile the most coveted items and resell them at a profit. As the babushka unzipped the suitcase with her knobby hands, Tanya prayed for the snowsuit.

"Bought something for my granddaughter, dearie, and it turned out the wrong size," the babushka said, twisting her head, on the lookout for the police.

She held up a pink rabbit coat with fur balls on the ends of the zippers.

"I have a son," Tanya said. Disappointment settled acridly in her stomach.

The toothless babushka proved to be a real shark when it came to persuasion, and in the end Tanya bought the coat. She could try to exchange it for something else in Magadan, although in all likelihood Pavlik would end up wearing it. Luckily, he was still too young to be teased.

At the National Department Store on Red Square, Tanya secured a lacy East German bra, which was so much more delicate than the gray, industrial Soviet make, built for sturdy kolkhoz girls. Also: a box of Polish toothpaste and lotion, stockings, and three Czechoslovakian shirts and a quality photo album for Anton. He would be so happy. A tube of French lipstick was passed to her over the heads of others in exchange for money. Its color was a mystery.

In a shopping frenzy, Tanya snapped up the last Yugoslavian silk dress without trying it on. Although its limited availability was its most important quality, she later discovered that it was also beautiful: the color of a lily pad with contours of large-petaled flowers embroidered in white thread at the shoulders and side seams. The neckline plunged bravely deep. She didn't know where she'd wear it: the dress was too light for Magadan, even in the summer. To a house party, maybe, with a shawl.

Tanya set out for her last shopping destination, the House of the Book on Arbat, stopping every twenty steps to rub her reddened palms and switch around the heavy bags. She imagined the headline in tomorrow's newspapers: "Woman Found Drowned in Moskva River, Still Clutching Bags."

She walked and thought. Despite the official State philosophy that the USSR was the best country in the world, Russians were always on the hunt for *importny* things. The best you could get was from the Warsaw Pact countries—especially Yugoslavia, which was almost half capitalist and bordered with Italy. Polish cosmetics were good but not comparable to French. Those you could get only in Moscow, only at the National Department Store. The appearance of Italian shoes was an event. People from the Eastern bloc looked better, too, and people from the capitalist West seemed to be made from higher-quality material altogether: whiter teeth, broader shoulders, happier faces.

Luciano had grown up surrounded by beauty. Tanya knew from studying art and from the travel programs on television that Italy was full of well-preserved palazzos and facades decorated with paintings and stone cupids. Hundreds of nude sculptures sunbathed in the piazzas and cooled off in street fountains. Maybe Luciano's eyes were simply better trained to see a woman's beauty?

Why couldn't Anton see it? After all, he could appreciate a pair of three-hour-line shoes for their ordinary, magnificent shoeness. Had she succumbed to him too easily? They had dated during their last year of university, and Tanya didn't want to be the last unmarried girl at the graduation.

❦

Auntie Roza opened the door and took some of the bags off Tanya's numb hands. One naked lightbulb in a row of five burned furiously in the hallway. Pea Soup's slouchy husband was smoking by the communal telephone. His hair was a violent red—a comical contrast to his straw-yellow eyebrows and eyelashes—as though his fiery crown had drawn out all the pigment from below. His sons (their hair the same Red Banner hue) rattled back and forth down the hallway, the elder on his indestructible bicycle and the younger, about Borya's age, with a saucepan helmet and a soccer ball. The Ivanovs' baby wailed. The poodle barked behind Sergeich's door. The hallway smelled of old cigarettes, fried meat, stewed cabbage, more pea soup, and something putrid—perhaps the dog's revenge on its neighbors.

"I'm just waiting for an intercity call. Do you need the phone? It should come any moment now," Pea Soup's husband muttered.

"Relax, Lyosha. I'm not your wife," Auntie Roza said. "Please tell your boys not to ride over the shoes."

When they reached the haven of Auntie Roza's room, Auntie Roza said, "*Shto,* got lucky?"

"Oh, yes. Now the shower."

"Not the best time, Tanechka. Everyone's cooking dinner, you see. We only have one heater between the kitchen and the washroom."

"You said it would be your turn in the evening."

"It is my turn, but—"

"You let them bully you?"

"What can I do? They've lived here longer than I. You could try tying a dishrag around the kitchen faucet—that's our sign for hot water needed in the bathroom—but I doubt it'll work."

"Oh, Auntie."

The kitchen was in midbattle. The laundry had been taken down from the ropes. The three female household heads and Sergeich, the lonesome penguin, were cutting, shredding, frying, boiling, meat grinding, and dough rolling at their stations. The oil hissed, the pans banged, the radio yowled like a frantic mother calling for her child in a crowd of strangers. Sergeich winked at Tanya. She tied the dishrag around the faucet and escaped to the bathroom. As she showered, the water went hot and cold every few minutes, then just as she was washing off, it shut off completely.

"For your rendezvous?" Auntie Roza said when Tanya

returned to her room. She was holding up the new dress to herself in front of the wall mirror.

"What rendezvous?" Tanya tried to keep her voice dispassionate. "I'm dog tired. I'd rather spend the evening with you." This, too, was true. "Tell me stories about when you and Mama were girls."

"You've heard all of our stories a million times, Tanechka," Auntie Roza said. "Straighten out your shoulders and try to make yourself a little happier. If you don't, no one will."

"I'm not sure this would make me happier. Honestly."

On the one hand, she didn't want to disturb the precarious balance of her life. On the other hand, there was the beautiful dress—a *defitsit* to everyone else and readily wearable to her. "I'll just try it on. If it's too big, I'll leave it for you."

Tanya slipped on the dress and looked at herself in the mirror. It fit as though tailor-made, accentuating her waist— not as small as in her youth but still workable—her narrow, sloping shoulders, her diminutive but adequately perky breasts.

"Look at you," Auntie Roza exclaimed, but Tanya had already grabbed her makeup bag and dashed out of the room.

The washroom was occupied. She couldn't go back to her aunt's room, not yet; she knew what Auntie Roza would say. She ran to the bathroom. Free! She switched on what she hoped was Auntie Roza's lightbulb, sat down on the toilet, and put her makeup bag in her lap. Squinting into a hand mirror, Tanya put on some blue eye shadow and mascara. The new French lipstick turned out to be a clownish shade of orange, so she wrapped the tip of a match in a piece of cotton ball, something she always kept handy, and scraped out left-over coral paste from her old lipstick tube.

Someone hammered on the door. The bleary-eyed young father of the restless baby, clutching a roll of toilet paper to his chest. Tanya got out of his way.

Back in her aunt's room, she sat down at the table, from which she could see herself in the mirror. She put her hair up in a bun. The hairstyle showed off her small ears, the only part of her body she'd consistently liked.

Neither the makeup nor the hairstyle had altered her features, yet she hardly recognized herself. The exhaustion in her eyes lit up her face with a kind of wistful nobility. She wanted Luciano to see that he was right to pick her from a plane of other dusty people. Tipsy off this sudden metamorphosis, some romantic essence of her separated and floated above her tired body like those happy lovers in Chagall's paintings. She wouldn't get in trouble with the KGB for one time, would she?

"Go, Tanya. Go," Auntie Roza said. Before Tanya could duck, Auntie Roza spritzed her with the unfashionable Red Moscow perfume and made the sign of the cross.

It was seven o'clock. As Tanya skipped down the five flights of stairs, even the clicking of her heels seemed brighter.

"Ah, Tanechka, I forgot to feed you!" she heard her aunt yell from the top of the stairs, but her hunger had already evaporated, along with her shame and fatigue.

Tanya's skin tingled pleasantly in the evening cool that had descended on panting Moscow. The tram came right away, and she sailed the two stops humming quietly to herself. She was walking to the metro entrance when she saw that at the fruit stand by the station they were selling bananas.

Bananas! Golden crescents, honeyed smiles, the fruit of sun-soaked dreams. They were even more rare in Moscow than Italian shoes. Seven-year-old Borya had eaten bananas only twice in his life. Chomping off the thinnest disks one by one to prolong the pleasure, he ran around the apartment pretending to be a monkey on a whirlwind adventure. The bananas were right out of the cartoons about Africa, right out of Mowgli—evidence of a world beyond Magadan's snowy winters and cold summers. Pavlik had never tasted them.

The line curved around the block.

Tanya lingered, then took a few steps toward the metro, which made her feel like a criminal. She took her place at the end of the line. Maybe there would still be enough time, maybe Luciano would wait. She stood, pelting the backs of fellow line standers with all the anger and frustration accumulated in her line-standing life.

Thirty minutes passed. Her whole being itched with indecision. Flecks of her new beautiful skin, the ones blessed with Auntie Roza's pungent Red Moscow, fluttered across the vast, indifferent city toward Hotel Rossiya, to Luciano, with his shiny hair and olive oil–rubbed lips. She understood that bananas would have a relatively small impact on the bright future she hoped for her sons. Yet, their future would begin when she returned home, and she had the power to make it a little sweeter. Gradually, the romantic kite of her soul descended back to her body. She felt tired and overdressed. Like herself.

When at last it was her turn, Tanya saw that the sales clerk was drawing bananas from two different boxes. One contained taut yellow bunches, while bananas from the other box were covered with brown spots.

"Excuse me, are you selling rotten bananas?" Tanya cried out.

"And what else am I supposed to do with them, *grazhdanka*? Throw them out? I have to move the product. If you don't want them, I have plenty of other customers who will take them with joy and be grateful."

Tanya bought three bunches—the allotment per person. Only one was in the early stages of rot. She looked at her watch: seven fifty. It would take her at least forty minutes to get to the hotel by metro. She could try catching a taxi, though she doubted there'd be any in this area. Surely someone would pick up a hitchhiker.

Twenty minutes later not a single car had stopped. Was her dress scaring people off? Clutching bananas to her chest, she turned the corner to a poplar-lined street and sat down on a bench. The pollen swirled around her like snow. There had been a time when the distinctions between right and wrong seemed indisputable, and doing right felt good. When all the decisions had been premade and in her best interest. Back when she didn't need so much to be happy.

She remembered sitting once as a girl on the bank of the Volga River. She had just finished a shift of volunteering at the kolkhoz with her Young Pioneers brigade. Soon it would be dark, and the Pioneers would build bonfires and sing songs about loyalty, valor, and honor. Tanya remembered how her hands hurt from pulling carrots all day. She knelt and dipped them into the river. The water was so cold, a shudder ran up her arms and jolted her heart. She tried in vain to scrub the black soil from under her nails. She lifted up her eyes in time to see the last sunray strike a little fire on the golden cupola of a country church on the opposite bank. She felt at the center of her life then, separate from the world only in a way that could allow her to improve it. Although her future seemed vague, its every mysterious facet glimmered with light and possibility.

༄

Early the next morning Tanya loaded up on several kinds of sausages and cheese, ham, smoked meat, good Hungarian wine and canned fruit, good vodka for Anton, and fresh produce at the grocery store near Auntie Roza's. She found two sturdy boxes sitting by the garbage dump in the courtyard. One of them, Tanya was shocked to discover, was from a color TV, a *defitsit* unavailable in stores even in Moscow. Luckily, the foam forms were still intact—perfect for fruits and vegetables. She hurriedly repacked everything again for optimal transportability.

At the airport, the loudspeaker announced that the eight-hour nonstop flight to Magadan was delayed because of adverse weather. The terminal swarmed with passengers, stir-crazy from the foul-smelling bathrooms and insufficiency of places to sit. Various personages of questionable intent, particularly gypsies and persons of Caucasian nationality, trolled the waiting halls, panhandling, selling trinkets, and soliciting fortune readings.

Tanya had too many things to carry all at once. She dragged her suitcases up to the end of the check-in line and asked the woman in front of her to keep an eye on them. When she returned for the boxes mere seconds later, the one for the color TV was gone.

She lost her breath, as if punched in the stomach. The bananas. She spun around and around: thousands of people, thousands of boxes of every stripe in continuous movement like atoms. How could she have not foreseen this?

Tanya shuffled back to her place in line. Now she knew with absolute certainty that she'd been happy just a moment ago, steadily on her way home, with presents for everyone. She began to cry. And she couldn't stop, not when the woman in front of her asked her what was wrong, and not when, pushing her remaining luggage centimeter by centimeter, she reached the counter and handed her passport and ticket to the check-in clerk.

Everything felt wrong, like she was living in a parallel universe, separated by one crucial degree from the one containing the life she was meant to have. This other, true life was visible to her, even palpable at certain instances—like during the births of her sons—but impossible to occupy. She cried from pity for herself, and because of the stupidity of such pity. She cried for Luciano and for Anton. She cried because she'd only loved one boy with the follow-you-over-the-edge-of-the-earth kind of love—at fifteen. She cried for her mother, who had died two years ago, and whom she still missed every day.

For the rest of her wait Tanya haunted the airport, looking in every corner for the missing box, in the weak hope that, upon opening it, the thieves had discovered no color TV and abandoned it. It was eight in the evening when the plane finally took off.

She landed the following afternoon. Wet snow fell in clumps from the chalky sky. After an hour on the washboard Kolyma Route—the infamous road built on the bones of Gulag prisoners—Tanya began to recognize familiar streets, decorated with red flags along the May Day parade route. Banners with noble yet unrealistic proclamations hung from the most important buildings. The snow kept falling and falling, covering muddy slush from the recent thaw, last year's yellow grass, and the garbage on the sidewalks—masking, for a short while, the old sins.

The taxi driver parked by Tanya's building and helped her carry the luggage up to the fourth floor. Their apartment was small, but all their own. Anton was supposed to be at work and the boys in kindergarten, but as she opened the door and right away stumbled over a vacuum cleaner in the hallway, she knew that everyone was home, waiting for her. It smelled deliciously of fried potatoes.

A soccer match played on TV in the living room. Various articles of clothing hung over the backs of chairs, and socks were piled in little nests on the floor. Anton and Pavlik were napping on the couch, Anton's face raw from a recent shave. She bent down to Pavlik's bottom: his pants appeared to be clean. She looked at them again. They were a perfect subject for Mary Cassatt, had she painted in Russia. Tanya felt a twinge of pleasure and shame.

She went into the boys' room. Borya sat on the floor, tinkering with his metal construction set. He wore his favorite orange flannel shirt and briefs. His feet were bare. He looked up at her, first startled, then astonished. His imagination winged back from the distant magical city he was building, and he smiled, baring a gap in his milk teeth. He jumped up and hung on Tanya's waist. She could feel the angularity of his knees through her coarse traveling pants. As she kissed his head, she noticed a cluster of new freckles on his nose.

"Borechka, put on some socks. The floor is cold."

"I'm hungry."

"Papa hasn't fed you?"

"Papa said to wait for you. We cooked together. I cut a potato myself."

Tanya pressed Borya to herself so tight that he cried out, but he didn't try to wiggle free.

"Wait here, kitten."

Before waking up Anton and Pavlik, she tiptoed into the hallway. The bananas were gone, as she'd suspected, along with the tomatoes, oranges, cheese, Anton's favorite smoked meat and sausages, and the wine. She rummaged in the suitcase and pulled out the green Yugoslavian dress. Made of high-quality silk, it had hardly gathered any wrinkles on its long journey east.

Closed Fracture

2012

~

This morning, a phone call from an unfamiliar foreign number interrupted my game of golf. I winced, recognizing Russia's dialing code, and let it go to voice mail. I would have done the same with any unidentified caller. You never know what guise the past might put on to haunt you. I had my habitual postgame round of cocktails with my golf partners, all California retirees like me, and returned to the condo I shared with my sister, Angela. She wasn't home. I took a long, cool shower, then went to the patio and looked out for a long while at the red terra-cotta roofs of our condo community, which, if not for the palm trees that stuck out here and there among the old Cadillacs and swimming pools, almost succeeded in looking Florentine. I listened to the voice mail twice. The message was from my former best friend. We hadn't seen each other for twenty-eight years and hadn't spoken for twenty.

"Tolik, is it you or is it not you?" his message began. His voice was thin but cheerful; he must have been putting on airs. He'd gotten my number through an improbably coiled chain of acquaintances, he went on to explain. "How are things? Family? It'd be nice to talk of our old adventures. Do you still play tennis? I'm in Voronezh, still." I waited to hear what he wanted, but perhaps this was something he was saving for the conversation proper. He gave his number with the country and city codes and hung up.

I went back to the living room, sat down on the couch, and took some deep breaths. Sputnik, my salt-and-pepper schnauzer, jumped up next to me, wagging his joystick tail. Then he hopped back down and planted his muzzle on my knee. Behind his bushy eyebrows his black eyes begged for a walk, and a snack, and love. For everything at once and right away.

Tolyan and I had been through the trenches of youth together, his loyal presence a watermark of authenticity on so many of my best memories. I should have been happy to hear from him. But what I felt was acute annoyance at this rather minimal invasion of my privacy. Maybe I've become too American. Or not yet American enough.

As I go about my long day, performing tasks I don't mind, thinking either about what I now have the time and mind space to notice—a beautiful flower or an intricate cloud formation—or the people who matter to me—my daughter, Sonya, my sister, Angela, my wife, Marina—I am sometimes shocked into a fleeting physical weakness by the realization of how fast the time has galloped by, each winter marked by the increasingly passionate moaning of my once broken shin. And by the fact that I am here and Tolyan is still there, whereas we started out together and young.

ஃ

We were both named Anatoly; I was Tolik for short, and he Tolyan. We were born a year before Stalin's death in a small town on the coast of the Sea of Okhotsk, in the northeast. Despite its isolation, every Russian of a certain age still shudders at the mention of our hometown, Magadan, which was once the gate to the most brutal Stalinist labor camps—the most remote island in the notorious Gulag Archipelago. Besides mining gold, tin, and uranium in the permafrost basin of the Kolyma River, the prisoners were engaged in extensive civil works, building the first roads and houses, as well as the Park of Culture and Leisure, the cinema, and the stadium, with its adjacent Palace of Sport. I still remember a brigade that worked on a five-story building across from mine. The construction site was blocked off by a fence—rows of barbed wire strung between eight-foot-high wooden beams. Several makeshift watchtowers were positioned around the perimeter. Canvas-top trucks brought the prisoners in the morning, when I was on my way to school, and carted them back to the camp at sunset. By then the security had been relaxed: the prisoners were not shackled, and the guards were not poking their napes with Kalashnikovs.

Although my mother had reprimanded Tolyan and me when she caught us talking to the prisoners through the fence, we became friendly with many. The scent of the Khrushchev Thaw was in the air; their hopes for freedom were high. At night we snuck in through the spaces between the barbed wire and hid cigarettes in agreed-upon places. In return, the prisoners carved toy guns out of wood and left them for us in secret spots.

By the mid-sixties, half of the town's population consisted of ex-convicts, some living and working side by side with ex-guards. Many former prisoners were criminals, but there were equally many people with higher education who were not allowed to leave Magadan—doctors, teachers, geologists, engineers. My father knew and worked with many of them. He was in charge of the petroleum supply for the whole region. Whenever I asked him what those people had been imprisoned for, his response was: For having a long tongue. Writers, artists, and musicians of national fame had sat in the Magadan camps, and productions at the local theater were on par with those in Moscow and Leningrad, but back then we kids didn't understand. Schools until recently didn't teach this layer of history. Besides, our heads were crammed with mischief. There was no space for anything else.

Tolyan and I were unruly but quick-witted enough to get through school with minimum effort. And we were lucky. Our skinny backsides were forever saved by bells, snow days, and convenient illnesses—our teachers' or our own. We were called to the blackboard only on the days when we had, on a hunch, prepared our lesson. Everyone smoked in the bathroom, but only Tolyan and I never got caught. We skipped piano lessons and went sledding on our folders, leaving our parents to puzzle over why our sheet music was always wet.

We crawled through the small underground tunnels by the old cinema, which we called "the catacombs." What with the mysterious trapdoor at the end of one tunnel—behind which there surely lay a chest of Kolyma gold guarded by the ghost of the first prospector, Bilibin—the risk of death by suffocation or drowning didn't enter our minds. We stole still-hot bread from the city bakery as the slow, fat baker loaded the trays into the truck bound for grocery stores. Tolyan was my upstairs neighbor, and I spent hours at his place watching music programs on TV and staring at the blurry black-market photographs of Swedish porn magazines that had been confiscated from the photo lab at the university by Tolyan's father, the senior detective at the police headquarters. We also played with his spare revolver, until one day it shot and shattered the crystal chandelier. Now that I think of it: that massive *defitsit* chandelier was probably a very serious bribe.

In eighth grade, we were suspended from the Young Pioneers brigade for bad behavior and, free of "volunteering" duties, spent the summer hiking and grilling *shashliks*. In those days, my big passion was zoology, and on weekends I helped out at the small zoo in the Park of Culture and Leisure. There was a yellowed polar bear named Yulka, an emaciated fox, a balding eagle, and a sad-eyed deer. Though Tolyan didn't care for such proximity to the creatures of the north (the cages were rather stinky) he tagged along, unable to bear exclusion from any of my activities.

In the last year of school, all the girls in our grade, at once, gained weight and developed acne. Self-conscious and closed in, they were useless for either friendly or romantic purposes. On top of that, the stadium where we played soccer in the summer and hockey in the winter was put under yearlong renovation, leaving us with nothing else to do but study for university entrance exams.

In the spring, a recruiting commission from the Riga Red-Bannered Civil Aviation Engineers Institute of the Lenin Komsomol arrived in Magadan. Riga was not Paris, but it was as far west as any of us had dreamed of getting back then. "Civil" sounded good, patriotic without trying too hard. "Aviation" sounded even better—steel wings and navy-blue uniforms, an exhilarating touch of grandeur and freedom.

Five hundred students competed for thirty spots reserved for recruits from the Magadan region. There were several *facultets* at the Riga Institute, and everyone wanted to get into automatics, the precursor of computer science. No one knew what it entailed exactly, but everyone wanted to dive into the stream of progress. Tolyan and I had passed physics, mathematics, and chemistry with an identical number of points. Together we crammed for the last exam—literature— and could, as far as I remember, tell Dostoyevsky from Raskolnikov.

The weekend before the literature exam, my parents and my younger sister, Angela, went for a walk in the Park of Culture and Leisure, the same park that used to house the now extinct zoo. There they ran into the head of the Riga recruiting commission, a Jewish fellow named Ginzburg. My father had already managed to meet him and mention me as a promising young aviator. So when this Ginzburg heard that I, along with the rest of the student herd, was storming the walls of the automatics *facultet,* he advised my parents that I should instead apply to be an economist. Next, he delivered the famous analogy that would change the course of my life.

"Here's the difference between economics and automatics." Ginzburg addressed my mother, a woman of rare beauty, with ashen hair, blue eyes, and the shapely yet sturdy figure of the *Venus de Milo.* "The economist sits in front of the calculating machine, while the automatics specialist sits behind it. With a screwdriver! Who do you think makes the decisions?"

My parents rushed home. Without taking off her astrakhan hat, my mother told me about the screwdriver. I hated screwdrivers. I associated them with my bike, which had to be fixed all the time as I rode the thing down hills, stairs, curbs, and through just about anything in my way. I took my mother's cold, velvety hands and warmed them with my breath. She laughed brightly. Her gold tooth gleamed in the back of her mouth like a little bell. Back then, I saw her as a conservative, middle-aged woman whom I had to beg to add one more centimeter of flare to the hem of my fake jeans. Now I am astounded at how young she had been that spring, only thirty-eight. "Don't worry, Mamochka," I said, "I'll be all right." I passed the literature exam and, as a highly ranked candidate, had my first choice of the *facultets*. Ginzburg transferred my application from one pile to the other.

Tolyan's parents had also gone for a walk in the Park of Culture and Leisure that weekend, and his mother was just as beautiful as mine (gymnast's figure, curly blond hair, dimples). But they didn't run into Ginzburg. At the time I was still able to tamper with Tolyan's destiny. I told him to quit automatics and become an economist, like me.

❧

We blazed into Riga in black trench coats. Pins with Magadan's coat of arms—a golden deer flying over the turbulent blue water against a scarlet background—burned on our lapels, just above our hearts. Right away we were sent to pick potatoes for a month at a local kolkhoz. Upon our return, we received navy-blue uniforms and caps and were made to cut our long hair and nascent mustaches.

At university we excelled in the economics of civil aviation, army logistics (our required military specialization), and caught up on sleep during the lectures on Marxism-Leninism. Our dorm room, which we shared with six other guys, stank so much of sweat, feet, cigarettes, vodka, and food we had forgotten to refrigerate that in order to fall asleep, we put handkerchiefs soaked in cologne over our noses.

But outside was Riga, so European and clean, so different from Magadan and even Moscow. Only a fool would sleep all night in such a city. Around every corner were coffee shops with five-kopeck espressos and cheap restaurants decorated in grand style and named after Riga's sister cities: Amsterdam, Bordeaux, Dallas. Street kiosks sold Polish and East German newspapers full of pop music charts, photographs of beautiful models, and of the Beatles—our paper window into the West.

To supplement our student stipends, Tolyan and I worked part-time jobs. First, at the candy factory, which we were fired from for stealing candy. Then, at the vodka distillery, which we were fired from for getting massively drunk. Finally, I settled as a night guard at the glass container storage. While Riga, the captive European princess, slept dreaming of freedom, I listened to the Voice of America, the BBC, and Radio Liberty, broadcasting news from around the world in Russian. The container storage was located on the Daugava River, where reception was the clearest in the whole city. Tolyan worked on the chipping floor of a match factory, inhaling sawdust all day. For the damage to his lungs he was given a free bottle of milk daily. His lips were constantly coated with a film of fine sawdust, and at the most inopportune moments he would break out into a violent cough. But we made enough money to finance our modest student fancies: Elita cigarettes, *holodets* at a favorite café, an occasional ticket to a car race or an organ concert at the Dom Cathedral, and copious amounts of vodka, wine, and the famous Riga Black Balsam.

Tall, blue-eyed, and wavy-haired, we were at the peak of our boyish handsomeness. Latvian girls looked at us with admiring fear of our seeming worldliness. So what if we got roughed up by the Latvian guys a few times? There were plenty of Russian girls in Riga, too. We barely noticed how five years of lectures, exams, dances with live bands, and standup comedy competitions clattered past and disappeared around the corner.

We graduated with red diplomas and the rank of junior lieutenant, having passed even the Marxism-Leninism exam, and received priority distribution back to Magadan because of our family roots. My family by then had moved west: my parents to Ukraine, the country of their birth, and Angela to study chemical engineering in Moscow. Through my father's connections, they left me the best thing a young bachelor could ask for: not just a room in a *kommunalka*—which would have been the allocation for a single person without children— but a private one-bedroom apartment with its own bathroom and kitchen. All this without having to wait in line!

We were glad to be back. Magadan, in those days, was the third-most coveted place of employment, after Moscow and Leningrad. Now that there were no Gulag prisoners, someone had to develop the region, and the government encouraged permanent migration with double salaries and benefits that increased every year. The town experienced a real boom as young people streamed in to take advantage of the "long ruble" and the stores stocked better than those "on the continent," which is what we called the rest of Russia. I got a position as a schedule engineer at the Aviation Administration. Tolyan began working in the passenger relations department at the airport and moved to Sokol, the airport township fifty-four kilometers from Magadan's city center.

Our mustaches had finally asserted themselves. Mine approached the coarse bushiness of the "walrus," while Tolyan braved the slight curvature of the "petit horseshoe." With the cool Baltic wind still whistling in our heads, we set out to stretch the balloon of our reckless youth to its limits. We played tennis and went to the movies with the prettiest girls in town, quickly earning the nicknames "tennisists the penisists." In the winter, we sledded down the glaciers on oilcloth mats, then spent hours searching for lost hats, mittens, and boots. People in Magadan said about me: Tolik, he's a good guy, smart, handsome, reads books, has a good job. But he has this friend in Sokol, Tolyan, who will be the ruin of him. Tolyan's neighbors in Sokol said the same about the good, handsome, educated Tolyan and the bad influence of his debaucherous friend in Magadan—me.

Time rushed by slowly. Historians and journalists coined catchy terms: Khrushchev's Thaw, followed by Brezhnev's Stagnation. Tolyan and I still juggled the same activities: tennis, skiing, drinking, blurry days at work, and girls, with whom we broke up as soon as their slippers and bathrobes appeared in our bachelor apartments. Minimal responsibilities, minimal rewards. By the time I was twenty-seven, a sense of my own stagnation began to nag at me. When will my real life begin, I wondered, and what was it, exactly, this real life, the one I'd spent so many years preparing for in school? I didn't share these thoughts with Tolyan; he was wholly in his element and happy.

One Saturday in March, when we were twenty-eight years old, Tolyan and I went skiing with several of our friends from the Aviation Administration. This particular slope, our favorite, was in the near wilderness and could only be reached by a rope lift. Over the years we had built a cabin up top and with every trip hauled food, alcohol, and gasoline from the bottom of the hill.

March was my favorite time to ski. The snow was still powdery, yet the sky was already bright blue and high. Compared to February's temperatures and ferocious winds, it seemed almost tropically warm. The deep-frozen dwarf birches and low spruce shrubs were beginning to straighten their shoulders and push through the dense icy crust, buzzing with the electricity of the new sun. We buzzed with them, drunk on the heady spring air. The town was visible from the top of the slope: a white matchbox labyrinth cradled in the snow leopard–colored mountains. As we conquered the hills and drop-offs and caught sight of Magadan during the brief moments we were airborne, it felt as though we were flying toward it. And a part of us, the young, dreamy part of our souls, escaped and beat in the wind awhile longer after our skis hit the ground.

By five o'clock, everybody was getting ready to leave. Tolyan and I skied down first to have the mountain to ourselves. I led the way.

The air was thickening fast. Unexpected bumps lurched from under my skis. Gangs of dwarf birches sprang up out of nowhere on the turns. My heavy backpack was disrupting my balance. Halfway down the slope an invisible force tripped me. Before I fell, I heard a crunch like splintering dry wood. My skis had snapped off. My left boot was facing backward. It wasn't pain, but the sight of that bizarre angle that made me nauseous. I pulled up my unharmed leg to my chest and began to moan.

Tolyan skidded by me a minute later. When he saw my leg, for a millisecond, a spark of anger animated his alarmed expression, the way he flicked the ice from his mustache and threw down his hat. (He had realized that we wouldn't make it to the dance that night.) Then, just as quickly, his face took on the noble grip of determination.

"Don't move." Tolyan picked up his hat and jammed it on my head with its woven visor backward. I'd lost mine during the fall. Then he took off his skis and began the trek up the slope to the cabin to alert the others.

It was quiet. The world was expressed solely in shades of gray, as though somebody had sketched the scraggy trees and slope curves on white paper with a graphite pencil. I felt a sharp pain in my elbow and my back was sore, but the leg didn't hurt. I barely perceived it as a part of my body. The snow Tolyan had picked up with his hat was dripping slowly down my neck. I was dizzy, yet I also felt a feral, jealous ownership of my body. My blood rattled as if I'd been plugged into a giant central life support system. I was hot and unafraid.

Dark fog saturated the air. Suddenly, I became convinced that the encroaching shadows of the mountains were about to absorb me into their indifferent landscape, make me a flat, black figure—of a man or just a log—invisible to my rescue party. This thought made me tranquil. If only I could send my parents a message that they shouldn't worry, that I would continue my life, except not as Tolik but as an acorn or a little shard of ice.

I spotted a fallen cone next to a tuft of spruce bush needles. The composition looked remarkably like a miniature palm tree, and, for some reason, making this simple connection moved me to tears. I wanted to take a whiff of the spruce, a smell I associated with magic since childhood—probably because of the New Year tree—but I couldn't lean far enough to reach it. I stared at the petals of the cone until they began to quiver, drawers about to open into another world. I felt like I was about to faint and began to hum under my breath. "*Michelle, my belle . . .*" And then I heard the voices of my friends calling out my name as they descended the slope.

Somebody had already skied down to call the ambulance from the bus stop, they told me. They hoisted me onto a wooden board and tied me down with rope. Tolyan and tall Oleg picked up the front end, and the shorter Slava and Artyom picked up the back. We inched down. When they ran out of war songs, they sang the discotheque anthems of the day, liberally interpreting the English lyrics: *Shizgara, yeah baby Shizgara* for Shocking Blue's "Venus" and *Just give me money, that pha-ra-on* for the Beatles' "Money." It was getting darker every moment. My pain came to from the shock and began to howl. Finally, I saw the headlights of the ambulance flash from the bottom of the hill.

The last thing I remember before the operation is pleading for the doctors not to cut my ski boot. My Yugoslavian skis and boots were my most prized possessions and had cost a month's salary. The diagnosis was closed fracture of the fibula and tibia, spiral, comminuted. Tolyan had stayed with me in the hospital late into the night.

This all happened on March 8, International Women's Day. We had planned to attend a big dance at the Palace of ProfUnions later that evening. While I was enjoying the post-bone-setting morphine haze, Tolyan tried to call our girl-friends to let them know what had happened. But they had already left for the dance.

Mine was Lily, a little hourglass-shaped Jewish olive, with amber-clear eyes and a bead of a birthmark above her lip that drove me crazy. She was engaged to a rising Jewish academic, which I didn't see as a problem at the time, at least not my problem. Lily ran to my apartment every other night. Who was I to stop her?

She visited me at the hospital three times. Each time the sight of me in bed with my broken leg in traction, supported by various slings, weights, and levers, brought her to tears. Poor Lily would put her bag on the stand near the bed— although many of my other, less mindful visitors simply hung their bags right on the weight—and stand shyly by my side. Then, her hands would hover above my full-leg cast, brush against my arm, and land over her mouth. She would kiss my forehead so tenderly that a wave of itching sensations rushed down my broken leg. I would seize my metal scratcher, insert it down my cast, and poke about savagely, moaning from pleasure and pain, which would trigger another bout of tears from my beautiful Lily.

The fourth time, it wasn't Lily who came but her mother. Our affair had come out.

"You almost ruined my daughter's life," her mother yelled in a deep, operatic voice. She was fat, almost a perfect square—the kind of woman Lily would probably become in her older years, after having children. "I'd kill you if you didn't look so miserable. I'd make sure you're an outcast in this town."

Suddenly I wanted to laugh, though her threats were far from empty. Lily's father had a high position in the local Party Committee. In Magadan, where everyone knew everyone's business, reputation was important.

Lily's mother went on detailing my lack of morals, of sympathy for a young girl's heart, of respect for their family and my family, of respect for myself. Lack, lack, lack. But the blade had narrowly swung clear of both Lily's head and mine, and I wanted to celebrate. My broken leg had saved my career. Moreover, it provided a blameless, romantic exit from my relationship with Lily. I knew all along that she wasn't the girl I'd marry even if her engagement broke up, and our inevitable separation, if protracted, could have taken a much uglier form.

Tolyan wasn't so lucky. He was smitten with Anya, an airheaded girl with a lean figure and a voice that went with campfire guitar as smoothly as vodka goes down with salted herring. While Tolyan nursed me at the hospital, Anya let herself be swayed by a former classmate of ours, a certain Seryoga, at the Women's Day dance.

"You didn't have to stay at the hospital. You could've just gone to the dance," I said when he told me the news.

"That didn't occur to me." Tolyan gave me a shaming look.

"Well, she showed her true nature. Why do you need a girl like that?" I said.

"It doesn't matter. There're always more. Seryoga will play with her and dump her soon enough. That's the way he is," he said, picking up my metal scratcher. "What's this for?" He put it in his mouth and chewed, making a disconcerting sound. "Brutal age, rough manners, *nyet romantismy*," he concluded with a quote from one of our favorite films.

I spent another month at the hospital. Tolyan and I grew out our hair, mustaches, and beards, which made us look like nineteenth-century Russian merchants. When he visited, we drank tea in character—out of saucers—and flirted with the nurses. After I'd been moved home, friends and girls stopped by to help with groceries and laundry, and to make sure I followed doctor's orders of three hundred drops of vodka daily. I enjoyed three more guilt-free months of reading. I was a big fan of Thornton Wilder then. While reading *The Bridge of San Luis Rey*, I wondered, just like Brother Juniper does in the novel, whether there was any logic in who got into accidents or became the victim of various unfortunate events. Of course, breaking a leg was a disaster not on the same scale as dying in the collapse of a bridge. Still, maybe I'd been plunged into this parallel, slower life to learn a lesson. Maybe Lily's mother was right: it was time to grow up. That meant getting married. Surprisingly, this thought no longer threw me into panic.

But I don't want to give the impression that I suffered unduly in heavy self-reflection. Apart from a few physical inconveniences, I loved living in my favorite striped mohair robe, away from my job, which didn't prove to be as exciting as I'd imagined when I went off to the aviation institute in Riga. I was often awake at five in the morning after reading all night to hear the first birdsong of the day. The Eagles' "Hotel California" had just made its way to the northeast and played from the radio in every open window. Sometimes, when reading or watching soccer on TV, I'd forget about my white underwear boiling in a giant pot. The water and bleach would spill onto the stove and then the floor, and this way the whole kitchen would clean itself in minutes. Life was good.

In July, the doctors removed the cast. Later I'd find out that the fibula had grown back at a slight angle: the soles of my left shoes would now forever develop holes before the right ones even showed signs of wear. I hobbled outside on crutches to exercise my legs. The stream of friends and well-wishers thinned. Everybody had gone on vacation. Tolyan and I played Battleship over the phone, unable to do any of the things that made the cold summer in Magadan bearable. (Tolyan couldn't, or wouldn't, find another tennis partner.) Finally, his father helped us obtain two-week passes to a sanatorium on the Black Sea and off we went to seek a cure for our bachelors' ennui.

It was there that I met my future wife, Marina, who was on vacation with her friend Lenka. I still remember my Marina's green bikini and the giant sagging straw hat, which was quite ridiculous, but on her seemed utterly stylish. Under the hat she had fantastic bangs. On top of it all, she was that mythical creature—an actual pianist and a piano teacher—whereas Tolyan and I, and everyone we knew then, had quit the fashionable, parent-ordered piano lessons after a year of family-wide suffering. A funny story: when I had first asked her what she did for a living, she said that she worked as an instructor. I, however, heard "on a tractor" and was considerably impressed, for days picturing her astride a tractor in the fields of golden wheat, her cheeks red and eyes shining.

Marina didn't take me seriously. I fell in love. While I crabbed after her through the toe-wrenching Crimean pebble beach, trying to impress her with my intelligence and wit, Tolyan was stuck with the plain Lenka. When he found out, though, that her father was a high-ranking Party apparatchik in Voronezh, with money and connections, she at once became a lot less plain. I realize now that Lenka was the type of girl whose beauty would have been awakened by a truly great love, which Tolyan could neither give nor inspire.

At the close of two weeks we said good-bye to the girls and spent the following months clogging the phone lines with long-distance calls. As soon as my leg was strong enough to bear the weight of a bride, Tolyan and I decided to visit Marina and Lenka in Ulyanovsk, their and Lenin's hometown. I arrived in my most fashionable outfit: a blue plaid blazer, plaid shirt, and navy pants I still had from my European days in Riga. I told myself that as soon as I saw Marina again I'd know. And I did. She met me at the airport in a scarlet dress with white polka dots and giant horn-rimmed glasses, her chestnut hair in a thick schoolgirl braid. The now legendary welcome dinner awaited me at her apartment: meatballs that had congealed overnight into one pot-sized meatball mass and had to be cut with a steak knife.

We married the next month. Tolyan married Lenka because if one must have a wife, it might as well be an apparatchik's daughter, he had reasoned. Perhaps I should have foreseen trouble. But the little sense I possessed at twenty-eight was hopelessly drunk on Marina. I wanted Tolyan to have what I had—the wedding, the young wife. We, after all, had known our brides for the same amount of time: two weeks plus the phone calls. Our chances seemed equal.

The weddings took place on the same day. Back then it was a simple affair: you signed the book at the civil registry office (I remember a big oil portrait of Karl Marx on a white-washed wall behind the officiant), took pictures next to the war memorials in town, and partied at a restaurant until morning. It was the first time my parents met Marina and I met Marina's mother, Olga, who was the chief doctor of a *polyclinika* in Syktyvkar, a city in the north. I remember being a little bit offended that she'd brought an extra pair of wedding rings, in case we'd forgotten to buy ours. She didn't trust me yet. She'd also brought a family album for me to catch up on my bride's family tree. They came from the Terek Cossacks, with a wild-card Mongolian babushka somewhere down the line. Marina didn't know her father; Olga had left him because of his gambling addiction when Marina wasn't yet two.

I still remember a particular photograph in that album. Marina's grandmother, a chubby, smiling woman in a floral dress, points out something in a book (her finger raised in a teasing, teacherly manner) to Marina's step-grandfather—a much skinnier, tired-looking man with a curly cowlick and linen pants pulled up high above his waist. And he looks at her with the most perfect mixture of attention, humorous suspicion, and love. Marina said she'd seen the ghost of this grandfather after his death—her grandmother's second husband; the first one had been accused of being a Japanese spy during Stalin's repressions and had sat in one of the camps close to Magadan.

What touched me most in that picture was Marina's grandmother's ear. It was the exact shape as Marina's: long and narrow, the lobe the same width as the top. It was then that I felt Marina and her whole lineage of feisty women, including the Mongolian babushka, were now my family.

After our honeymoons—mine in Bulgaria and Tolyan's back in Riga—we took our brides northeast. At first, Marina and Lenka complained about how far Magadan was from the continent, from their parents, and marveled at how close it was to Alaska—a fabled place that was once Russia and now inaccessible America. Soon they acclimated to the weather and began to love, like us, the quiet white days after the snowstorms. They noticed that despite Magadan's extreme remoteness, they were surrounded by intelligent, professional people, who were always willing to help. Survival in the harsh north, especially back in the Soviet times, was impossible without friends and reliable acquaintances.

Marina found work as a piano accompanist in the wind department at the local arts college. On the weekends, we all went mushroom and lingonberry picking, grilled *shashliks*, and sang songs, accompanied badly on the guitar by Tolyan. He'd learned a few chords back in his days of courting Anya. With the first big snowfall I was back on the slopes and teaching Marina, who had never skied before.

My newlywed life was not without surprises and discoveries. That happens even if one makes a proper acquaintance first and then signs the marriage registration, but we were good candidates for getting used to each other. Tolyan and Lenka weren't so lucky. It was clear from the start that they were catastrophically incompatible. At first, they tolerated each other because of the novelty of marriage. Later, Lenka tolerated Tolyan because she wanted children. He was still a flirt and a heavy drinker. When he wasn't playing tennis with me, he lay on the couch and watched soccer. Sometimes Lenka called me to whine about Tolyan's behavior, as though I'd sold her a defective product. What could I do? I had lost my power over him; he was now her responsibility.

৪৯

Three years later, Marina and Lenka gave birth, within weeks of each other. Perestroika was taking root in the country and at home. We named our daughter Sophia, after my grandmother, Sonya for short. Tolyan's son sustained an injury at birth and, the doctors said, would be severely disabled for the rest of his life.

Tolyan and Lenka were devastated, and so were Marina and I. We couldn't shuttle between Sokol and Magadan as often with the newborns. And when we did see each other or talk on the phone, Marina and I couldn't fully express our joy about our daughter, nor did we know how to sympathize properly with Tolyan and Lenka. How could we ever come up with the right proportion of understanding, concern, and encouragement? How could we ever truly relate?

When their son turned one, Tolyan and Lenka moved to Voronezh. I didn't try to talk Tolyan out of it, though I knew he would be unhappy there. It would have been me against Lenka and her family. And what could I offer him in practical terms? Now he would be unhappy anywhere. The few times I've thought back to our separation, I am always struck by how undramatic it was. I remember picking up Tolyan's skis at his place for safekeeping and how he had held on to them a moment too long. In the background, Lenka was screaming on the phone, and his son was wailing. I couldn't wait to get out of there. My real life had already begun and was waiting for me back at my apartment, whereas Tolyan's was slipping out of his hands.

In Voronezh, Lenka's father had arranged for a two-bedroom apartment, which by the standards of the day was shockingly spacious for a family of three. He helped Tolyan get accepted into the Party and found him a position at the local aviation agency. Tolyan, I could tell from our still-frequent phone conversations, was miserable. All of his life he'd lived in pursuit of his own pleasure. Now, the care of a sick child—a child, he said, he wasn't crazy about having to begin with—was like a second, more stressful and time-consuming job. It soon became apparent just how spoiled and selfish Lenka was. Her papa could solve only so many of her problems.

Tolyan's unraveling progressed quickly. He drank earlier and earlier in the day, slept at his desk at work. He and Lenka started having affairs. Eventually, their new paramours moved into the separate bedrooms in their apartment, and the kitchen became a veritable battlefield. When the Union collapsed, Tolyan's father-in-law lost his Party power. Without his patronage, Tolyan and Lenka were both fired from their jobs. They exchanged their apartment for two smaller ones and finally divorced. Tolyan was picked up by a good woman, who, for some reason, decided to save him. (Oh, Russian women! Many of them still live by the principle "Doesn't matter what he is, as long as he's mine.") Lenka took on the custody of their son.

The last time I heard from Tolyan was by phone in '92, shortly before I moved to America. His second wife had sobered him up, and they tried to launch a business importing knockoff brand clothing from Poland. Tolyan refused to cooperate with the local mafia for his "protection" and was beaten up. The business folded. *Brutal age, rough manners*, indeed. On top of that, he got into a car accident and couldn't walk for a year.

I was surprised at how adamantly he interrogated me on the subject of tennis. Did I still play? At our old courts in the Park of Culture and Leisure or at the Palace of Sport? How often and with whom? Since my daughter's birth, tennis wasn't my tenth or hundredth priority, I said, though not dismissively, in honor of our good memories on the court. This seemed to disappoint him gravely. Then he asked after his skis and we talked about the skiing accident. How young, strong, and healthy we were then, with our whole lives ahead of us. In fact, looking back over his life, Tolyan said, he didn't know what it all had been for. He was a failure at work, at being a husband and a father.

"What about your new wife? Aren't you at least a bit happy with her?" I asked.

"You're going to laugh. I keep thinking about Anya."

Anya, the one who got away and was caught in the memory like a fly in amber.

"You stupid old goat."

"Have you heard anything about her?"

"No." The lie jumped off my tongue instinctively. Anya was still in Magadan, with two daughters. The older one was Seryoga's, although neither he nor the father of her younger daughter, Asya, were around. Asya and my daughter, Sonya, attended a ballroom dance studio in the same Palace of Prof-Unions where Tolyan and I used to go to dances. I had recently run into Anya at one of the ballroom competitions. She was heavyset, her hair faded, her eyes tired and wet. We talked for a few minutes, mostly about our children. Her older daughter was studying piano, she told me with pride. She didn't ask about Tolyan.

I contemplated whether this information would make Tolyan feel better or worse. "Well," he said, "at least it worked out for one of us. Imagine if you hadn't broken your leg then?"

I could have told him that nothing was his fault or mine, that he was simply unlucky. I could have asked him whether there were any medications prescribed for all his bruises or anything else he couldn't get in Voronezh that I could try to procure for him in America. I could have invited him for a visit. But something inside me turned cold and protective. I was wary of dragging so much bad luck into my new life, nervous about Tolyan's dormant alcoholism, the possibility of his wanting to involve me in some dubious business scheme. A good-for-nothing childhood friend was better left in childhood.

We exchanged a few more reminiscences and hung up.

૪ର

It was a beautiful afternoon in Southern California, and I decided to take Sputnik to his favorite beach. As I drove, Sputnik breathing fast into my ear, I continued to think about how luck is distributed among the living—a subject I've been ruminating on often lately. I began to understand why Tolyan might be so eager to get in touch with me. For him, the years when our paths ran parallel to each other were the peak of his life. I could only imagine to what legendary proportions our youthful friendship had grown by now in his imagination. For me, however, those years were a takeoff strip, not the flight.

While Tolyan and Lenka hit each other over the head with frying pans in Voronezh, I was living out a happy routine in Magadan. Work, home, grocery stores, day care (then kindergarten and school). Marina cut her thick, dark hair into a bob, which sat on her head like a thatched roof. Sonya was growing up healthy, beautiful, and ambitious. She shined at school, which in time would be converted into the English Lyceum, with an emphasis on learning English. She studied piano at the special section for gifted children at Marina's college (the poor child was not allowed to quit) and pursued passionately a hundred other interests from basketball and ballroom dancing to theater, figure skating, and astronomy. She often talked about becoming a doctor, like her grandmother Olya. I could never get her to love tennis as much as I did, but she liked to ski. When I showed her the fateful spot where I had fallen and broken my leg—the accident that led me to her mother—she bent down and whispered "thank you" into the snow.

In the summers, we took Sonya to the Black Sea or sent her to her grandparents, Marina's mother in Syktyvkar or my father in Ukraine. My mother died when Sonya was eight. Two years later my father met another woman and moved with her to a small village outside of Kiev called Milaya—"darling." He now had a vegetable plot, a chicken coop, and a goat.

By the time Sonya was born, I was vice president of the Department of Commercial Transportation. Due to my youthful misadventures with the Young Pioneers, political reservations, and, in large part, lack of desire to invest time and effort, I'd never joined the Party and that made further promotion unlikely. I developed good relationships with the head of my department, Vasily Lavrentiev, and the vice president of the Aviation Administration, Afanasy Prokhorov. I could barter my access to distribution of airline tickets for favors and *defitsit* items. My hours were leisurely. I had plenty of time to spend with my daughter and to appease Marina in the kitchen by frying an occasional fish and potatoes.

In '85, a new man from Moscow, Davydenko, was appointed president of the Aviation Administration and immediately set about getting rid of the old guard. He stirred up half-fictitious criminal cases against a slew of heads of various departments, accusing them of faulty accounting. In those days, the economy was mostly on paper; it was easy to find evidence of just about anything. Prokhorov and Lavrentiev were sentenced to two years of "work for the development of the national economy." Prokhorov, a bear of a man, served out his term as a truck dispatcher, cramped all day in a tiny radio booth. Short and rotund Lavrentiev, on the other hand, was comically appropriate as a loader at the bakery, the same one from which Tolyan and I used to steal bread when we were boys. The town was outraged by the injustice, but we could do nothing.

In the end, the legal drama turned out for my benefit. When several of Davydenko's men, having no prior experience in Magadan aviation, failed to handle the position of the commercial transportation VP, I was appointed to fill it.

In '87, perestroika began in earnest. Food shortages started to occur even in Magadan. I stood in endless lines for meat, milk, and butter; then, just as my turn was coming up, I phoned Marina to bring Sonya to the store to show to the sales clerk. Three meat coupons, three family members accounted for. Marina got a mushroom haircut and highlighted her hair with ashen streaks. Prokhorov and Lavrentiev were acquitted and restored to their former positions—and I had to give my post back to Lavrentiev. There were no job openings, so Prokhorov created a nominal position for me: director of special programs. I had no official duties and absorbed the overflow. In my free time I studied English. In '89 and '90, a passage to America opened via none other than Alaska. The first charter flights were organized to Anchorage, Juneau, and Seattle. Children's choirs and sports teams began exchange programs. Rotary and Lions Clubs and the Seventh-day Adventist Church descended on our backwater shores in a flurry of philanthropic and missionary activity. Americans wanted to invest in Magadan's gold and fisheries, and see the ruins of the ill-famed Gulag.

In time, the agency developed an international aviation department, and I happened to be just the right man to head it. After I had translated one or two short documents (looking up every word in a dictionary), I was hailed as the resident English-language expert. And, as I wasn't tied up in any other projects, I flew to Moscow to take a course in international aviation and then to Alaska to study the American side of the operation. For the first time in my career, the fact that I'd never belonged to the Party was beneficial; my work visa application was processed without a hitch. I think of my first encounter with America aromatically: the coffee and cinnamon of the hotel lobby, the lilacs of the bathrooms, the deodorant of people unadulterated by sweat. Though, I must say, even the bright, smiling America could not eclipse the impressions of youth—the cobblestone streets of Riga, the view through my paper window.

In the fall of '92, I moved to Anchorage to become the airline's representative. Marina had grown out her hair into a bob again and dyed it red. This was shortly after I had talked on the phone with Tolyan for the last time, after his ridiculous intimation that my skiing accident had ruined his life. I was tempted to argue that I did well because I worked hard and planned far ahead. But I knew I'd been helped along by a string of coincidences, both personal and historical, which to this day continues to thread lucky pearls.

Marina and Sonya remained in Magadan. Since we didn't know how long I'd be in Anchorage, we decided it would be better not to interrupt Sonya's school and music education, friendships, and activities. At the time, Magadan was suffering a mass exodus to the continent. With the collapse of the Union, social and economic infrastructure also collapsed. Power outages occurred weekly, schools weren't heated, inflation soared. The shops were finally full of imports, but only the New Russians could afford them. For everyone else salary was delayed for months, and Marina was paid with a few coupons for the local grocery store. I thanked my fortune to be able to send a big box of food with the pilots on the short flights from Anchorage—a weekly Christmas for my family. Sonya was crazy about sushi, strawberry milk, cream-filled toaster strudels, yellow legal pads, and highlighters.

In '96, just as I thought that my life couldn't get any better, there was another power shakeup at the Aviation

Administration. As soon as I had finished setting up the business from scratch—every detail, from the American way of de-icing airplanes to the printing of tickets—the new bosses fired me. A few months after I returned to Magadan, Marina left me for a TV journalist of local semifame. Her hair was long and red. Sonya was thirteen, too old to lie to about certain things.

For a year I floundered. Then I decided to prove to Marina that leaving me was the biggest mistake of her life. I joined one of the young airlines that cropped up during the first fertile years of capitalism, contacted several investors I'd met in America, and worked with red-eyed determination. After a couple of years, we had a fleet of five planes. By '99, I was back in Anchorage on my own terms. So, in a way, I was fortunate that Marina left me, too.

I took Sonya with me so she could attend the last two years of high school in America. She catapulted to the top of her class and went to Princeton on a full scholarship. In college, she entertained ideas of becoming a film director, an actress, a photographer, and, briefly, even a fashion designer, but in the end she stuck with her childhood dream of following in her grandmother Olya's footsteps. She's twenty-eight now, an oncology resident in New York. When she finds the time, she dates. She is not the kind of girl who'd jump into marriage after two weeks. In America, young people are cautious, afraid of the losses that may come with marriage and love. While in the USSR, most of us had nothing to lose but innocence—and even that we usually managed not to lose much of. Sonya is wiser than Marina and I were at her age.

And if she makes a mistake, I hope that luck will come to her rescue, just as it has always come to mine.

Marina moved to Anchorage a year after Sonya. By then her relationship with the TV journalist had disintegrated. She let her hair grow out to her natural color and cut her bangs, which made her look so much younger. I hadn't divorced her because, having no official relations in America, she wouldn't have been able to immigrate, and Sonya needed her mother. We are still not divorced; there was never a hard-pressed need for it. Marina still lives in Alaska and is friends with many other Magadan expatriates. We often speak on the phone. She has almost forgiven me for the ways in which I had disappointed her, and I have almost forgiven her betrayal. After all, she'd been nothing but a positive influence in my life.

In 2011, our little airline company ceased flights between Anchorage and Magadan—there was no longer a market. Perhaps Americans had become disenchanted with the way Russians did business. I wouldn't blame them. The portal of friendly associations and opportunistic marriages had shut. Instead of taking a four-hour nonstop flight across the Bering Strait, those who wanted to visit relatives now had to connect through Seattle, Seoul, Vladivostok, or through Los Angeles and Moscow—all the way around the globe. In the summers, it would probably be easier to paddle over in a canoe, fingers crossed and betting on the old Russian *avos*— "what if."

What if, what if.

My partners and I disbanded the company, paid our debts, and called it a good run. Then, after more than fifty years of snow, vicious winds, and icy nights, I moved to California, where Angela had been living for years and working as a manicurist. Hers is a whole other story. I live quietly now, minimally, in the golden land of dreams, which to Tolyan and me had once seemed farther than the moon. I manage a few properties. I try not to tax my luck.

৯৯

I'd been walking on the beach for almost an hour—my exuberant Sputnik so wet and happy—thinking about how readily I always dismissed Tolyan's disabled child. I'd tucked that tragedy between a hapless first marriage and a failed career. But, surely, this misfortune had influenced his life in ways I couldn't imagine. How was the boy now? I almost didn't want to know.

On the other hand, knowing Tolyan, I could as easily see him as an emotionally and physically absent parent to a healthy child. Children were not one of his great interests, nor was his career. Though, how many blows on the head could one take until one finally decided it was safer to stay on the ground?

Perhaps I had misinterpreted Tolyan's comment back in '92, and he didn't blame me for what had gone wrong in his life. He simply wanted to reconnect, and that was what today's phone call was about as well.

How much of my life did he know? What news, what rumors had reached him?

Or maybe he wanted to ask for a favor. If he had sought me out, the favor was probably big. Russian people had a notion that all Americans were rich and powerful, and definitely all Russians who had made it in America. First, it wasn't true. And second, he didn't know what it had really taken, all the dirty details. My family didn't know. He couldn't just show up and pick the fruits.

I was getting a headache. These were silly things to get so worked up about. Like a wound-up toy, Sputnik jumped up over and over to a stick I held at shoulder level. For the next three days he would have to lie stretched out on the carpet "without hind legs," as we say in Russia.

Tolyan had been present at the pivotal moments of the first thirty years of my life. But he was incidental, not critical to my progress. A mere cobottler. I would have achieved all the same things with another ski- and tennis-obsessed man-child by my side. If I hadn't broken my leg and Tolyan's father hadn't gotten us tickets to the Black Sea sanatorium where I'd met Marina, I would have met someone else. There has always been a surplus of good women in Russia.

On the other hand, maybe luck was like a magnet, and to function my positive pole required his negative one. The prospect of calling him back made me angry. I hurled Sputnik's stick into the ocean, and he took off after it.

I felt a stab of pain in my chest, and at once I was certain I was about to die. I will die.

I sat down slowly.

All my senses had burrowed deep into my body, and I knew that if I opened my mouth I wouldn't be able to speak. I felt as if I were holding my naked heart in the palm of my hand and it was pumping there, laboriously, trying its best but not making any promises. I held it as carefully and tenderly as I could, with awe and fear, like I once held my newborn daughter. I needed to take a breath but was terrified that if I did, I'd drop it. I'd drop my heart on the hot sand and die.

This horrible feeling lasted for about three minutes. Finally, the pain loosened its choke hold. Was that my first heart attack? I'd have to see the doctor. Luckily, I could afford it.

Sputnik was yelping and licking my knees and hands. He'd retrieved the stick and brought it to my feet. I grabbed his wet neck and kissed him on his bearded snout. I was overwhelmed with relief; it flowed into my past and reinforced its stitching. I've forged a good life.

The platinum waves broke on the shoreline and retreated, broke and retreated, leaving ribbons of froth and trash in their wake. A plastic bottle without a label filled with water and leaking. Green and brown seaweed. A feather. I closed my eyes and took a full-bodied breath.

No, the magnet theory of luck is a preposterous idea.

I have to take better care of myself, that's all. I'll swim laps in the pool when I get back to the condo and call Sonya afterward. She'll be happy to hear about my cardio efforts. I won't mention the heart incident; she has enough to worry about as it is. I won't tell her about the cognac and the good chocolate I have every night, while Angela and I watch Russian news and talk shows on satellite TV. Though Sonya probably knows; somehow she always knows everything. I'll spend half the night reading from *The Next 100 Years* by George

Friedman, a book I highly recommend. Sputnik will snore next to me and kick me from time to time, dreaming of the chase.

I narrow my eyes and, instead of white California sand, see the snowy mountains of Magadan. Skiing in those young days of spring felt like flying high above life, a sensation duplicated when one is newly in love. It is a pleasant reminiscence. But only in solitary confinement does memory become a merciless editor, cutting a bearable story out of the ever-accumulating mess of days.

The Witch

1989

~

We set out for the witch's house in the still-gray morning. Babushka drove, squeezed behind the steering wheel of our boxy yellow Zhiguli. Mama sat in the front, fumbling with my migraine diary. Over the last year, the doctors had failed to establish any correlation between the excruciating pain that assaulted me weekly and what and how much I ate, when and how much I slept, what I did, the season, the weather, or my geographical location. No medication had helped. The witch was our last resort.

Although my babushka, a nurse at the Polyclinika, had assured me that this witch, a good witch, a healer, had cured her friend's heart disease, I was scared. I kept picturing the fairy-tale Baba Yaga, who lived deep inside a dark forest in a cabin held up by chicken legs. Her home was surrounded by a fence of bones, on top of which human skulls with glowing eye sockets sat like ghastly lanterns. Baba Yaga flew in a giant iron mortar, driving it with a pestle and sweeping away her trail with a broomstick, on the hunt for children to cook in her oven for dinner. Were Baba Yaga and this good witch sisters? Were all witches sisters? How often did they visit each other for tea?

The car smelled of gasoline, and a cauldron of nausea was already brewing in my stomach. I didn't need the migraine diary to predict another cursed day. Soon the world would be ruined by blobs of emptiness, like rain on a fresh watercolor. Everything familiar would shed its skin to reveal a secret monstrous core. And, after a tug-of-war between blackness and fire, an invisible UFO would land on my head. The tiny aliens would drill holes on the sides of my skull, dig painful tunnels inside my brain, and perform their terrible electric experiments. I'd rather get eaten by Baba Yaga.

We took the same road out of the town as for our frequent mushroom-picking trips. The trees grew in two solid walls, the leaves silvering in the windy sun like coins. Mama stared out the window. After whispering late into the night, she and Babushka hadn't said a word to each other all morning. This was a strange summer. Mama would usually accompany me on the three-day train from home to Syktyvkar, spend a week at Babushka's, then head back to Papa and work. This time, she showed no signs of planning to leave. In fact, she hadn't been herself all year: all the time awake, eyes and cheeks burning, telling me to remember that she loved me most of all in the world, as if she was about to die or move away.

Often, after an especially long bout of migraine, I imagined myself an orphan. How miserable and sad I would be without Mama, how feeble and helpless, and how lucky Vasilisa the Wise was in the fairy tale. Her mother had left her a magical doll, who, when fed, became alive and told Vasilisa to go to bed and not worry about anything. While Vasilisa slept, the doll did all the impossible work that was demanded of Vasilisa by her mean stepmother and stepsisters or by Baba Yaga. Oh, how I wished for a magical doll of my own.

"If you decide on it, at least make sure you don't bring them the same gift, like your brilliant stepfather, Lev Davidovich. Twice," Babushka said in a brash, joking tone. "Did I already tell you this story?"

Mama ignored her.

"Goes to Sweden, brings me a watch," Babushka went on. "I look at the receipt in the box: two ladies' watches. Gets all nervous, says they made a mistake at the register. Yes, very likely—a mistake at a Swiss register. One of the best lawyers in town and a complete idiot in life. A few months later I'm unpacking his suitcase from another business trip—two nighties. One small, one big. I leave them, see what happens. Surprise-surprise, he gives me the bigger one, the small one disappears. He wasn't sure what size I wore, he says, so he got two. After sixteen years of marriage he wasn't sure!"

"Quit it," Mama said and turned back to me. "How are you feeling, kitten?"

"Another one's coming," I said. I missed my old, understandable illnesses—coughs, stuffed noses, ear infections. And I missed the gamelike remedies: mustard chest compresses, an orchestra of little glass cups tinkling and tingling on my back, a night spent in a headscarf soaked with vodka.

"Of course, I later gave him and that witch such a beating they took turns writing complaints to the regional Ministry of Health. Fools," Babushka cried out. "I always had more friends than him because I am a good person. Our chief doctor, Olga Nestorovna, bless her soul, looks out for her women, always has. She knows that most men are dogs, as I say as well, except for one." She shot Mama a look.

"The witch?" I said.

"That one's another witch, Alinochka," Babushka said. "A bad witch."

"Enough. This is not helping. You're scaring Alina."

"I just don't want you to do something you might regret for the rest of your life."

"You don't think I know that? You don't need to torture me!" Mama yelled. My heart winced. "Stop it now. If it passes, you'll be the first one to know, I promise. Please, let's focus on Alina."

"Precisely," Babushka said.

Mama climbed over into the backseat and curled up next to me, her head on my lap. This made me uncomfortably hot, but I was too weak to move.

"Don't listen to us, Alinochka. The most important thing is for you to get better." She kissed my hand and put it under her cheek, which was pink and covered in fine hairs, like a peach.

❧

We stopped for a picnic lunch; I was too nauseous to eat. I wanted to crawl into a cool, dark hole and stay there with my eyes closed. My ears burned—two red signal flags for the incoming UFO.

After lunch Mama returned to the front seat, and I lay down in the back. From time to time she turned back and looked at me with worry, circling her lips with her finger. She and Babushka kept arguing, but I no longer heard them.

Soon we arrived at the witch's house. Instead of the cabin on two chicken legs like I had imagined, it was a regular *izba* on the edge of a small village. The airport inside my brain pulsated with light. The UFO beamed its invisible radioactive rays at Mama and turned her into a gray rabbit, while Babushka became a brown bear. At least this was one of the less scary of their transformations.

Babushka the Bear got out the plastic bag for the witch, and Mama took my hand in her soft paw. The three of us went up to the witch's doorstep. Babushka crossed herself and knocked. My forehead shook under the UFO's landing gear. I closed my eyes and braced myself for the pain.

The door opened. "Hello. Come in, come in." The witch's voice was low and kindly. I felt a light touch on my head and opened my eyes. Instead of an old hag with rotten teeth and eyes like live coals, before us stood an orange fox in a blue housecoat. She wore metal-framed glasses on her long, thin snout and a headscarf. "So, this is Alinochka, our little patient. Does your head hurt now?" I nodded. My temples had just begun to throb. "*Nu*, don't be so gloomy. We'll cure you."

We went in. It was pleasantly dark inside. The room was dominated by a giant old-fashioned stove, on top of which Ivan the Fool, the youngest and laziest of the three fairy-tale brothers, usually snored away his days. And where Baba Yaga cooked naughty children for dinner! Orthodox icons hung in the far corner; the gold halos around the stern faces of the saints shimmered in the glow of several church candles. An episode of *The Rich Also Cry,* Babushka's favorite Mexican soap opera, played on a small black-and-white TV on a bookshelf in front of the bed. I recognized the two-tone spines of the World Literature Series, the same one we had. Multicolored carpets covered the walls and the floor. It was a disappointingly ordinary home for a witch.

"Welcome. Please sit down." The Fox turned down the volume on the TV and motioned to a table with a samovar, several teacups, and a plate laden with honey cakes. Mama smoothed her denim skirt. She looked so pale next to the lustrous Fox. I was getting a bit suspicious: in the fairy tales, foxes were crafty, treacherous creatures—probably not without a reason.

"Thank you. This is for you." Babushka offered her the bag. I'd seen her pack a bottle of vodka and a box of chocolates along with the money.

The Fox waved it away. "Afterward, afterward. Alinochka, why don't you sit on the bed while I talk with your mama and grandma?"

As I settled on the scratchy plaid throw, the Fox poured them some tea and added a coffee-colored liquid from a brown bottle. The black label was covered with ornate golden designs and lettering, some not in Russian. At once a sharp herbal smell filled the room, which made me nauseous again. "Now, tell me about your daughter from the beginning, from birth."

Mama laid out my migraine diary in front of her, then hesitated for a moment, looking around the room and at the Fox with reservation, as though she'd forgotten how we got here and why. "All right. Alina was born in the winter and caught pneumonia when she was two weeks old. She skipped the crawling stage and began walking at seven months. She had already begun talking at six. Chronic sinus infections."

She gave the dates and durations of all my colds, flus, and childhood illnesses. The Fox listened attentively, wrinkling her nose after each sip of tea. From my shadowy corner her fur appeared almost flat, like freckled human skin. Her hind paw, clad in a high-heeled slipper, danced under the table. Babushka took a big bite from a honey cake.

"As a toddler, prone to tantrums. Often in a bad mood. The migraines started a year ago, but Alina still finished first grade with all fives. The doctors advised to keep a diary." Mama slid the diary toward the Fox. "The average episode lasts four hours, the auras before are . . ."

I tuned out. The aliens had begun drilling and pounding on the right side of my skull. Then they moved on to the left side. I took off my shoes and wound into a kitten ball. The Fox's pillow was uncomfortable: hard, cold, and pierced with stems of goose feathers. My vision was full of holes. A low choral humming came from the corner where the Orthodox icons hung. I squinted to see whether the saints were moving their mouths, but their dark, mournful faces only stared, flickering in and out of the candlelight's yellow fog.

White light strobed in front of my eyes, and the usual countdown began. Ten, nine . . . I jumped off the bed and stumbled toward the table, hoping to reach someone before the explosion. Babushka caught me. Eight, seven . . . She sat me on her sturdy knees and held me tight.

"You're forgetting Chernobyl, Vika," she said.

"I need to know everything before I can start the healing."

"Alina was in Kiev," Mama said to the Fox apologetically. "With her grandparents, on her father's . . . my husband's side. But the cloud didn't go over Kiev. There was no direct radiation. She wore that radiation meter for months."

I'd been four then, but I remembered that day at the zoo. I'd looked so many times at a photograph we'd taken: me sitting astride a big stuffed bear; Grandpa Sasha and Baba Lera, who had been recently diagnosed with cancer, on either side. A donkey flanked Baba Lera, and a monkey in a red vest and skullcap sat on Grandpa's shoulder.

Suddenly, my migraine lifted. The countdown stopped, and the aliens retreated. I saw them all clearly now: Babushka, Mama, and the red-haired woman in glasses and a blue housecoat. She was much too beautiful and young to be a witch. Her pink lips were lined with maroon pencil, and a small gold cross twinkled on her freckly chest.

"We never know the whole story," she said in a doctorly manner, the way Babushka spoke to her patients. "I don't trust the news. I don't trust anyone. These days we have to take matters into our own hands."

"Exactly what I've been telling her," Babushka said. "She doesn't listen to anyone's sensible advice. About anything."

Mama rubbed her nostrils.

"There are many causes for ailments. But, besides a few microbial and viral infections"—the witch nodded at Babushka—"the causes are rarely biological. For one, Russia . . . Well, what am I saying, the whole world, the whole world is full of spirits thirsty for revenge. Wars, revolutions, genocide. The crafty ones find their way into a new life. But most are too broken. They linger around, haunt the streets, haunt our homes, contaminate the minds and bodies of the most innocent. They hide in the hollows of the heart, warming themselves in the downy scarf of a child's soul, leaking poisons of old hurt."

"This philosophy seems rather—" Mama began.

"Listen carefully, Vika, and think," Babushka interrupted her, as though Mama were a disobedient child. "She is very sensitive."

I was about to tell them that it didn't hurt anymore when the witch called me over. She took out a measuring tape from her pocket and wrapped it around my head. I was nervous. With a magician's flourish she showed Mama and Babushka a thumbed number. Then she dug her cold fingers into my scalp.

"Ah yes, I can see the pain now, strong pain. You poor child," she chanted in a low voice. "The pain is like black ink, filling your head, and your head is a giant inkwell. All those spirits are floundering in the ink—I see them. They want to express their pain through you, but we will banish them out of your head—banish! banish! banish!—tell them to go and cry elsewhere!"

She encircled my head with her fingers and rubbed it, singing something folky under her breath. She smelled more like Mama than a witch—of dishwater and borsch and Lancôme perfume. She massaged her song into my head, hard and fast, now building my hair up into a crown, now letting it fall to my shoulders. "Into the forest they go! Into the forest! Into the forest!" she shrieked.

It felt good, but so what: this witch didn't know what she was doing. She had been wrong in her diagnosis of my pain, which was gone. I was doomed.

She lifted her hands and blew hot breath on my nape.

"How do you feel?" Mama said. She was pale, her big, gray eyes shining with fever. No, I never wanted her to die or go away, even if it meant I wouldn't get the magical helping doll like Vasilisa's. Instead of growing up, I would shrink, I would turn into a doll myself and ride in Mama's pocket everywhere.

"It doesn't hurt anymore," I said and smiled. "She stopped the pain."

Mama jumped from her chair and clutched me to her chest. "Oh God, thank you. Thank you, Galina Kirillovna."

The witch's name turned out to be just an ordinary Russian name. "You're welcome. This one wasn't too hard because she's so young," she said. "May your daughter grow up healthy and happy. And remember that the child's health depends on the mother's."

She measured my head again and showed the mark to Mama and Babushka. My head had shrunk two centimeters. I touched it all over. Ears, mouth, nose, eyes—everything seemed intact. Maybe something had happened after all. Maybe she'd somehow altered the surface of my skull so it was now impossible for the UFO to land. I wouldn't know until the next attack.

"Galina Kirillovna, do you by any chance do card readings?" Mama asked.

"Card readings? Of course. I do everything."

"I wouldn't trust the cards with such matters," Babushka said but didn't make a move from the table. She handed Galina Kirillovna the payment and took another honey cake.

"Alinochka, drink this and go lie on my bed. You need to rest now," Galina Kirillovna said and gave me a cup of tea. Its bitter herbal smell made me sneeze.

My eyelids became heavy once I lay down. The bed didn't feel as uncomfortable anymore. Through the syrup of sleep I heard the familiar incantations of the fortune-telling: *For you, for the home, for the soul. What was. What will be. What will calm the heart.*

❧

I woke up in the back of our Zhiguli on the way home, nauseous again, this time from hunger. Babushka drove, occasionally dropping her head forward to stretch her neck.

Beneath the neckline of her striped red dress she had a small fatty hump. Mama was asleep in the front seat, her face turned to me. Her lips were smiling. But whatever had calmed her heart was most likely a lie or a mistake. This Galina Kirillovna could be a healer witch or an evil witch, like the one in Babushka's story. Or not a witch at all.

The morning is wiser than the evening, Vasilisa's doll always said. And if the doctors can't help and the witches can't help, and Papa and Babushka can't—who else is left?

The ink of the night was leaking from the corners of the sky onto the day's bright canvas, as Galina Kirillovna would have probably said. She liked talking about the ink. Maybe she'd make a better poet than a witch.

Birches, birches, birches forever. The notches on their white trunks looked like sad black eyes. They had long tired of staring at the world without blinking, but they could never close and go to sleep.

Strawberry Lipstick

1958

~

Olya lay in bed between her younger sister, Dasha, and her older sister, Zoya, feeling that, at eighteen, her life was over. For what was life without love? A never-ending shift at a factory assembly line. Left and right, her friends went to the dances at the Palace of Youth, fell in love, and got married. They moved out of their parents' tiny apartments and no longer shared a bed with their sisters. They lived real lives. Plus, as married women, they could wear lipstick without attracting judgmental stares from nosy babushkas on the street. Olya was dying to wear lipstick.

The room was hot and stuffy even with the windows open. She sat up and looked at her sleeping sisters. Dasha's lips were pinched by a secret smile. She always seemed so much happier in her sleep. Zoya gripped her corner of the sheet and ground her teeth with the same intensity she applied to her waking activities, from stirring sugar into a cup of tea to expounding the virtues of the Party over dinner. Olya was fed up with Zoya's lectures, fed up with the poverty and having to put in hours and hours of work at the three different vegetable plots her parents had. She was fed up to death with everything in this town.

She climbed out of the bed and tiptoed into the living room. The old wooden floor creaked in betrayal. On the pullout couch, her mother and stepfather groaned in their sleep. She'd already heard one of them use the chamber pot—a big metal bucket in the hallway—earlier in the night. She was sick to death of that bucket. The nighttime deed made the kind of shameless trickling sound Olya imagined woke the neighbors not only in their house but also on the other side of the courtyard. It gunned the message into the metal: I am alive and I don't care what you think of me.

Which was very different from Olya's current state of mind. First, the love of her life, Kostya, had jilted her. Second, she had been denied admission to the Nutrition Institute in Odessa, where Kostya was now stationed. And third, she'd just found out that her tall and handsome Kostya, the dark-haired and green-eyed Kostya, a newly graduated officer of the Stavropol Military Academy, witty Kostya, guitar-playing and campfire song–singing Kostya, had married Olya's former classmate—she wasn't even that pretty—and taken her with him to Odessa.

On top of this, another graduate of the military academy, a

certain Alek, whom Olya had met just two weeks ago, had unceremoniously proposed to her. He was a communications officer and had been assigned to Petropavlovsk-Kamchatsky, a port city on the Kamchatka Peninsula nine hours away by plane. He didn't have to say it, but this was his last chance to secure a wife before the lonely military life in the Far East swallowed him whole. Olya always had so many friends, so many admirers from school and the academy. She was the most popular girl in her neighborhood and the star at the dances. How had it happened that her choice now came down to this?

Zoya laughed when she heard of the proposal.

"He can't be serious about this," she said. "He hardly knows you."

"So what? A man can't fall in love with me at first sight?"

"A boy. You don't know him at all."

Olya had known Kostya well, and where did that get her? So she considered ending it all.

She could cut her wrists, she thought now as she put on her sandals. A slow and painful way to go. That bastard Kostya wasn't worthy of so much suffering. She could jump off a building. It would have to be high enough so that she perished instantaneously. Life as an unmarriageable invalid was even worse than death.

She could hang herself, but she'd have to rummage in the closet for a rope or a belt, which would wake everyone up. It would certainly wake Dasha. Dasha thought Alek's proposal was romantic. Poor Dashen'ka, she would never get over her death. Eventually the news would reach Kostya in Odessa.

He probably would be too busy with his new wife to give poor, dead Olya a second thought. Such a possibility set off another wave of self-pity.

Olya knew she shouldn't grumble at her personal circumstances. The war had ended only thirteen years ago, and everyone still incanted: "Anything but the war, anything but the war." And her current life could hardly be compared to her parents' life before the war, at the height of the Terror and famine. Her mother was accused of stealing a loaf of bread from the grocery store where she worked. For this, she was arrested and sent to a work colony in Turkmenistan, where Olya and Dasha would be born. Her father, who had worked at the Anti-Plague Institute as a medical researcher in charge of developing vaccines, was accused of spying for the Japanese. He was tortured, his nails peeled off to the all-deafening accompaniment of a song from the film *The Children of Captain Grant*: "Captain, captain, smile! For a smile is the flag of the ship!" After several years in the Gulag, he returned home a sick and broken man. Throughout childhood, when Olya and her sisters would, in their ignorance, break into the ever-popular song at home, their father would pale, and their mother would scream at them to stop. She didn't explain why until each girl turned eighteen, and then only in a whisper and after swearing them to secrecy. Dasha still didn't know. Their father lived for another four years.

Stalin was dead now; food was almost plentiful. People had finally taken a deep breath.

But Olya had had enough of such reasoning.

She found a flashlight and picked up a cloth bag with cut-up newspapers kept by the door for trips to the outhouse. Two flights of stairs later, she plunged into the warm cocoon of the summer night. Her own building was too low for a fatal jump. The almost full butter-yellow moon hung in the sky like a giant river pearl. It seemed to her she could smell a hundred different flowers—most ardently, jasmine. Two opposite windows were lit up on the dark faces of the ancient *izbas*. Perhaps secret lovers had stayed up all night to relay messages via curtain Morse code, Olya mused, though she knew that those windows belonged to two querulous old hags. Either way, it was a night for secret rendezvous with one's sweetheart, for kissing so long you didn't need red lipstick, for not being able to fall asleep. Not suicides. In her small, crowded home she felt forsaken.

She used the pitch-black outhouse, then sat down on a homemade tree swing and looked at the moon again, its big-eyed, mournful face frozen in a cry or a grave request. Maybe Alek wasn't so bad. He was short but good-looking enough, especially in the dress uniform he'd worn at graduation. His gray eyes were playful, his cleft chin optimistic, his wavy hair shiny like his parade boots. He drew well. He'd shown her an album of his caricature sketches before proposing.

No, Olya wanted something death couldn't give her—a revenge on love and life, and on Kostya. She wanted to wear lipstick without the gawks from babushkas who sat cracking sunflower seeds on the courtyard benches all day, gossiping about the past and predicting the future. She wanted to be the mistress of her fate.

૪ə

They married ten days later, on Alek's twenty-third birthday. At the wedding Olya noticed with disappointment that his lower lip was sizably puffier than his upper lip, and five minutes after she lost her virginity, she threw up next to the bed. The physical act itself had revolted her, and she lay awake all night, wondering whether it would have been different with Kostya. At sunrise, she decided she needed to hurry up with her progress of love.

The day after the wedding Olya bought herself a lipstick the color of a ripe strawberry. It was the first object she had owned that wasn't a hand-me-down, and putting it on felt as wondrous as she had imagined. In another ten days Alek went off to Petropavlovsk-Kamchatsky to report for duty. She was to join him two months later, after he was done with training.

At first Olya wished she could've spent more time strolling down the leafy boulevards with her new husband, holding on to his arm and flashing her gold wedding band. Then, she realized she could enjoy her new status more without the discomfort of wifely duties. People no longer pushed her in lines, men gave up their seats on the bus, and everyone, even the grouchy babushkas, looked at her with respect and hope. Even her parents allowed her some leeway when it came to domestic chores and working on the vegetable plots. Olya sauntered around town with Dasha, talking about her plans. She would have her own kitchen, with her own pots and pans and knives and plates and a blue embroidered tablecloth, and she would cook whatever she wanted—however she wanted to cook it. And if Zoya didn't like the taste of it, well, she wouldn't be there to criticize her. She and Alek would vacation on the Black Sea, but not Odessa, of course. Odessa was an awful place. She would have a vanity dressing table in her bedroom and a separate little box with a cushion for each ring. Dasha looked at her with reverence. Just don't tell Zoya, Olya said.

By the time Olya celebrated her nineteenth birthday and began to pack for Petropavlovsk-Kamchatsky, she found out she was pregnant.

An exuberant southern fall was lazily taking over Stravropol. Caught in a chestnut hail, the park hummed and groaned. Giant red maple leaves appeared on the sidewalks like tracks of phoenix the firebird, joining the green leaves that had been patiently waiting since early August. The city was rolling out a crunchy welcome carpet. The warm wind rustled the leaves and the nylon raincoats of the hurrying passersby, and Olya's soul rustled too, anxiously and excitedly in her chest.

She packed everything she owned: three cotton dresses, a pair of woolen tights, a pair of shoes and old winter boots, a rabbit-fur coat, and her late father's black doctor's bag. Olya gave her fourth dress to Dasha, who had long coveted the yellow number with violet floral print and a lace collar.

"Won't you need it there?" Dasha said. "For military dances?"

Olya threw her head back in laughter, the way she'd seen an actress do in a movie. "Trust me, I won't need so many summer clothes in the Far East. It's cold there. Besides, I'm sure Alek would buy me more if I ask."

In the days before Olya's departure, Dasha wore the dress

nonstop. It looked beautiful on her but seemed to have a strange destabilizing effect. Usually dexterous and sure-footed, she dropped bags and parcels, cut herself while cleaning potatoes or chopping onions, and walked into furniture. And every time Olya took Dasha's small, clammy hands and said to her, "Dashen'ka, my soul, I'm not leaving forever," Dasha, her beauty a paler, once-copied version of Olya's, burst into silent tears.

Zoya, meanwhile, acted like she didn't care whether Olya left or stayed. A sturdy girl with orange hair and the same dark blue eyes that Olya had, she kept herself busy at the library of her teacher's college and with her various Komsomol obligations. At home, her already upturned nose stuck up higher still. She was jealous of Olya's marrying first, Olya concluded, and not just anyone—an officer. In a gush of magnanimity, Olya bought another tube of strawberry lipstick and tucked it under Zoya's pillow, wishing for a quick improvement in her sister's romantic life.

With the commotion of the wedding and excitement about the pregnancy, and now preparing to move across the country, Olya hadn't completely forgotten Kostya. But she found that focusing on his treacherous double-cross made her feel she was doing the right thing.

Alek returned from Petropavlovsk-Kamchatsky with cans of red caviar and a mustache strip that looked like a pencil stain. He closed his matters at the local military branch, packed up the few possessions he'd stored at his mother's, and on a bright mid-September morning headed with Olya and her family to the airport.

At the terminal, after offering last-minute words of wisdom and household advice, Dasha and her mother began to cry. Towering over him, Zoya briskly shook Alek's hand, then turned to Olya and locked her in an iron hug, the way she used to tame Olya's tantrums when they were children.

"Good luck, Olya," she said. "You're going to need it, but you'll be all right. You've always been the luckiest of the three of us."

"You're going to need it, too," Olya said, annoyed. She wasn't lucky—she was brave. Courage was needed if you wanted to live your life and not just hold forth about it at meetings and demonstrations.

On the plane Alek sat straight, like a real officer. He looked out the bright window and for a moment his gray eyes washed out to almost-white. It frightened her.

"You are so beautiful," he said and smiled shyly, as though she were not his wife but a fellow passenger at whom it was not polite to stare.

"You think everything will be fine?" One fears what one doesn't know, her mother always said. Alek was a good man, Olya knew that much in her heart.

"The flight is long," Alek said. His gray-again eyes glinted with mischief. "There's a small chance we'll crash. But don't worry, you won't miss much in Petropavlovsk-Kamchatsky."

Alek took Olya's hands in his. She liked his hands, with their long, thin pianist's fingers, the river network of veins. They were a tall man's hands.

⁊ఎ

They settled in ramshackle barracks in a military neighborhood across the bay from the city proper. The sparsely furnished room was tiny, but Olya was happy to share the bed with just one person. Alek left for work at dawn, came home for lunch and a nap, then returned in the evening, wolf-hungry and exhausted. During the day, he sent the soldiers from his squad, mere children themselves, to haul buckets of water from the neighborhood pump and chop firewood for the stove. They helped Olya with grocery shopping, too. She saw now that red caviar was the only thing one could bring from Petropavlovsk-Kamchatsky as a present. Pyramids of caviar cans stood on nearly empty shelves like miniature defense installations. There wasn't much in the way of vegetables and fruits, compared to Stavropol, and she doubted she could maintain a garden in this cold, wet soil by herself. At least she didn't have to carry that burden, too. Pregnant and therefore unhireable, Olya mostly stayed home. Something always needed cooking, cleaning, washing, ironing, darning. She liked gossiping in the communal kitchen with the other officers' wives. The nights she was unable to fall asleep because of Alek's snoring, she read—like her mother told her to—and thought of the nights back home. She and Dasha had often stayed up late waiting for Zoya to return home, and though they read different books, it felt like they were enveloped in the comfort of the same dream of other lives, of other possibilities. Back then, in their minds and bodies they were free.

One night, a month into her sojourn in Petropavlovsk-Kamchatsky, Olya woke up in alarm. She had distinctly felt something scurry over her pregnant belly. She jumped off the bed and turned on the lights just in time to see two rats rounding the corner.

"Alek!" she screamed. "Rats!"

"What! Who's there?"

"A rat just ran over your future child. We have to move out of here. You have to talk to someone about this first thing in the morning."

Alek made a sour face. "I'm still new here."

"What does that matter?"

"Well, unfortunately it's my duty to put up with the inconveniences. I'm a soldier first and an officer second," he said without conviction.

"Yes, that might be the soldier's duty, but not his wife and child's. There is no war going on. I didn't follow you here like some—" She wanted to say "Gulag prisoner's wife" but caught herself. It wasn't safe to yell such things in the middle of the night, especially when the walls were thin enough for rats to chew through. "Like a Decembrist's wife! Do you want your baby to be eaten by rats?"

Alek put his head in his hands and stayed like that for so long, Olya thought he'd gone back to sleep. He wore a holey undershirt, which she hadn't yet mended, and, generally, did not look like a husband at all.

"Why don't *you* talk to them?" Alek said through his hands, then looked up. "It will be more effective. They'll take one look at you—your condition—and do anything you say."

Olya went to the housing office the following morning and yelled at the director, a bald, glistening fellow in an ill-fitting uniform. She never did pay much attention to rank.

He listened, leering at her thin shoulders, legs, ankles. He even grinned when Olya said she was afraid to go to bed at night because of the rats. She almost threw up in disgust after leaving his office.

A week later they were moved into a room in the two-room communal apartment with a shared kitchen. Their neighbor was an old army doctor, Vasily Petrovich, who kept to himself. This place was newer and had no rats, just cockroaches. It even had an indoor toilet, though no running water.

ஃ

I love it here very much. It's not for the weak of heart . . . Olya described her new life in vivid detail in her letters home. She knew her mother would read them aloud over dinner, and she hoped her parents, overwhelmed by pride, and Zoya, dumbfounded by jealousy, would talk about her in the stores' waiting lines and at the Komsomol meetings, and eventually the news would reach Odessa. She didn't love Kostya anymore, but she wanted him to know that her life didn't end when he left. On the contrary, it had only properly begun.

Olya found much to like about Petropavlovsk-Kamchatsky. Yes, its streets and squares were not as wide and lush with trees as those of Stavropol. Even the standard five-story *khrushchyovkas* seemed lower than back home, huddled together in tight neighborhoods to take cover from the long winter's callous wind. Yet she felt invigorated and alive in a city surrounded by active volcanoes. Anywhere she looked, she saw their pyramidal outlines in scarves of clouds, white and mystical against the blue sky. During her first earthquake, the ceiling lamp swung wildly and the teacups tumbled from the table. Alek had warned her that mild earthquakes happened about once every three months, and after that first one Olya was thrilled like a rookie sailor after his first big storm. Nothing this exciting ever happened in Stavropol.

Alek came back from flights to inspect the radio towers in the mountains full of admiration for Kamchatka's nature. Such beauty! Such romance! He told her about the Uzon Caldera, the site of a giant extinct volcano. The hollow, surrounded by steep walls, was a veritable museum of Kamchatka, with poisonous mud cauldrons, hot springs, and bogs. Enormous bears bathed in the cold rivers and swans honked near the small, warm lakes. One time, as a very special present, Alek snuck Olya with him on one of these trips. It was strictly forbidden for civilians, but the commander of the helicopter owed him a big favor, Alek had said. When Olya saw from the air the famous Maly Semyachik, she held her breath and thought of her sisters. On the one hand, she felt guilty that they couldn't see the crater, with its black beach and the unimaginably bright, sometimes turquoise, sometimes green acid lake. They had never even been off the ground. On the other hand, she was vigilantly possessive of her new experiences. Maybe that made her a bad person—a selfish Soviet citizen in the eyes of Zoya—but now that Olya was married, she wanted to be the first in everything, she wanted every sensation for herself. Her soul, dislocated from its warm nest, had become a more sensitive instrument. Back in town, she would pick up on a deep underwater humming whenever she approached the bay. She felt it churn the blood in her veins, raising her body temperature and levels of optimism. She thought it was the surge of adrenaline due to the rapid changes in her life: the pregnancy, the marriage, the new city. Decades later, after declassification, she would find out that Russia's largest atomic submarine base had been just across the bay.

Petropavlovsk-Kamchatsky's seasonal capitulation was sudden and intense. The surrounding tundra burned with scarlet until October, and the birch forests stood drenched in gold. The temperature dropped overnight. On her way to the grocery store in the mornings, Olya could hear the hoar-frosted leaves falling with a jingle. The gusting wind brought the scent of sea and winter. First snow fell in early November.

In the first few months of marriage Olya learned the following about Alek. One: his father had died on the last day of the war. His mother, doubting she could raise two boys by herself, had sent Alek and his brother to the Stavropol branch of the Suvorov Military School, not uncommon for so many fatherless boys of the postwar years. Two: as long as there was hot dinner on the table and a pack of Belomorkanal cigarettes on the bureau, Alek was content. And three: he loved to play *preferans,* which his mother had taught him on his breaks from the military school. One of his card buddies was the helicopter commander who had flown Olya over Maly Semyachik.

When Alek won, he came home cheerfully tipsy, with presents for Olya—usually chocolate bars with white, blotchy coating from the canteen on base. He gave her all his winnings, danced her around their little room, and felled her on their little bed. His veiny hands hovered centimeters above her swollen stomach, then slid between her legs. His eyes filled with glassy determination. His paltry mustache tickled her unpleasantly, and she kept whispering, "Not so loud, just not so loud, please. Vasily Petrovich will hear."

After Alek fell asleep, she crashed back into her sore body. She must not have been in love just yet. But she would be soon, when the baby came—at the latest. It was hard to think of either Dasha or Zoya doing this with a man, and even more impossible and revolting to imagine them enjoying it. And yet she couldn't stop thinking about it. She was scared for them to find out the truth on their own and blame her for not warning them.

If Alek came home with a short smile and headed right for the kitchen, Olya knew that he'd lost. He smoked in the dark, without taking off his overcoat. He didn't look up at her even when she held his head against her round stomach—which, she knew, he didn't like touching—and stroked his black, wavy hair. She felt disappointment but also a kind of power in his guilt. She assumed that Alek would either quit when the losses became too big, or go on losing a little and winning a lot. She didn't mention his gambling to her family. It seemed unpleasant but manageable, like the flu. Besides, what could they do? She was already up to her elbows in marriage. Aside from the cards, it was hard to pick on Alek. He hadn't cheated or raised his hand to her. Not when he was sober, not when he was drunk. Not even after a loss. A gambler but an officer nevertheless.

Every few weeks Olya received a thick envelope from home. Her mother's letters were full of recipes and stories from Olya's childhood, stories Olya had heard a hundred times before. Her stepfather wrote about the vegetables he and her sisters were planning to plant on the plots. Dasha's pages about the new school year, her last one, were streaked with tears. She already missed her classmates and she missed Olya even more. From Zoya, Olya expected lecturing. Instead Zoya sent proverbs.

To marry is not to put on a bast shoe. Bride has an axe, groom is barefoot.

Olya didn't know what to make of it, though she didn't think about it too hard. Her pregnancy was going well. She felt strong; she could haul water from the pump by herself when Alek and his soldiers were gone on training assignment or to inspect and repair the radio towers.

The winter dragged along. After the first blinding snowstorm in December, she understood the purpose of the ropes that had appeared stretched between buildings at certain strategic crossings. You couldn't make any progress in the sudden whiteout without holding on to something solid, a wall or a rope. You could freeze to death meters from home. There were days in the perpetual twilight of January and February when Olya didn't leave their room at all, relying on Alek's soldiers for sustenance, water, and wood. She had her own small army to take care of her, she wrote in her letters. Alek, too, stayed home more often, his passion for cards having gone into winter hibernation. Some snowy evenings, Olya looked away from her knitting of baby socks and watched contentedly as he read a newspaper in the yellow glow of the floor lamp, his brows drawn in concentration but his mouth bunched to one side in a smirk, as though, as entertained as he was by all the lies, he could see through to the truth. One day she might even admire him, she thought—when he rose through the ranks and stopped gambling. One day.

The baby was born in mid-April. The labor was short and easy, the only thing that came easy to her, Olya would say in the years to come. The girl—they named her Marina—had eyes of indeterminate color, chipmunk cheeks, and a full head of chestnut hair. Olya spent hours staring at her small face, hardly believing that Marina was real and hers. Sometimes, she wondered what her child with Kostya might have looked like, but the only image that rose in her exhausted mind was that of her new daughter.

In a recent letter from home, Olya was shocked to learn of the romantic developments in both of her sisters' lives. Zoya was seeing a Party functionary fifteen years her senior, her mother wrote with palpable glee. Dasha, meanwhile, confessed on her own that she'd met an engineering student. They had danced at the Palace of Youth and gone on long walks around the melting city together. She wrote with so little of her habitual shyness about how much she adored her suitor that Olya became suspicious. Her little sister was changing in her absence. She tried hard to be happy for Dasha and Zoya, and for her mother.

Husband with fire, wife with water, Zoya wrote in her letter without mentioning her new boyfriend.

୨ৡ

One rainy Saturday night in May, Alek stumbled home late from a card game, the drunkest Olya had ever seen him. Marina had been screaming for hours, and Olya, in her delirium, was ready to throw the baby out the window. Her arms were sore. Her headache had wiped out all the emotions besides anger and frustration. Vasily Petrovich, the army doctor, had already come twice to their room to complain about the noise and attempted to calm the baby. Marina's silky face was scrunched like a soiled handkerchief as she continued to screech.

Alek took several uncertain steps toward Olya. The corners of his eyes still flickered with his usual impishness, but the pupils were black holes of fear. He stretched his arms to the baby, and Marina stopped crying. Olya gave the stunned baby to her father. Alek and Marina stared at each other for a moment, as if confused who the other one was and what had brought them to this cramped, cold room. Then Alek began to cry, soundlessly but with a boyish abandon. His daughter resumed wailing. He returned her to Olya and shuffled to their lumpy little couch, where he continued to cry with his eyes closed. Soon he passed out in his coat.

Olya worried all night. Had his mother died? Was another war about to begin?

She found out in the morning. Several exceptionally good players, new to the group, had ganged up to squeeze Alek down to the last ruble. A month's salary in one night.

"I don't understand. What are we going to live on? And the baby." It was both a relief and worse than she thought.

Alek was sitting at the table in their room, eating a piece of buttered black bread with tea. His hair was dirty and matted.

"I'll quit as soon as I pay off my debt," he said, not looking at her.

"And what are we going to live on, Alek?" Olya heard herself say again. "Meanwhile."

"They can't just come over here and raid your wallet. Although, they're such dogs, they could. We'll hide it under the mattress in Marina's crib."

"I don't keep our savings in my wallet."

"We have savings? Where?"

"In the birch-bark box, in the bureau," Olya said. His cluelessness shocked her. But she was also moved by his neediness, his complete, childish trust in her.

"How much?" Alek said into his tea.

"For food, another two weeks, maybe. Please don't play anymore. Or maybe without betting so much. Can you?" She put her arms around him from behind, like a good wife would do.

Alek turned back, clasped her hips, and pressed his head to her stomach, which he was no longer afraid of.

"Such a shame," he said through his teeth. "I'm a good player, I am. If my mother found out . . ."

One less girl, one more broad.

"Are you deranged? You can't bet on winning. You're an officer, for God's sake. You're educated. How can you be so stupid? If you don't stop playing, I'll leave you. I'll take Marina and go."

"I'm doing this for Marina and you."

She slammed the table with her fist. Alek's cup of tea jingled in its saucer. He lifted his head and stretched his lips, as though getting ready to smile. Did he think this was a joke? She struck the table again; she didn't know what else to do.

Marina began to cry and Olya ran to her. Alek followed and stood close without touching either Olya or the baby. The smell of alcohol and cigarettes and acrid male sweat was making her sick. She was afraid he wanted to sleep with her.

"Wash yourself," she said.

"We don't have any water."

"Bring it then!" The echo of Zoya's righteousness in her voice made her shudder, but the results were swift. In a few moments Alek was clunking with the buckets in the kitchen. Before going out to the pump, he came up to her.

"I will stop, Olya, I promise. I promise this time," he repeated until she told him not to talk to her for the rest of the day.

She cleaned up the dirt in the hallway while Alek heated up the water and splashed in the bathroom. She wished she could complain to someone. She knew that her mother, despite teaching her girls to count only on themselves, was relieved that Olya got married. One less mouth to feed, one less body to clothe. A village girl, she had married Olya's father at sixteen and found out at the civil registry office on their wedding day that he was twenty-five years her senior, when she saw his passport for the first time. She had said nothing. She was grateful to him for pulling her out of the peasants and into the intelligentsia. Olya wished that they could have talked heart to heart about those early days of her mother's marriage—and about everything. Her mother had worked around the clock when the girls were growing up and never had time for much more than a good thrashing or an occasional saying. One of her favorites was: *Live with your husband for a century but never show your backside*. But how could she not? Olya was at a loss. She wanted to be a good and honest wife.

She couldn't disappoint Dasha, she couldn't spoil her new romance with the engineer. As for Zoya: her voice with the proverbs was running through Olya's head almost nonstop. *A wife is not a gusli; you can't hang her up on the wall after playing*.

That day, in self-imposed penance, Alek washed the dishes and changed Marina's diaper for the first time in Marina's life.

శ్రా

Nothing changed. Alek kept playing and losing. He came home drunk; often he didn't make it to the bed. He didn't defend himself when Olya yelled. He didn't complain or hit her back when she came at him first with her fists, then with pots and pans or anything else within her reach, and he no longer promised to quit. She was ashamed when Vasily Petrovich caught them fighting in the kitchen or in the bathroom. Zoya's proverbs crawled, like roaches, out of the cracks in the walls, from the corners of the cupboards and the holes in their socks, from the cold bubbles in Olya's dishwater, screeching their nonsense. Couldn't anyone else hear them? *The thread follows the needle. The thread follows the needle. The thread follows the needle*.

To pay off some debt, old and new, and to buy food and other necessities, Olya and Alek had no choice but to borrow money from Vasily Petrovich and the same officers Alek had lost to. Begging was below his rank, Alek said, so Olya put on her strawberry lipstick, whipped her hair into a coif, and went knocking on doors. She couldn't bear the looks of the young soldiers when they brought water and wood to the apartment. The old army doctor seemed completely indifferent as he opened his wallet; her domestic drama was nothing compared to what he'd seen on the battlefield. A marriage, she had discovered, was a deep trench inside which festered a hundred previously concealed details about the person in whose company you had enlisted. She wanted to caution her sisters, but before that, she would have to admit her own defeat.

Olya remembered how Zoya had once organized a charity concert to raise money for the families of veterans, how she convinced every music ensemble and dance group in town to perform on Victory Day in the park. She had several schools put on short plays, pantomimes, and gymnastics routines and persuaded shy poets to declaim their patriotic works on stage. Olya had insisted that, though she had nothing against the veterans, of course, no one would come to see a concert without a single professional performer. Zoya took Dasha and went knocking on doors to invite half the town personally. The show was a huge success. Thousands came.

Only now Olya began to appreciate the magnitude of Zoya's power. If Zoya was able to subjugate that many people to her will, how easy it would be for her to tackle just one husband.

❧

I was tired of sitting home, Olya wrote, *so I now work as a second-shift cashier at the Bread and Bread Products counter at the grocery store on the base. Like you said, it's good to have your own money, just in case. Count only on yourself. A very nice lady from our building watches Marina in the evenings. Marina is getting big and has a loud voice, maybe strong enough to become an opera singer.*

The full horror of reality ambushed Olya at home, in two variations. The first featured a mise-en-scène of Alek and his officer friends at a card game engulfed in cigarette smoke. A vodka bottle stood on the table. Marina sat in her crib, covered with tears and snot. In this scenario, Olya went to the kitchen to pick up a frying pan and chased everyone out, disregarding the differences in height, weight, and rank. *A young wife cries till the morning dew, a sister—till the golden ring, a mother—till the end of times.*

In the second variation, Olya returned from work to an empty room. This meant Alek was playing at one of his friends' and Marina was with the babysitting babushka. The dinner she'd made earlier would be gone, and Alek would sometimes leave a humorous cartoon to explain the mess in the kitchen—for example, a cat with its tongue out sitting by a bowl of dumplings, sketched on a piece of paper he would leave next to a sinkful of dirty dishes.

In both cases, Olya was shocked and mortified anew as she crossed the threshold of her room, as though she kept accidentally walking into the neighboring apartment, the neighboring life, to catch its inhabitants at something shameful. She yearned for a break, for a summer vacation at the Black Sea or, at least, back in Stavropol. But Alek told her that he was allowed free tickets to the continent only every three years, so they must be patient and wait.

That November, when Marina was seven months old, an earthquake much stronger than what Olya had become accustomed to shook the town in the middle of the night. While Alek snored drunkenly on the couch, Olya rushed outside with Marina wrapped in a thin blanket, the first thing she could grab. Marina caught a chill, and it developed into pneumonia. Olya spent weeks with her at the hospital. As she wrapped the legs of Marina's crib with rags soaked in roach repellent, she cursed the earthquakes and Petropavlovsk-Kamchatsky, she cursed Kostya, Alek, and her marriage, she cursed Zoya's proverbs. Marina coughed for months and months afterward, and with each wet heave Olya imagined someone scraping a layer of tissue off her baby's lungs, tender like the inside of her chipmunk cheeks.

On the rare occasions when Alek won, he still brought home presents for Olya, but she only yelled at him for wasting money on nonessentials instead of paying their Hydra-like debts. He had stopped pushing Olya into bed, and at least for this she was thankful. She was still puzzled, however—in a sociological kind of way—how Alek could continue doing something that was so destructive to the family. Even without love, they still constituted an economic cell of the Soviet society. Shouldn't that mean something to an officer?

More and more Olya thought about home and her childhood. Sitting in a field as a toddler, when the grass was as tall as she, and watching a bee circle a flower bush round and round. *Bzzzzz—bzzzzz* was the only sound in the world, the happiest sound, and in that moment nothing else existed or needed to exist. That must have been one of her first memories. Bathing with Dasha in the fountain across from Lenin Square on hot summer days. Twirling with Zoya on a tiny patch of ice in front of their father's Anti-Plague Institute, imagining themselves world champions in figure skating. Speaking a made-up nonsense language with Dasha and pretending to be foreigners, until their mother categorically forbade it. And then there was the time when she, Dasha, and Zoya had walked twenty kilometers on the train tracks by themselves at night in Turkmenistan. Dasha must've been no more than four then. Olya remembered standing on a hill and Zoya pointing south: "That's Iran over there." And the time Olya and Zoya decided to heat up paraffin for a hot compress to cure Dasha of her cough, and it exploded in the kitchen. The whole ceiling was black, and they were charged with whitewashing it. And when Olya went with Dasha and Zoya to a Malenitsa fair in Stavropol and ran into a boy she had a crush on in seventh grade. He asked her where she was going, and she replied, too mortified to think straight, "Looking for pancakes." She was still a chubby girl back then. Zoya laughed about this for three days straight, and one night, when Zoya was sleeping, Olya cut off a thick chunk of her hair. In revenge, Zoya threw Olya's most treasured possession, her grandmother's gold locket, into the hole in the outhouse. The locket was retrieved grudgingly by their poor stepfather. How many hours she'd spent weeding those stubborn vegetable plots with her sisters and walking, walking everywhere, and whispering in bed. And all that time of just staring at the snow. It all seemed so important now.

೫௨

One evening the following spring, when Marina was almost a year old and looked like a copy of her father, Alek stumbled home after another gambling loss. His coat was open, his cap fixed on his head at an inadvertently jaunty angle. His features swam, now forming an idiotic smile, now an unsure frown.

When she saw his condition, Olya jumped at him with a book she'd finally just found a moment for and welted him tiredly in the stomach, chest, shoulders. Marina began to holler. The chronic phlegm slurped in her sinuses with that awful heartbreaking sound.

"You're killing us," Olya yelled. Her voice had been pitched to a high roof months ago and refused to come down. If only she could beat him hard enough that he would stop ruining her life.

Alek twisted the book out of her hands and carefully set it on the floor. Then he rose, holding on to the bureau, and slapped Olya in the face. In her shock, a proverb Zoya had yet to mention popped into her mind: *If he beats you, he loves you.* He hit her skinny upper arm, at first tentatively, as though measuring resistance of the muscle, then harder. He looked surprised and vacant, as if his arm were a separate object from him, something for which he wasn't responsible. His expression scared Olya more than the beating. He could kill her and not notice.

He struck her back as she broke free, then lurched after her and pummeled her backside with particular viciousness— perhaps for all the times she didn't let him touch it. She ran into the bathroom, hoping that Vasily Petrovich wouldn't hear them. Alek barged through the flimsy door and pushed her to the floor. He kept beating her, then throwing fists at her. Then just hands. His eyelids drooped unevenly. Abruptly he turned and staggered back to their room.

After a few minutes Marina's wailing registered again, and Olya ran back to the room. Alek was passed out on the floor by the couch. Underneath his unbuttoned coat his fatigue-green officer's shirt was soaked with sweat. She picked up her daughter and carried her in a small circle as though in a dream. She took many, many steps. A new kind of ache seized her arms cell by cell.

Eventually Marina drifted off to sleep. Olya sat down with her on the bed. She should get up and turn off the light, she thought, but the baby was so warm and heavy on her lap. A soft anchor. She closed her eyes for a minute.

Olya woke from a sudden movement of the bed. Not another earthquake!

Alek had revived and was kissing Marina's forehead.

"Don't touch her!" Olya screamed.

He jumped away from her. "What's wrong with her?"

"You beat me."

He squinted in playful disbelief. Olya knew that look well.

"Don't you dare make this into a joke." His mustache and the dimple on his chin repulsed her. And those pathetic Belomorkanal cigarettes. For what kind of person was that enough to be happy?

Shaking from anger, Olya carefully transferred Marina off her knees and onto the bed. The girl curled up into a ball, bracing herself, even in sleep, for yet another skirmish between her parents. Olya showed Alek her arms. They were covered in bruises, blots of dark water under thin ice. Then she pulled up her housecoat and showed him what he'd done to her backside.

He looked at his hands. His face drew back to reveal a panicked rawness. His features reconstituted immediately into a sleepy, drunken grimace, but Olya had already seen that he, too, was terrified of himself, more terrified than she was. Marina woke up and strained her face in preparation for a wail.

"This is what you did," Olya said and began to cry. "Like a drunken peasant."

Alek stared at the floor without moving.

A bad husband's wife is always an idiot.

He hobbled to the kitchen. There was a violent banging of drawers, then silence. In a few moments he returned with a knife. He placed a chair in the middle of the room, sat down, and slashed both of his wrists. As he bent forward to put the knife on the floor, blood began to spout out of the cuts. It was a surprisingly bright hue of red.

Olya turned away. Everything settled within her and retreated. She picked up whimpering Marina and rocked her, staring at the dark window. A few more months and her daughter would no longer be a baby. She wondered whether anyone was still awake, curled up with a book or huddled in the kitchen over tea and secrets. Marina kept sobbing. If Olya fell asleep now, she would sleep through this noise, too, and the ambulance sirens. She would happily sleep through the rest of her life, she thought.

A heavy sigh blew like a ghost from the chair. Alek sat slumped, with his eyes closed. His hands hung at his sides, lifeless as oars. The blood flowed steadily. Olya rocked her baby from side to side. They were out of milk. She would have to go first thing in the morning. Marina liked her semolina porridge thin, with lots of milk. Lots of milk and sugar.

By the time Vasily Petrovich burst into their room—he'd had a premonition about the silence that followed half a night of fighting—there was a puddle of blood next to the chair.

"Why are you sitting there like a statue? Waiting for him to bleed out?" the old doctor yelled. He rummaged through their room. "Nothing. What kind of wife are you? Prepared for nothing."

"And what kind of doctor are you?" Olya said.

Vasily Petrovich grabbed a pillow off the bed and tore the case into strips. Cursing and groaning, he tied Alek's wrists. Alek didn't shift, but he didn't fall either.

Olya still hadn't moved from the bed when the ambulance came and took Alek to the hospital. Marina had at last tired herself out and dropped off to sleep. Soon Marina would get hungry and start up again. This thought didn't bring on the usual desperation in Olya. Her daughter was solely hers now. Every problem and burden hers alone. Relief was spreading warmly through her body.

A few hours later Marina woke up and Olya fed her. Then she put her daughter into the crib and began wiping up the puddle of blood, the edges of which had already congealed into a maroon jam.

✿

The following day Olya went to the base to see about the plane tickets home and was surprised to learn that Alek had paid leave and free tickets available for himself and his family every year. "The defender of the Motherland must have quality rest to maintain the highest degree of combat readiness," said the friendly lieutenant at the transportation department. So Alek had kept her prisoner in their smoky room because he couldn't return home broke. Because it would be shameful for an officer.

She divided their meager marital possessions into honest halves, assigning herself the last unpaired pillowcase, since its mate had been sacrificed in Alek's botched suicide. There was no time for a painstakingly calibrated letter, so she went to the post office to call home. Zoya picked up the receiver; no one else was around.

"Marina and I are coming."

"For a vacation?" Zoya said.

Olya detected underwater mines in her tone. "Yes."

"Well, it's about time we all met your little chipmunk."

"Zoya, already for a while I wanted to ask you. Why did you write those proverbs in the letters? If you wanted to tell me something, you could have just written that. I'm used to your lectures."

"I never lectured you, Olya. It's the voices in your head." Zoya laughed, not maliciously. "It was for a joke, from Dasha's library book. I thought you of all people could tell. You teased me about Komsomol, so I thought I'd tease you back. At a safe distance."

"I never teased you about anything," Olya said. She'd been afraid to.

❧

As the days passed and her departure date grew closer, Olya's euphoria swelled. She felt as happy and light as in those first fall days in Petropavlovsk-Kamchatsky, when her growing belly seemed to be the one thing that kept her from flying off into the sky. At first Alek thought that her plan to leave was a ruse. Then he begged for her forgiveness and promised to quit whatever she wanted him to quit. "You'll be the general," he said over and over, trying to hook her with his wobbly smile. "Everything will be the way you want. Just tell me." To Olya, his pleadings were a faint prattle on a radio someone had forgotten to turn off. She and Alek had failed at not remaining strangers.

Alek still couldn't believe Olya and Marina were leaving when they said good-byes at the airport. Vasily Petrovich had come, too, probably to make sure Alek didn't do anything else stupid. From the bus that took them to the airplane, Olya spotted Alek's slumped gray figure in the crowd of passengers' families. He was waving along with the others. He wore the winter greatcoat to conceal his bandaged wrists, which made him look especially sad on such a bright spring day.

As the plane was about to take off, Olya looked one last time at the volcanoes in the distance. For a second, it seemed as if the clouds had thickened above one of the tops. She squeezed Marina tighter to her chest. Petropavlovsk-Kamchatsky was even grayer from the air than from the ground. The naked trees on the snow-covered mountain slopes looked like patchy stubble on a giant's sallow cheek. The plane broke through a layer of clouds and the city, the crater of her marriage, disappeared.

※

Back home, everything was understood and all the questions were now asked. Olya's sisters were ecstatic to have her back and fought over who would get to babysit Marina. One of Olya's classmates was taking the entrance exams to the surgical *facultet* at the Stavropol Medical University and dared Olya to try, too. What if? She needed to move on—and quickly. Besides, she already knew she wasn't afraid of blood. All summer Olya reviewed the old chemistry and physics textbooks at the library. Zoya's boyfriend had to pull some strings: Olya got in. The surgical *facultet* ended up with an overflow of qualified candidates, and she was offered a year-long deferral or a transfer to the dental course, which was four years shorter. The choice was clear.

While in school, Olya lived with her parents. Both Dasha and Zoya had married soon after Olya's return (although she had counseled them about the perils) and moved out. That first summer back was sweltering. In the evenings, Olya studied on the bench in the courtyard while Marina slept in her stroller under a jasmine tree, clearing her chronically stuffed sinuses of volcanic ash. Then came the opulent fall again, with its maple-leaf tracks of phoenix the firebird. Every morning, when Olya went to medical school, her mother took

Marina to the nursery under a shower of golden leaves and chestnuts in the park. In time, Olya's stepfather taught Marina to ride a bicycle. Olya and Marina slept together for years in the sisters' big old bed and were happy.

In her thirties, Olya moved to Syktyvkar, in the north of Russia, and soon became the chief doctor of a *polyclinika*. It was considered improper for a woman in her position to be single, so she got married again—this time to a doctor, a man of another so-called noble profession. Her second husband chased every skirt at his hospital and had a five-year affair before they finally divorced, but it was his miserly ways that offended her most. The days when she would open the fridge and see his name written on cartons of milk and packages of cheese and ham that he had bought on his salary, she thought of Alek—how he gave her all his money and was content as long as he had his Belomorkanal cigarettes.

Many more years later, Baba Olya, as she was now called, retired from her post as the chief doctor and returned to Stavropol, to live closer to her sisters. They got together often at one of their apartments or Zoya's dacha and talked of the past. All three agreed that their childhood and youth had been happy. Zoya never did have children, and Dasha, poor little Dashen'ka, had in the same year lost her husband, the engineer, to a heart attack and both of her grown children. Vityok, her son, was poisoned by a drug addict friend, who knew that Vityok had money in the house after selling his car. Her daughter, Tamara, was stabbed by a boyfriend in a drunken fight.

Now and then Olya's thoughts drifted to Kostya and her second husband, but most often she thought of Alek. It was inconceivable to her that she, who spent her whole life taking care of people, had once almost let her husband bleed to death in front of her eyes. His good and open heart seemed like the most important quality a person could possess, and she now felt something for him akin to loving pity. Maybe, in due course, Alek would have gambled away his youthful folly.

Other times, she shuddered at the tragic cliché that was her first marriage.

Olya saw Alek again once, several years after their quick divorce. He was in town visiting his elderly mother and turned up at Olya's to beg her to return. She was about to go grocery shopping and had just put on her signature strawberry lipstick. He looked at her with a stranger's voracity, as though he was seeing a beautiful woman for the first time. She refused. Her mother had always said, *If he hits you once, he'll hit you again.*

He asked whether he could see his daughter. "She's on vacation on the Black Sea with my parents," Olya lied. Marina was doing her homework just two closed doors away.

"Next time, then," Alek said. His eyes were still mischievous but tired.

Olya never tried to find him. She didn't want his money. She didn't want anything from him. A few months after his visit, she heard through the town's rumor mill that some woman had come to Stavropol in search of Alek, claiming to be pregnant by him. Another naive soul trying to capture an officer.

To entertain your wife, become a soldier.

The Uncatchable Avengers

1993

~

"**T**ak, children, we are almost ready to begin. Let's go over this again," the mustachioed producer said. "When I say 'Silence in the studio. Cameras rolling. Action!' the performer Anna Glebovna calls should come up to the piano, say your name and age, the piece you're going to play, and who it's by—"

Dima snorted. A couple of the other children giggled.

"Oleg Borisovich, it's the Children's Festival of Tchaikovsky, so every piece will be by none other than the esteemed Pyotr Ilyich," Anna Glebovna said to the producer. Dima had recognized her from prior citywide competitions and recitals. She was the director of the Magadan Children's Music School #1.

The producer scanned the list on his clipboard, as if looking for Tchaikovsky's name. He wore tight black jeans, a green turtleneck sweater, and, over this, a black corduroy blazer.

There was something cockroachy about him. Dima cringed. He was the first on the list, and he just wanted to get it over with. He had more heroic things to do after the taping.

"Tchaikovsky, Pyotr Ilyich Tchaikovsky," Anna Glebovna sang out. The children laughed again but were quickly shushed by their parents and piano teachers from the back rows.

"Yes, yes, of course. Say your name, your age, the title of your piece. Sit down at the piano—please, try not to drag the stool across the floor—and play. When you're done, take a bow and go back to your chair. That's it. Don't run. And please, audience, nobody talk until I say 'Cut.'"

"Any questions, children?" Anna Glebovna said. "Let's show our TV station what we can do, ah? Oleg Borisovich here will also send the tape to Moscow, and Moscow might broadcast clips from our little festival to the whole country. How would you like to be famous?"

Dima's piano teacher, Faina Grigorievna, had once told him that Anna Glebovna was the worst pianist ever to hold an academic position in the history of musical education, and that she was a hack. Dima wasn't sure what a hack was, but in her ruffled red dress Anna Glebovna sure looked like one.

"One more thing," the producer said. "Audience, very important. Don't forget that you are on camera, too. Please look like you're enjoying the music. In the final segment, we may cut to reaction shots at any time, so children: no making faces or picking your nose."

Dima realized that at that very instant his own finger had been inching toward his nose.

"*Bozhe moi,* Oleg Borisovich, who do you think they are?

Monkeys from the zoo? You are underestimating us," Anna Glebovna said, waving her hands as if they were fans. "These are not just some street children who spend their days chasing neighborhood dogs. These are the most talented and dedicated young musicians in all of Magadan."

Dima craned back his neck. Faina Grigorievna sat in the last row, her gaze frighteningly calm, as usual. She wore her famous mustard shawl and giant amber earrings, into which he had stared so many times while she scolded him during lessons—he'd seen his whole life in those caramel globes. She was one of the largest people in the room and definitely had the largest head. Her short, yellow hair made it look as if she were wearing a hat made of fox fur.

Dima's small mother sat next to Faina Grigorievna, slightly leaning away. When they had first come in, his mother sat down in the front with Dima and all the children, and wasn't noticed until halfway through the producer's first round of explanations. She had to be escorted to the back row while everyone watched.

She gave him a fugitive smile, then lowered her head. Poor Mama, she'd always been afraid of Faina Grigorievna. It shouldn't take long. Playing time was under a minute, and he knew his piece forward and backward.

"All right, Anna Glebovna, let's begin," the producer said. They made an awkward bow to each other and took their respective positions: the producer behind an arsenal of monitors in the left corner, and Anna Glebovna on a chair in the right corner. The producer, boom operator, and both cameramen put on their headphones. "Control room ready?"

A young woman, who'd been napping behind a glass window in the back, started. With her face blue from the monitors' glow, she looked like a fairy. "Ready, Oleg Borisovich," her voice crackled over the intercom.

There was a pause.

"Anna Glebovna!" the producer yelled.

"Oh." Anna Glebovna jumped off her chair. Its legs scraped shrilly against the floor. "First up is Dima Ushakov, from the Magadan College of Arts. The special section for gifted children," she added with a smug smile.

"Silence in the studio," the producer yelled. The cameramen stuck their faces into the viewfinders. "Cameras rolling. And action!"

Dima stood up—no floor scraping—and marched confidently to the piano, even though the pattern of black-and-white four-leaf clovers on the studio floor made him dizzy. He looked into the camera pointed at him, then at the camera pointed at an angle at him and the audience, then back at the first camera. Breathe. He saw the boom operator move, and the microphone lowered closer to his head, like a big, hairy spider dangling from the foliage of lights that covered the ceiling. He fought every urge to look up. Breathe.

"Dima Ushakov. Nine. Nine years old," Dima said, looking somewhere between the main camera and the blue-faced girl in the control room. The microphone crept closer to his head. "'March of the Wooden Soldiers,'" he said louder. Anna Glebovna nodded maniacally in the background.

He sat down and was immediately blinded by a panel of lights. Another microphone had been snaked into the innards of the piano. So much fuss over such a short piece, the march. He looked at the keys: white black white black white white black white. A row of tombstones. Stop, must not think of tombstones or snakes, he thought. Spiders either.

He took a deep breath, then caught himself halfway through the exhale, remembering that he was not supposed to make any noise. He noticed a big round clock on the wall, as obvious as a harvest moon: 12:04. Stop looking, Dima thought, and squeezed his thigh. Yesterday, he'd lied to his best friend, Genka, that he would be absent from school because he was going to the dentist to fix twenty cavities. He said he'd be knocked out under anesthesia all day. Genka had swallowed the fib; he was so naive. Maybe Genka wasn't qualified to be the leader of their new gang, after all. The Uncatchable Avengers, oh. Just thinking about it made Dima's skin all goose-bumpy. But not now, not for the next minute. Afterward. Save it for their inaugural meeting at the abandoned construction site behind the school—their secret headquarters. Genka said they would make up secret hand signs. It was a start.

Still 12:04. A piece of black wire stuck out above the dial like a curl. Head, heart, hands, ears—Dima went through the preplay checklist and cupped his hands around his knees to give them the proper shape. He imagined the vast green field where the soldiers would be marching, the sun like a big golden shield sending fiery arrows into his chest to activate his *nutro,* which is not a muscle or an organ, though sometimes it acts like both. Or either. Faina Grigorievna said to think of it as a little clay oven that hangs between the stomach and the heart. It's where the stories and ideas about each piece of music are converted into a winged feeling, a bubbling fuel that makes the black dots on paper come alive. Whenever Dima felt his arms begin to tire, Faina Grigorievna sensed it. She got up from her chair at the back of the classroom and, if she'd been filing her nails, poked his lower spine with the sharp tip of the nail file. This always woke up his sleepy, sometimes frozen *nutro*. His arms felt immediate relief, the notes began to string together again. Sometimes she clapped above his head or banged on the higher or lower register as he played. One time, she knocked down the keyboard cover so suddenly that Dima only just managed to pull out his fingers. She knew how to set him back on track.

Nonpianist people had a *nutro,* too, Faina Grigorievna said, but for most it remained underdeveloped and underutilized. As was obviously the case with the whole Children's Music School #1. Dima wondered whether his *nutro* could be used for the Avengers business as well, whether it could make him a better, stealthier Avenger. Genka would laugh. His *nutro* must be like last year's shriveled plum.

Dima held his hands over the keys. Ears, head, et cetera. All systems on. Three, two, one . . .

Plop. He got the first chord right.

—TaTaTatitati TaTa Tatitati . . .

The soldiers are marching across a wide green field. Faina Grigorievna told him to imagine the field, though the real soldiers must've had better things to do than march through fields. For example: march through the town square, where they could keep an eye on the unruly citizens and flaunt their military regalia. Genka talked about making a badge they could pin on their school uniforms to distinguish them from the common troublemakers and hallway racers. Then what? The soldiers had war; the Avengers had nothing to avenge. Yet.

Dima forgot whether the upcoming drumroll of six-teenths in the left hand was to be played by one finger or different fingers. His fingers went on playing, though, of their own accord.

—Ta Ta Ta Ta Tatitatita tititata . . .

As soon as he played the drumroll with one finger—a poky second—he knew it was wrong. It had to be first, fourth, third, second, then first!

His wrists clamped up; the rest of the march's familiar topography crumbled. He stopped.

"Cut!" the producer yelled and yanked off his head-phones. "Anna Glebovna!"

Anna Glebovna slid off her chair and waddled up to Dima.

"Ushakov," she said. She had a mole on her nose that sprouted fine yellow hairs.

A hack.

Dima now remembered Faina Grigorievna talking about treating your fingers with respect and giving each one a little deserved rest. That's why, after all, you had ten of them, not two. The moon clock showed five minutes past noon.

"Ushakov," Anna Glebovna said again. "Ushakov."

Whispers hissed from the audience, legs swung, backsides fidgeted.

Dima's cheeks began to burn; the rest of his body shud-dered against the clammy studio air. Poor Mama.

"Now, Ushakov. Such an easy piece. *Tok tok tok tok* and let's ride." Anna Glebovna snapped her chubby fingers. "Look how many of you I have to get through."

March. March. March, Dima pleaded with his *nutro*. He knew it; his fingers knew it. March now, avenge later.

"I'm ready," he said. The clock's minute hand rolled lazily to six. The second hand marched on without a care in the world. In the wrong tempo.

"Silence in the studio," the producer commanded from behind the monitors. The audience held its breath. "Cameras rolling. Action!"

Fingers, head. "Sorry, do I have to say my name and age and what I'm playing again?"

"Cut! Cut! You don't have to say your name again. You've already said those things very well, now you just have to play."

Dima nodded.

"Silence in the studio. Rolling. Action!" Dima could only see the producer's mustache moving.

He began to play. The green field. The soldiers. The sun in the silver sky.

—TaTaTatitati TaTa Tatitati Ta Ta Ta Ta Tatitatita tititata.

Drumroll avenged! He knew the piece. The musical footprints laid themselves out before him, and all he had to do was let his fingers run, the phrasing guided by the steady burn of his *nutro*. So easy. The way he'd done hundreds of times before: at home for his trembling mother and in front of Faina Grigorievna, while she filed her nails in a little white cloud.

—TaTaTatitati TaTa Tatitati Ta Ta Ta Ta Tatitatita
tatatata . . .

The knees in identical navy-blue uniforms shoot up in
unison to the chests shining with medals. Despite the heavy
boots, the soldiers' step is sharp and exact. They march in
tight formation, yet they never (unlike Dima's fingers) trip
each other. Would the soldiers march through the field with
medals on, though? They certainly weren't as vain as Genka,
who wanted everyone to know he was a hero even before he
knew what heroic things they should do. Dima didn't know
either. When he suggested they apprehend the older boys
who smoked and confiscate their cigarettes—thus avenging
those whose clothes, or worse, had been ruined by cigarette
burns—Genka rolled his eyes. Maybe Genka was afraid of the
upperclassmen. It had been Dima's idea to form the gang in
the first place and name it after their favorite movie. And just
because Genka was three months older and taller didn't
automatically make him the leader. Stop thinking about
Genka.

Dima's mind turned a blank page, his *nutro* sputtered.
Not again, not again, please.

"Cut, for God's sake!" the producer yelled. "Anna Glebovna!"

Anna Glebovna was already tottering toward Dima. The
big hand of the clock was now halfway to the seventh minute.
Only three minutes had passed. Already three minutes. He
could've been done ages ago.

The parents and teachers started to whisper. He turned

back to look. His mother sat hunched over, her eyes darting about the floor as if in search of an escape. She was like that at the school cafeteria, too. A mouse. Sometimes it took several moments for Dima to recognize her among her fellow white-coated lunch servers. And when he spotted her, he would quickly nod, but he wouldn't come over.

She had stayed up late last night starching his performance outfit. His pants felt like iron. The collar of his shirt cut into his neck. If it weren't for the yellow bow, he could pretend he was wearing a knight's armor. Though the Uncatchable Avengers wouldn't be so uncatchable in armor. Stop, he yelled to himself inside his head. Stop, stop, stop. He wished he could put knight's armor on his thoughts. Poor Mama.

Faina Grigorievna sat stone-faced. She was the best teacher in the Magadan region, no, the best in the whole northeast, and everybody was afraid of her, even the other piano teachers. Non–piano teachers didn't need to be afraid because, for her, other instruments didn't even count as real instruments. She would kick him out now, Dima thought. His mother would cry, but he would sleep better at night. Eventually. His mother cried a lot, anyway.

Anna Glebovna banged on the piano's raised lid, a black lacquered sail. Dima wished more than anything in the world to sail out of this tomb and into the bright spring day.

"Ushakov, gather your brains, would you? If I was your teacher . . ." Anna Glebovna looked in the direction of the audience. "Well, our esteemed Faina Grigorievna is here, of course. Don't embarrass her, Ushakov. She hasn't gotten that many of you left to pin her hopes on," she said, her voice saccharine.

A hack, a hack.

He'd never had a problem with the march before. He'd practiced so hard he could sometimes hear the soldiers marching along his teeth and up his spinal cord, and through his ear canals. He could play the piece with his eyes closed or in the dark, as he'd done many times during electricity outages. He could play it from the middle. He could tap it. He could hum it, though he never did. Singing was for girls, not Avengers. He could play the right hand's part with the left hand, and the left with the right.

Now he only had to play the march once.

"Silence in the studio!"

Anna Glebovna scuttled back to her chair. He'd show her.

"Cameras rolling. Action!"

Mind, mind, hands, mind. Dima felt Faina Grigorievna's stare. He counted down from ten, breathing shallow breaths so the iron grip of his collar wouldn't cut into his throat. These keys were so flawlessly white and shiny, unlike the keys on their home piano, which his mother had rescued from the arts college dorm. Some of those keys were chipped. At the far right of the high register several cigarette burns gaped, like craters from tiny hand grenades. Piano was always a battlefield—between fingers and tempo, pedal and sharps and flats, chords and staccato, fifth fingers and forte, first fingers and pianissimo, scales and laziness, *nutro* and Genka. And this was before Faina Grigorievna got involved.

The dumb policeman clock showed 12:09. At 12:10, Dima could be done. Then, he would think about what to do heroism-wise; maybe he could even get something accomplished while Genka was still at school.

Ready and . . . the field, the sun, the shiny knees. Or the medals. Shiny medals. High knees. He transferred the domes of his hands onto the keys.

—TaTaTatitati TaTa Tatitati Ta Ta Ta Ta Tatitatita tititata. (Whew.)

With the first mine avoided, Dima's hands marched on toward freedom.

—TaTaTatitati TaTa Tatitati Ta Ta Ta Ta Tatitatita tititata.

Now the regiment comes upon a dark forest at the edge of the field.

—TuTuTurururu TuTu Turururu Tu Tu Tu Tu Tututu-tutu roo roo roo.

The soldiers are stumbling over the crags and roots of the tall black trees. This was a stupid story. The only reason for the soldiers to march into a dark forest would be to fight a forest monster. He should've made up his own story instead of listening to Faina Grigorievna.

—TuTuTurururu . . .

Dima's mind drifted back to all the things that had happened in Magadan in the past year. The teachers' hunger strike. The gas explosion at the hospital. The three bank robberies. Of course: the mayor's murder! The killer was never caught. And never would be, his mother insisted sadly. A whole marching army would scare the murderer further into hiding. The task required stealth, surprise. The huntsman would have to act incognito, someone the culprit could never expect. Someone like the Uncatchable Avengers! How did he and Genka not think of this earlier? They would be in the newspaper, on the evening news.

Dima felt his *nutro* overheating, spewing steam. This venture will require sleuthing, breaking into government offices in the middle of the night, stealing documents, reexamining evidence, and reinterviewing eyewitnesses. The shots were fired in the middle of the day, on the steps of the municipal building. The murderer had been hiding in plain sight. Too bad the teachers' strike was over. He felt bad for the teachers, sure, but free from school, the Avengers would have had so much more time to investigate their first big case. Plus, all the parents and the whole town would have been distracted. Dima remembered the poor teachers, lying on the foldout cots under heavy blankets day and night, haunting the school hallways like ghosts. He had seen his favorite teacher, Rita Pavlovna, faint in the hallway when he came to visit with his classmates, and all he could think of were the funny names of flower parts she'd taught in Nature Studies just a week prior. Pistil, stigma, ovary. Stamen, sepal, peduncle. Now he felt ashamed. Some hero he was, wanting to be on TV, and wishing such terrible things on the teachers.

Then it dawned on him: he was on TV. Now. And his legs were itching like crazy.

He stopped again. The audience began to buzz even before the producer yelled "Cut!"

The cameraman closest to Dima stood up. "Enough time to get a smoke?" he said.

Again Anna Glebovna was upon Dima, her heaving neck covered with red spots.

"Maybe someone else could play first and then we let Ushakov try again?" one of the parents piped up.

"My students can go first," said another teacher from the arts college. Dima knew Faina Grigorievna didn't like him either. He, too, was a hack. "They have their pieces drilled down to the last note. We've got all the dolls, 'Sick Doll,' 'Doll's Funeral,' and 'New Doll.' We'll be quick."

Full-voiced conversations sprang up throughout the audience. The producer milled in front of the lights panel, looking at his clipboard.

"My daughter practiced very hard," cried out one of the mothers. "We have a doctor's appointment later in the afternoon. We can't be here all day."

Tik tik tik tik tik . . . 12:12 already. The plate-faced clock smirked at Dima with its unnatural brow.

"Silence! Silence in the studio," the producer said. "Maybe we should call his mother? Or his teacher? Where are they?"

"Futile," Anna Glebovna said and looked at Dima as if she were about to bite his head off.

He imagined his mother being dragged away from her chair and onto the stage, under the projector lights. He had never seen her speak in public; he'd never seen her do anything in public. Poor, poor Mama.

Something salty began to pop in his nose. He wasn't going to cry now, was he? His stomach gurgled. His mother had cooked him a special Tchaikovsky Festival breakfast this morning. They didn't eat eggs often, and he couldn't remember the last time they'd had meat. For months now his mother was paid in barter with cafeteria food, which—he had to admit—tasted considerably better at home. But this morning she had conjured a warrior's meal. Two sausages were the sturdy cannons, pink-rusted from their heroic participation in the Napoleonic Wars, also the Great Patriotic War, and the American Revolution. The peas were the cannonballs. If Dima asked for the whole jar, he would get at least half—there was no such thing as too much ammunition. The two eggs, sunny-side up, were enemies, which, once pierced by the five-pronged lance, spilled their blood all over the battlefield, showing everyone that no enemy blood would be spared in the fight for . . . against the fascists. Yes, the fascists! Their blood was yellow like poison. Tadadadadadadada pshaw, tatatadadadadadada pshaw poohhweeea!

"We should call someone," the producer said. "Ushakov! Ushakov? Somebody do something."

Stop, stop, stop! Dima pleaded with himself. He stuck his head into his hands. Whose idea was piano anyway? His mother's, who else's. And what for? Nothing heroic came of it, and everyone only suffered. When Dima struggled, squished flat under Faina Grigorievna's teaching, his mother would get a worry flu. When he did well, he would sometimes notice a blink of suspicion and fear in her eyes. Once, he caught her sitting at the piano at home, with her elbows on the keyboard cover, her eyes closed. She sat like that for a while. He was going to ask her whether everything was all right, but the silence in the room was like the silence after the orchestra conductor had raised his baton. Thick with the future, or the past. Uninterruptible. So he closed the door and tiptoed to the kitchen.

It was too late now to uncoil the chains of fate. Dima was handcuffed to the piano, sinking down down down, through the floors of the studio and into the dark catacombs under the city, where the old Kolyma gold was buried.

Eureka! The Uncatchable Avengers will find the legendary treasure guarded by the ghosts of the first prospector, Bilibin, and the ten helpers he killed to keep the gold all to himself. Genka can't disagree with a plan like this; he can even keep some of the gold. The rest—chests upon chests of it—they will distribute equally among the people of the town. His mother will be happy. She will finally buy a new winter coat and beef to make her famous "snowstorm stew." He will give some gold to Faina Grigorievna, too, so she could visit her family in Germany. The Avengers will give some of the gold to the school so the teachers never have to go hungry again. Well, only if they wanted to. He felt warmth spreading from his *nutro* to the rest of his body. His ears rang with distant music. Cymbals and timpani. He will hire private detectives from Moscow or London (like Sherlock Holmes!) to find the mayor's killer. A hundred buzzing violins and violas were circling in on him like a swarm of bees. He will buy mountains of coal. He will melt the city so that spring and summer would come early and stay. Or not stay: he loved playing hockey with Genka in the winter, too. He began to rock, like he'd seen the pianists do at the concerts on TV, their hands springing about in gymnastic contortions. He'd been embarrassed for them before.

Without a doubt, his inability to play his piece through was more than a problem of concentration. Under the bright projector lights and the stares of the audience and the camera, the soldiers marching through the field were amplified to the size of the world. It clogged his still-young *nutro*. To play the simple march, he had to forget all about the Uncatchable Avengers, the murdered mayor, the hungry teachers, the Kolyma gold, and his poor mama. Or play another piece—a virtuoso concerto with full symphonic orchestra. He could already hear the way such fortes and such pianos could sound, as if the instrument were made not of wood and metal but of something alive and breathing. He wasn't good enough of a pianist yet.

"This is your last chance," Anna Glebovna growled. Some of the parents were still talking. The children, however, were quiet. They knew that no matter how much they'd practiced, Dima's fate could befall them all.

"You are embarrassing Magadan's entire musical community, Ushakov," she continued. "Your so-called gifted program as well as my music school. This is unacceptable. Any fool with half a mind can play this march. Don't play it well. Just play to the end, for God's sake. I don't know how else to tell you."

"Are we ready?" the producer said. He had taken off his corduroy jacket. His face was red, his mustache twitchy. "Last take, then we're moving on to the next participant. Audience, return your chairs to their original places and be ready for the camera. Pleasant faces, content faces. Art is the beauty of life, et cetera. Crew, stand by."

He walked toward the monitors in the back, tugging on the collar of his turtleneck. "Silence in the studio!"

The microphone lowered above Dima's head like a bomb on a string. The light panel seemed to have lit up even brighter. Suddenly, he felt a heavy presence behind him. Sandalwood perfume. Faina Grigorievna. He turned around to face her. Her green eyes were unreadable, like windows in an ancient abandoned house.

She bent toward his ear. At the same time that she said "Play," Dima felt a sharp pain on the top of his left thigh. He looked at his lap: there was a small tear in the fabric of his pants. The spot around it was growing wet with something sticky. Blood. He looked up at Faina Grigorievna, but she was already gone.

"Silence in the studio!" the producer yelled again. He hadn't noticed anything. Nobody had noticed that he'd been wounded. "Cameras rolling. And action!"

Dima began to play the march. His heart thumped in the gash.

—TaTaTatitati TaTa Tatitati Ta Ta Ta Ta Tatitatita tititata.

The soldiers marched and marched. He felt the pain bury deeper into his leg, spread to the rest of his thigh, then his calf and foot.

—TaTaTatitati TaTa Tatitati Ta Ta Ta Ta Tatitatita tititata.

He picked up and kicked out his fingers, pushing forward. He was losing blood. He had to finish before it began to drip on the cloverleaf floor.

—TuTuTurururu TuTu Turururu Tu Tu Tu Tu Tutututu Tu BAbaBA.

His hands marched on across the black-and-white desert, tired and weary, bleeding. He wanted to crawl to safety, key by key.

—TaTaTatitati TaTa Tatitati Ta Ta Ta Ta Tatitatita tititata.

—TaTaTatitati TaTa Tatitati Ta Ta Ta Ta Ta-tita-TITA.

Applause . . .

He was done.

"And cut!" the producer hollered from his corner. "Cut, oh saintly father, Lenin and Cheburashka!"

The clock read 12:14.

Dima stood up and walked to his seat in the first row. The applause died down. Did he do well? He was afraid to look at his mother or Faina Grigorievna. He pulled on the fabric of his pants. It hurt. The material had stuck to the cut. He had forgotten to bow.

"Next up is my Rita Larina and after her—Sonya Koval-chuk. Gather your brains while you have a chance, Sonya and all the rest of you, so we aren't here till evening," Anna Glebovna said.

Sonya was another one of Faina Grigorievna's surviving students, and she was good.

"Silence in the studio," the producer said. "One second, one second. Ushakov, be so kind and leave. We've had enough of you for today."

Dima looked at the producer's red face. He almost pitied this simple man, with his simple life. Sonya, who sat next to Dima, grimaced sympathetically and offered him a handkerchief.

He didn't take it. He bolted from the studio, overturning

his chair, and ran down the hallway. His mother caught up with him by the exit.

"Dimochka, your coat." An unsteady smile swung across her face like an out-of-control dancer, bumping into her nose and ears.

They were outside now. Dima squinted at the fuzzy air and the pink sun. He wiped his flooding nose. Pink and yellow dilapidated buildings. Gray and white peeling *khrushchyovkas*. Everything was bathed in touchable light.

"You played so well, Dimochka," his mother said and rubbed her eyes.

"Did you see that she stabbed me? She stabbed me with her nail file or maybe a knife!" His voice came out high and squeaky.

"Faina Grigorievna?" His mother was trying to get him to put on his coat.

Dima pushed her and took off. It was snowing, snowing in May! He ran half-mad, half-happy, delirious. The snow smelled like freshly cut cucumbers, like summer at Grandpa's. At once he remembered that more than anything in the world he wanted a bike, one that had a tire-patching kit with the special glue. He bumped into passersby on the streets and shoved those who didn't get out of his way. He overturned a trash can with glee, ran across the intersection in front of the honking traffic. If he had a bike, he would fly on it through Grandpa's village in a cloud of dust.

He was running to burn last year's yellow grass in the courtyard, before the snow and Genka got to it. He'd get the matches the Uncatchable Avengers had hidden at their secret headquarters the other day. He kicked a stone toward a stray dog. The dog barked and chased after him. As he ran, he thought of the inquisitive cows at the village and the uppity goats, the earthy carrots, the cold river with tickly blue fish, and the gang of dirty-footed kids his age who smoked cigarettes and could catch a goose with their bare hands.

Rumba

1996

~

Roman Ivanovich Chepurin first noticed her dollish hips during rumba at the spring competition. On the four-to-one and twist. The triangle of her panties, hugged by a slitted lime skirt, flashed then disappeared. Two, three, four—and twist. Away from him.

He had been standing at the back of the stage with the other judges, squinting under the lights. Headache, his cranky mistress, fluffed pillows behind his left ear, spurred on by three minutes of the same Latin music played over and over as the new dance pairs took the stage. Identical save for the colors of the girls' dresses, they walked through their identical elementary routines. Roman Ivanovich was bored.

He didn't know many of the children. He trained the junior and senior groups, while his teaching assistants waded through the endlessly replenishing pool of dancers under twelve. After twenty years of experience he knew what to expect. Some, for the life of them, wouldn't flex their joints. They walked around like compasses, arms windmilling all over. Others twitched their shoulders as though trying to shake off a parrot, or wiggled their behinds like Papuans high on sun and coconut milk. Some couples stubbornly stepped between the beats.

Roman Ivanovich was long past the point where the efforts of these awkward, mostly talentless children endeared him. He and Nata, his wife and former dance partner, had coached only one pair to any kind of stardom. Lyuba and Pavlik now competed in quarterfinals in central Russia and Europe and returned to Magadan once a year to teach a master class at the Chepurin Ballroom Studio and Chess Club. Roman Ivanovich clutched his scoring clipboard to the sweat spot between his breasts and his belly, willing the competition to be over so he could go home and surrender his mind to the custody of the TV.

Then he saw her. He checked the number on her partner's back against the list. Thirty-four: Nemirovskaya, Anastasia. To him she instantly became Asik. The little ace.

She was mostly leg. Her thighs were as slender as her calves, shades darker than he'd ever seen in still-wintry Magadan May. The ripe, gypsy-brown of her had to be natural: he prohibited the use of tanning sprays in her age group, six to eleven. Her bare back snaked without dragging in the shoulders. She moved as though her pelvis were suspended from the ceiling by an elastic string, weightless and pliable. Despite careless execution, her raw talent was hot.

The music had stopped and he hadn't noticed. Applause. The other judges scribbled on the scoreboards, and Asik was already pulling her tree trunk of a partner toward the quivering side curtains, where Nata directed the sequin-and-tulled traffic. Away from him.

He decided on the spot to give Asik a good boy and make her a star by next winter's competition. She'll be his next Lyuba, he thought. No, she'll go further. She had the mischievous sparklet that Lyuba—all step counting and obsession—lacked.

❧

After the competition Roman Ivanovich established himself on a chair outside his office. The eternally cold studio smelled of sweat and hair spray. The girls exited the curtained changing room, their bright dresses hung over their arms in clear-plastic cocoons like discarded butterfly wings. The boys swept the floor with their tuxes. One by one they came up to say good-bye and wish him a good summer. Where was Asik?

The chess boys were cleaning up the postcompetition detritus and bringing the music equipment, lost shoes, tights, pieces of costume, and fake hair from the concert hall. Roman Ivanovich had one more chess match to officiate the following week, and then he would be done for the school year. As in summers past, Nata would be preoccupied with their anemic vegetable patch on the outskirts of town and with redecorating the apartment, which no rearrangement of furniture would make bigger or—against the view of the gray *khrushchyovkas* from their window—more inspiring.

He noticed a plump woman in a faded fox-collared coat

trudging through the studio with a tall girl hooked in her elbow. They stopped by the black curtains of the changing room.

"How much longer? We're suffocating here," the woman yelled over the curtains. The girl looked with interest through the open doors of the office, where Nata was organizing a rainbow of rented dresses.

"Leave me alone," a high voice hollered back. Asik, dressed in jeans and a giant blue flannel shirt, ran out with her costumes—the lime one and a coral number with a balding feather boa for the standard set. She returned them to Nata and started bickering with the woman. Roman Ivanovich hurried up to them.

"Ah, and you must be Anastasia's mother and sister," he said and turned to Asik. "Do you go by Nastya?"

"Asya," Asik said. She looked frightened.

Up close she was snub-nosed and thin-lipped. Her eyes, big chocolate cherries. Her fake eyelashes had half come off, and strands of gelled black hair, released from her bun, stuck out around her head in question marks.

Asik's mother turned and regarded him. "And you are?"

"This is Roman Ivanovich. Chepurin. As in Chepurin Ballroom Studio and Chess Club?" Asik said.

"Hello," her sister said. Despite her long coat (vintage by necessity, clearly), he could tell she was well built. Her features were a watered-down version of Asik's: a straighter nose, smaller eyes with irises the green-brown of weak tea. Classic, honest. Yawny. She lacked her younger sister's playful slant, which sprang up now in Asik's eyes, now in the flick of her wrist.

"Congratulations on your daughter's success." He'd made sure Asik reached the finals. "She has the kind of talent I haven't seen here for the last ten years," Roman Ivanovich added, continuing his customary pitch. Only this time he meant it. "When she joins my junior group in the fall, she'll be eligible to have a personalized routine choreographed for her during private lessons. I'll partner her up with a capable boy. With much practice and private coaching, she's guaranteed to win first place here. Such talent. My wife will sew new costumes for her, order special fabric and rhinestones. Then take her to Moscow, the big races."

By this point in his pitch, Roman Ivanovich would usually see in the glimmering eyes of even the poorest parents the accounting machinery rebalancing the family budget to accommodate the incubation of their very own star. Asik's mother appraised him coldly, then looked at Asik, who was pumping up and down, her face a blur of runny makeup and thrill.

"We've had enough of this, Ivan Romanovich," the mother said. Her eyes were bloodshot.

"Roman Ivanovich!" Asik said.

"We hardly get by as it is. I'm raising two girls by myself."

So the mother was going to play that game. "I understand, of course. But dance is a very important part of a young girl's education. A real classical education. It's the Russian tradition. Everybody must learn to dance. Why don't you dance?" he asked Asik's sister.

"I took your adult beginner class last year," she said. "I liked it a lot, but I had to partner with another girl." She smiled shyly. Perhaps he could get her on his side.

"Inna's busy with something more useful. She's a piano student at the arts college," the mother said. Asik rolled her eyes.

"A talent like this must be nurtured," Roman Ivanovich addressed the sister. "We have a duty before the art—"

"Is there money involved, in Moscow?" the mother said. "If she could earn something—"

"At top places. Depending on the type of the competition. In the beginning it would be to cover the entry fees, costumes, plane tickets." He looked from one girl to the other. "If only I had such talented daughters. I'll even lower the tuition for Asya. Private lessons—half off. It's a unique opportunity."

"She's on the verge of failing several classes at school," the mother said. "Instead of shaking her half-naked ass around here like it's some Africa or Brazil, she should be locked up studying."

"Are you deaf?" Asik cried out in that wild, harsh falsetto young girls use in desperate moments. Her sister looked down. "He said I have a rare talent, too. It's not just your precious Inna."

Over the years, Roman Ivanovich had seen all strains of sibling rivalry. This one, he could already tell, was particularly toxic. The mother favored the older daughter. But Inna seemed too nice to exploit such emotional ammunition, thus withholding from Asik permission to fully throw herself into the rebellion she so craved.

Asik looked at him as if he were about to give away the last ticket to the Ark. He put his hand on her crown—her hair was coarse and sticky, like a cub's—and ever so slightly she buckled into the eave of his shoulder.

"I promise to study hard, I promise." Asik spoke only to him. "Honestly. Please take me."

"Fine, get her off my hands," the mother said. "One more bad mark at school, and she'll be too bruised to wear those skimpy dresses. Seriously, Roman Ivanovich, we can't pay."

"Deal," he said, matching her haggling stare. "She'll attend free of charge."

Eight minutes later they disappeared into the gates of summer. His headache had gone, too.

⁂

All summer Roman Ivanovich swung and turned his stocky but not yet hopeless physique around their small living room. Nata, rosy from working on the vegetable patch, sometimes joined him, testing the steps Asik would have to learn in the fall. Her blue eyes lit up with memories of a life well danced. She could still follow his lead effortlessly, although there was more flesh between them now. Her short, once-sporty figure reminded him of a hen's: ample bust and backside, drumstick legs. Those small feet that used to excite him.

He didn't ask for Nata's help with rumba, which he'd originally dreamed up for Lyuba and Pavlik but had never dared to stage. He feared the routine was too tantalizing for the Soviet standard. Besides, Nata was too heavy for all the lifts and dismounts.

"Are you sure she's ready for this?" Nata said one pale day, after Roman Ivanovich almost knocked a crystal vase off the shelf while practicing an imaginary lift. "Don't you think it would be more appropriate for a senior couple?"

She was right. "Asik can handle it," he said with irritation. Nata knew that her role at the studio ended at costumes and keeping the books.

"I'm glad someone's finally come along," she added. "You were beginning to waste away. And she has at least Lyuba's potential. At least. You're absolutely right about that."

※

Roman Ivanovich steadied himself against the mirror in his office. The first class with Asik in his junior group would begin in fifteen minutes. Time was a brilliant caricaturist, indeed. Over the years, his small gray eyes had become smaller. The bulb of his nose had ripened from overexposure to frost and vodka. His jowls drooped. His hair, once the wheat silk envy of even the girls, had deserted him clump by clump. He forced a smile: at least he still had his shallow dimples.

One of the chess boys barged into the office.

"How many times have I told you to knock before entering?" Roman Ivanovich yelled. Was this one Gleb?

"I just needed you to approve the player matchups." The boy pulled his thin neck into his shoulders. His trembling arm held out a piece of paper. Roman Ivanovich glanced over the sheet, made some marks, and handed it back.

"Tell everyone to be quiet at the tables."

The boy slinked out. Roman Ivanovich turned to the corner plastered with photographs of Lyuba and Pavlik in poses or holding up trophies. He made the sign of the cross, then tightened his belt and walked out into the studio.

The girls stood in clusters, twisting their feet on high silver heels. Some boys were observing the chess games. More loud voices came from the boys' changing room. Someone must've brought in the latest comic book or a Game Boy. What were those boys interested in? Certainly not the girls, not yet. The junior girls still belonged to him.

Asik sat on the windowsill, which Roman Ivanovich forbade, banging the expensive satin shoes he'd ordered for her from Moscow against the rusty radiator. Both her short bob and her outfit—a long-sleeved ballet shirt and jeans—violated the studio rules. He wondered whether the junior instructors had really forgotten to drill in the studio regulations.

He clapped three times, and the boys began appearing on the dance floor. Asik jumped down. She was thinner, darker, and at least two centimeters taller than in the spring. The chess section turned to watch.

"Girls, a dress code reminder. Tight skirts no longer than halfway down the thigh," Roman Ivanovich began in an impartial tone. "Black tights, no leg warmers. I need to see the lines of your body clearly. Hair no shorter than one-third down the upper arm, in a bun or a ponytail. If your other instructors didn't require it before, fine. These are the rules for the junior group," he added for Asik's benefit but didn't look her way.

"I'm sure I don't have to remind you about the no-dating policy. No boyfriends or girlfriends, no little love associations. Not the dancers, not the chess players. You will be expelled. Now, I'll be making some partner switches based on May's results. This is not up for discussion, so please spare me the whining. Igor," he addressed Asik's partner, "you will dance with Olesya." He was tall enough now.

The ballroom mothers (Olesya's mother the most involved among them) lobbied fiercely for the few talented tall boys. They invited the boys' mothers for dinner, bought the boys dance shoes and gifts, and bribed the poorer families. Roman Ivanovich, however, still had the final—often paid for—word in the matchmaking process.

"And Sasha will dance with Asya."

The room gasped. The boys moved obediently, like chess pieces. Asik looked up at handsome Sasha, then looked down, chewing a smile. Sasha's main merits were his height, a solid sense of coordination, and a tolerance for being bossed around, which Olesya had exploited with impressive results at the competitions.

"But Roman Ivanovich," Olesya began, her voice tripping over swells of injustice, "it's—"

"No discussions. Now, everyone, let's start with the basic samba walk to remind your lazy butts what it means to dance. And no sitting on the windowsills!"

The children formed a circle. Roman Ivanovich noticed Olesya creeping toward the exit.

"That'll have to wait till the bathroom break," he said. He couldn't stand tears.

He walked to the CD player, nailing his heels into the parquet, and turned on the music. And they were rusty, his little pupils, oh, they were rusty after the summer rains.

Sonya, who had once been his pet, seemed to have completely forgotten how to use her feet. Unable to delay it any longer, he found Asik in the bouncing roundelay. Her hips were indescribable—two distinct entities, each containing a delayed-action spring. When the right hip moved, the left hip lingered, teasing, then snapped to catch up. She walked swinging and swaying. For several counts she looked straight ahead, and then she looked at him and smiled.

🙥

As the fall term progressed, Roman Ivanovich submerged himself in the Asik project. For a month, she was a dream. She personalized every detail he pointed out on the competition tapes—syncopated click of the knee, degree tilt of the hips, pecking nod versus ladling bow. Even her ribbon lips danced, shaping words the true meaning of which she couldn't possibly understand, in languages she couldn't know.

Although she was a perfect china doll in the waltzes, foxtrots, and quicksteps, her hips were too impatient for the standard set. Latin dances were her forte. She danced paso doble like the daughter of Bizet's proud Carmen, little Carmenochka. A scarlet costume flower she insisted on wearing at practices gleamed against her bluish-black hair. Her samba was pure and easy, as though she'd shaken her backside in Rio de Janeiro's carnivals since she could walk. Her rumba was transfused with imaginary love and heartbreak. Whenever Nata passed through the studio, she stopped to watch Asik. Sometimes Olesya would run up to Nata and plead to be switched back to her old partner, but Nata only nodded and glanced toward Roman Ivanovich with blind faith.

For a month, he was happy. Everything was justified: the lost income, the unpleasant phone conversations with Olesya's mother, the gossip he knew was being chewed like cud behind the changing-room curtains and at the dinner tables.

Then, at the beginning of November, Asik became unpredictable and moody, an ungrateful little caterpillar. Some days she switched herself off. Her hip springs creaked. She yelled at Sasha and threw around her sharp-heeled sandals, the satin of which was already filthy from improper care. Sasha endured her moods with a calm that baffled Roman Ivanovich.

He could tell she was making mistakes on purpose. His usual tactic was to roar and spank the applicable backsides. But with her, he held back. During private lessons, he coolly drew loops and turns with her hips, feeling her sharp, small bones slide under his fingers. At group practices, he first ignored her tantrums, then broke down and asked Sasha to step aside. With him, she quickly corrected her errors and danced so tastily one could bite one's fingers off.

Asik kept breaking studio rules. She'd come in late, walk through the studio in slush-caked boots, slack off during warm-ups, wear baggy sweaters, and go to the bathroom whenever she pleased. He'd had to assign a special chess boy to mop up the street slush after her. Some days he could almost see the other girls bristling in her presence.

More and more Asik was becoming just another rude girl

of twelve, with stooped shoulders and a messy ponytail, angry at the cold wind for chapping her lips and stripping her summer tan. He'd always considered that handling cranky girls was a part of his profession. But with her, he was stumped. To punish her was to admit he'd made a mistake.

⁂

"You should be careful with that Nemirovskaya girl, Roma," Nata said to him one evening at the end of November. With less than a month to go until the winter competition, she was buried under a mountain of fluorescent satin and tulle, sewing new dresses for the rich girls and tailoring rentals for the others. "I know she's not just another one of your dancey girls. But you're alienating everyone else, and they pay. We've got plenty of couples who work hard, and who may yet hatch when they move up."

Stupid, naive, comfortable Nata. The senior girls were lost to him. Those who stood a chance of scholarships to universities in Moscow or St. Petersburg studied maniacally. The ones stuck in Magadan worked their assets on the local potato oligarchs in hopes of securing a warm, well-fed life.

"I know what I'm doing, Nata."

Behind gold-rimmed sewing glasses, her blue eyes were moist and vulnerable. In ten years or less she could've been a grandmother, if they had had any children. He'd never liked the haircut she'd settled into years ago, which concealed the lovely line of her nape. Or maybe it wasn't lovely anymore. Maybe now it was loose and wattley like her neck.

Their relationship began just as their ballroom careers got serious, when they were partnered as teenagers. On the dance floor, it was crucial that he led and she followed. She seemed content to follow him outside the studio, too. He often told himself that they were one of those couples who understood each other implicitly. But, as time went on, he became afraid to ask whether she was happy. He, unlike her, applied his love selectively. It wasn't that he loved one thing about her and didn't quite love another. That was natural enough. Rather, he stopped loving her entirely when a hint of coarse independence manifested itself: when she questioned him, when she told him he was wrong. This unlove persisted until the episode lived itself out and sedimented in memory. Only then, like a harbor cleared of the night's fog, the qualities that made his life bearable, her comfortable qualities, became visible again, and he slid back into his way of appreciation. Because— who was he kidding—it was not love, it was not love.

"Do as you know, Roma," Nata said and went back to her sewing.

He began to pace around the living room.

"We need eggs," she said. And within minutes he was out the door, embarrassed and thankful for her knowledge of him.

On his way back from the grocery store he lingered in a small park with a worn-out bust of Berzin, the first director of the Dalstroy trust and forced-labor camps in Kolyma. Naked trees stuck out of the tall banks of hardened snow. Theatrically-fat snowflakes streamed from the black sky. It was quiet. The cold air smelled of burning garbage—his childhood's scent of freedom and adventure, when he and his gang of ruffians would run through courtyards and set trash containers on fire to the grief of hungry seagulls. Before his mother bound his feet in dance shoes and shackled him to a girl.

He had a sudden craving for fried eggs with a particular Polish brand of cured ham, sold at a private shop in the town's center. It was his one evening off work; he figured he deserved a small indulgence.

He walked up Lenin Street. Its preholiday luminescence was even more radiant this year, more drunkenly optimistic. White lights lay tangled in trees. A shimmering canopy of pink garlands hung across the roadway. Up ahead, the dystrophic A of the TV tower, the Eiffel Tower's long-lost illegitimate child, shyly illumed its red and white stripes. The town clock, lit up in green, read half past eight. By now the junior group would be halfway through their weekly ballet class.

These classes weren't mandatory, but Roman Ivanovich had made it clear that no dancer should dream of correct posture without paying their dues at the barre. He considered the instructor, Gennady Samuilovich, too lenient, though, and preferred not to imagine the likely chaos of his practices.

The wind had picked up. He bought the Polish ham and walked, out of habit, to the Palace of ProfUnions. He crept around the back and hid in the shadow of a copse.

Through a single window Roman Ivanovich could see the ballet class. The vision, suspended in the darkness, seemed to him all the more brilliant and distant. Against his expectations, most of the junior group was at the barre by the mirrored wall, diligently knocking out *petits battements*. Gennady Samuilovich strode back and forth, whipping the air with his wrists. His white tights showcased the anatomy of his legs in excessive detail.

Pale Asik, dressed in a black leotard, with her hair up in a tidy bun, was merely adequate. Her butt kept sliding out of alignment, and she wobbled as her leg swung. But she was trying the hardest of them all. Roman Ivanovich was in shock. Who would she be now? Not his Carmenochka, not his fiery little gypsy. He watched her till the end of class. She was that hardworking average student he liked to praise to the parents. Effort over results. He breathed easier.

Gennady Samuilovich dismissed the class. Before wandering off, several girls—Olesya among them—trapped Asik in choreographed parentheses. They were saying something to her, something unpleasant, judging from Asik's pinched mouth. She crossed her arms and threw her weight to one hip. After they left, Asik was alone in the room. She turned to the mirror and performed an ironic half plié, half curtsey to her reflection. Then she put her elbows on the barre and worked her face through a series of smiles in different tonalities. A laughable sinner-seductress. Pierrot at a party. Piranha. She stomped—sloppily, neurotically—pitched forward and folded herself at the waist over the barre (against the rules! The barre wasn't made to sustain such weight), her leotarded backside the shape of a black heart. She closed her eyes and just hung there, like a piece of laundry forgotten in the courtyard.

Roman Ivanovich imagined the fragile basket of her hip bones rubbing painfully against the barre, all her little organs squished. He looked down. The snow was mildewing over a pile of cigarette butts and a green balloon scrap still attached to a string. She was nothing more than a body that danced.

⁂

"Remember, dancers," Roman Ivanovich said at the last group practice before the all-studio run-through. Less than a week remained before the winter competition. "Although in the junior group we call rumba the dance of friendship, in the professional world it's the dance of love."

Shivery giggles. The heat was off all winter, the town's clever way of rationing coal. Despite the chess boys' valiant efforts to bandage the windows, the studio was still an icebox.

"As I've told you all before," he continued, "rumba originated among the African slaves in Cuba. In the sugarcane fields, the barefooted slaves first stepped lightly, without bringing their full weight down, until they were sure there weren't any sharp pieces of cane on the ground. Once you make the commitment, make the step deliberate, like squashing a cockroach." More giggles. "Keep your shoulders and head still; the slaves had to carry heavy weights perfectly balanced on their heads. And try to show some passion. If not for each other, then at least for dancing. Controlled passion! Tension is in the promise."

He put on the music and sat back to watch his flock. The dancers grimaced and jerked their gawky bodies. Asik made a soap opera of her routine, complete with eyelash flapping, hair pulling, and clutching of poor Sasha's shirt. At every twist, she fished for Roman Ivanovich's eyes. It took the last of his willpower not to walk over and slap her.

When he came out of the office after the break, he saw that among the couples ready to resume practice Sasha stood alone.

"Where is she?" Roman Ivanovich yelled.

Sasha shrugged and looked toward the exit. As Roman Ivanovich crossed the dance floor, twenty-nine pairs of eyes followed him, vulturelike.

He walked into the hallway and knocked on the girls' bathroom door. No answer. He barged in. No one. The acrid smell of tiled walls, the floor toilets, and the flimsy wooden partitions was laced with cigarettes. The girls smoked, too? He felt betrayed. Three faucets dripped in echoey discord.

He found her in the boys' bathroom. Asik was pushing a scrawny chess boy against the dirty wall. Him? Couldn't she find someone better? It took a second to recall his name. Gleb. Released, he sprang away from her. Asik wiped her mouth with the back of her hand and looked defiantly at Roman Ivanovich. His face grew hot, as though he was the one who'd been caught.

The spin of his world slowed. He heard from the studio the *tak-chwoot-tak-chwoot* of the heels and suede soles of the ballroom shoes shuffling on the parquet, and the hollow thumps of the chess pieces landing on their felt feet.

"Please, don't kick me out," Gleb squeaked. "She made me do it."

"Get out of here," Roman Ivanovich said. The boy scuttled out.

Roman Ivanovich stared at a picture of a horse in a jacket and tie that someone had drawn with a black marker on the wall.

"I know it's against the rules," Asik said. She looked him straight in the eye, then hung her head. "But he loves me. I don't love him, but he loves me. What can you do in such a situation?" She sniffled.

The boy does. She was lying. Or not. What did either of them know about love? The claw-grip of anger loosened on his neck, and he felt a twinge of forgiveness and generosity toward the children, toward all of them.

"Please don't kick him out, Roman Ivanovich. It's not his fault." She was flat-chested, the front and elbows of her purple sweater covered with fuzz balls. The beauty marks on her gangly, pale thighs showed through her mesh tights. Little fishes caught in a net. "And please don't kick me out. I'll kill myself, I swear."

He came closer. She stood slumped, looking to the side, her eyes teary. She wiped them with the back of her hand, leaving black smears on her face. Makeup was against the rules, he thought wearily. He wanted to squat down and clutch her legs, to comfort her.

"So you won't? Roman—"

"Shhh." He looked at her without blinking until her image trembled like a reflection thrown upon water. He was struck by the whiteness of the razor-thin part in her sable hair. He couldn't resist drawing his finger down the length of the part, her forehead, the ski jump of her nose. Her skin was hot and smooth. Asik smiled brightly, as if she'd won a small prize.

He pulled some tissue out of his pocket and gave it to her, then walked out.

"Attention, dancers!" Roman Ivanovich roared back in the studio. The children started, like electrocuted mice, and quickly paired up. Asik took her place by Sasha. Her gaze hovered low.

"Aren't you going to kick her out?" Olesya said. They all looked at him expectantly. Gleb must've told.

"What did you say?"

"The rules. She broke all of them. Even the worst one." Olesya's tone was shaky but with a righteous core.

"I didn't want to," Gleb said. He stood in no-man's-land between the studio space and the chess tables. The chess boys pretended not to be interested in the scene.

"I've been thinking about this for a while, and I've made a decision. A while back," Roman Ivanovich said, inhaling and exhaling in the wrong places. "I am canceling the no-dating rule. You are not children anymore. Feelings should inform your dancing—as long as you're not distracted. It's not a secret that I met my wife in a class like this one. Love . . . Good, beautiful feelings deserve respect."

The children gaped.

"What? I can't anymore, like this. I quit," Olesya muttered and ran into the changing room. Asik threw her palms over her face and bent forward. Roman Ivanovich caught peripheral sight of himself in the mirror—a gray, blurry lump.

❧

At the final run-through on Friday Asik danced the way he had dreamt of since he'd first seen her on stage in the spring, in that little winking lime skirt. On Sunday she would be discovered, no longer his secret.

He stalled her after practice.

"You made me proud tonight," he said. "If you don't lose anything before Sunday, the first place is yours."

Asik smiled. Her teeth were small and crowded.

"Why would I lose anything?" she said. Her confidence annoyed him.

"It's important to keep moving, to keep dancing in your head tomorrow."

"I know." She lazily collected her face into a serious expression. "I'll dance in my head through my sister's piano banging and my mother yelling."

"The studio floor will be open."

"And packed with seniors and all those girls who hate me." She looked around to see who was passing by.

"Maybe it would benefit you and Sasha to have one last private lesson. You were wobbly on that dismount in rumba."

"Oh. For me it was okay."

"I have time tomorrow late evening. A lot to do before Sunday."

She shrugged. "Okay."

"Will your mother worry?"

"She doesn't care."

Asik's orange lip gloss failed to conceal how chapped her lips were. She could've been beautiful, if her nose was a bit smaller. "I'm sure that's not true."

"She'll care if I win the stupid competition." She caught herself. "I mean, I'm just nervous. We've worked so hard."

"Come at nine, then. Tell Sasha," Roman Ivanovich said, then went into his office and locked the door. He sat alone for a long time before the shrine to Lyuba and Pavlik.

※

The next day, as Roman Ivanovich took care of the final arrangements for Sunday's competition, a reel of Asik dancing looped in the back of his mind. He had visualized her routines so many times it seemed she'd already danced all of them flawlessly and won first place. He wondered what dresses she would wear. He hadn't asked Nata which costumes of the ones she'd been working on were Asik's, so as not to spoil the surprise. He'd spotted a black Latina dress with long sleeves and a low-cut back that he particularly liked.

When he had a free minute in his office, he took the new pair of dance sandals out of the box and inspected them. They were made of smooth gold leather, with rhinestones on the front strap. He'd ordered them for Asik especially for the competition, but they arrived too late for her to break them in. There was a danger of blisters now; plus, the heels were much higher than what she was used to. He turned the shoes over, contemplating whether to give them to her anyway:

they were so beautiful. He touched the virgin suede soles, still soft and creamy. The size was printed in gold on the shaft: 35. The same as Nata's, he realized. He still remembered the moment when that number had become significant to him. Minutes after they were paired up, Roman Ivanovich dared Nata to follow him through an improvised choreography. He appreciated her smooth movement, her lack of extra limbs. Girls usually grew at least one additional set of legs with the purpose of sticking them in the way of a new partner. He threw her into a dip, nearly folding her spine in two. She gasped but obeyed pliantly. Before his eyes lay the valley of her chest and the shadowy, aromatic hollow at the base of her neck, in which a silver wishbone pendant sparked. Farther down was the underside of her jaw with a faint trail of a vein, her blond ponytail juxtaposed against the black satin heel, the suede sole with the number 35, and her little toe sticking out from between the straps, the nail painted purple. He was impressed with the elegant way she'd responded to the dip. He pulled her up and appraised her with a smirk.

"*Nu*, you think you can handle me?" he said.

There was something of a young Catherine Deneuve about her, he thought.

"I almost peed myself," she said.

Nata always seemed older when they danced, more serious, and he was often surprised at the silly things she said after practices—when she would turn back into a girl.

৪৯

At nine o'clock Roman Ivanovich came out of the office. The chess boys had set up curtained partitions to accommodate the upcoming costume-changing frenzy of over a hundred dancers, aged six to twenty-one. The darkened studio resembled a military camp, still and quiet before battle. Asik and Sasha sat on the windowsill. Asik was dressed in all black.

They winged through the five standard dances with few mistakes. During the Viennese waltz, they shipwrecked one of the changing tents.

"Don't bend back as much, Asya, head at a forty-five-degree angle between his ear and the tip of his shoulder," he shouted over the music because he couldn't be silent. "Sasha, straighten your fingers, hand no lower than her shoulder blade."

The first two Latin dances—flawless. Then rumba. Roman Ivanovich had arranged for his favorite rumba song, "Loco," to be played during Asik and Sasha's turn on the stage. He turned it on now—though to the other dancers their competition songs would be a complete surprise—and sat down to watch.

At first Asik stands alone, dancing with just hips and arms. The man walks around her as she watches coyly. Sasha couldn't yet master the right seductive look. He circled her like a predator. On the first couplet of Loco, he takes her hand and gives her a light push, initiating the classic Hockey Stick figure. For several counts they dance Alemanas, Cucarachas, Chase Peek-a-Boos, Serpientes. She dances a little carelessly—a tease to his attention. Nothing more.

On the third Loco, she twists into another Hockey Stick, reaching out away from Sasha with her hand. She is ready to leave, but the man doesn't let go. He lowers her within a hair's breadth of the floor. She dares him to drop her. Then, she puts one foot on his high shoulder and he drags her across, her other foot slicing the parquet like a blade.

On the sixth Loco he spins her away from him, and she bends like a bow. This time she comes back to him herself. She holds his face as he dips her. Could she have changed her mind about wanting to leave? After a few counts he lifts her and turns with her. Then she rolls off his shoulder, down his side, and between his legs. He gives her a hard whirl and she swivels on her backside, away from him. On the floor, right leg pulled up, she arches back. She never surrenders.

"Stop, stop, stop," Roman Ivanovich said and turned off the music. "The dismount—Sasha, make sure you hold her with both hands when she's mid-hip, and then quickly switch the grip for the push-off. Otherwise you'll drop her."

"I've never dropped her," Sasha said.

"I am a little afraid every time, Sasha," Asik said. "To be honest." She flicked her weight from one hip to the other.

"Watch my hands," Roman Ivanovich said.

Sasha stepped aside.

Roman Ivanovich picked Asik up. She was heavier now than in the fall, when they'd blocked the choreography. And warmer, despite the chill of the studio. He wanted to coil her around his sore, tired neck. He rolled her down his side and pushed her from between his legs. She spun across the floor. One, two turns. It was so easy. Sasha could accomplish only one. They demonstrated the move several times.

"Your turn, Sasha," Roman Ivanovich said. He was sweating. There was something he didn't like about Sasha's complacent smile.

At eleven, Sasha's tall mustachioed father arrived. Both Roman Ivanovich and Sasha were exhausted. Asik remained on fire. She and Sasha ran through paso doble and jive. Sasha's father applauded after each take, puffed out with pride. So this was the source of Sasha's poise, Roman Ivanovich thought, his father. They adored each other.

"Anybody coming to get you?" Roman Ivanovich asked Asik after Sasha and his father had left.

"Nope. They're busy. Busy, busy, busy," Asik sang out.

He watched her small black figure slip into the changing room curtains. "I'll walk you home, Asya. Hurry up."

"If you want," she yelled back.

He walked to the office to get the new golden sandals, then remembered that he had decided not to give them to her yet. No need to distract her from what is important. He would give them to her tomorrow, as a present for winning first place.

Away from the glow of the town's center, the streets became emptier, angrier, underlined by violet ankle-snatching snow. The wind, with its erratic sense of rhythm, made it comically difficult to walk. Should he hold Asik's tiny mittened hand? She prattled on about some intrigue at her school.

The world felt like a small, black box.

"Make sure you get a good night's sleep," he said when they reached Asik's building.

"Roman Ivanovich, can you walk me up to my floor?

You're here already and it's dark and I'm scared of the drunken bums that hang around on the stairs. Please?"

He came in. The hallway stank of piss and God knows what else. Weak light leaked from the upper flights, illuminating the nail-carved and chalked graffiti on the walls like cave paintings. They climbed the stairs, holding on to the rails. Asik kept on and on about school. Sometimes he'd catch a word: home ec, burnt, two, so unfair. He tried to reel his mind back, for he could not help looking down on this strange scene—his bearish body, sweaty and cold, dressed in a sheepskin and a synthetic woolen cap, clambering after a little girl.

Asik turned to him abruptly on the fourth floor. "Are you very tired, Roman Ivanovich?"

She had a few steps on him, her wan face level with his. He was no longer tired, though he wanted to be.

"Yes. You?"

She took off her gray rabbit hat, and a scent of wet bread rose from her scalp.

"Not really. Actually, night is my favorite time. They finally stop nagging me."

"Isn't your sister home?"

"Inka? She's already in bed. She's a lark."

"I'm a lark, too."

"Good night, Roman Ivanovich," Asik said cheerfully. Neither of them moved. Then she threw her arms around the bulk of him. "You're the only person in the world who's on my side."

She pulled away. Her child's face was open. Tomorrow, she would pull back her hair, glue on the fake lashes, paint her lips red. She would put on the glittering dresses and go out into the floodlights. Her unbeautiful features already contained the drama of tomorrow's competition, all the disappointments of her future and its small moments of bliss. Already in them lived the Asik of ten years from now, and thirty, and fifty—long after Roman Ivanovich had gone.

He grabbed her folded forearms and covered her mouth with his. Asik's tongue fluttered like a butterfly under the net of his lips. He traced the uneven ridge of her small, cool teeth, flew up to the scratchy ribs of her palate, then swooped down and cajoled her tongue into submission.

Oh, his dancey girls! Their images flew before his eyes like a trick of cards: Anya with the dark curl tickling her ivory neck; the spattering of freckles on Oksana's neck and chest; Lara's chubby stockinged legs. Their cometlike flight over his gray planet had kept him alive.

Roman Ivanovich felt a gust of cold in his mouth and a dull tingling in his coated forearms. Asik was pinching him. Tears streamed down her blotchy cheeks. They should both be crying, mourning their innocence. Yet he was bellowingly happy. He couldn't understand how up to now he had managed to carry this feeling inside, like water in a sieve. He kissed her again, holding on with his lips, his teeth, his claws. Ah, how she tasted, of salt and metal.

Summer Medicine

1993

~

All my life I've been healthy, too healthy to ever go to a real hospital, naturally. But this summer break, I had finally hit on a perfect plan and I carried it out masterfully. First, while undergoing my annual physical at Baba Olya's Polyclinika in Syktyvkar, I told the gastroenterologist, Dr. Osip, that I had chronic epigastric pain. I had saved up raw mushrooms from a recent picking trip to the forest with Baba Olya and had been eating them every few days. I only had to throw up three times (with accompanying moans and shrieks) for Baba Olya to arrange an overnight diagnostic stay at the Big Hospital. She was in charge of me for the summer: I knew she'd take no chances with my health.

Compared to the two-storied wooden Polyclinika with lazy *polyclinikanese* cats warming themselves on the porch and lilac trees throwing sleepy shadows into the doctors' offices, the Big Hospital seemed like a whole different city. It was gleaming white and as enormous as an ocean liner—with columns, marble steps, and two wings extending into the green waves of the park. Patients in faded pajamas shuffled along the flower-lined alleys, holding on to walking sticks or the elbows of their visitors. Ambulances buzzed by, their sirens wailing. Doctors hurried in and out of doors like white cranes. All the chambers of my heart were aflutter. Helping out at the Polyclinika no longer satisfied my thirst for a bloodcurdling, bone-protruding emergency, but here I was sure to finally observe real medicine.

As Baba Olya and I walked down the hallway, I looked out for my summer friend Alina, whom I still hadn't seen this year. She had already been to the Big Hospital several times because of her migraines and didn't like it. But it was different for her—she was just a patient, while I was going to be the chief doctor, like Baba Olya.

Instead of with Alina, Baba Olya set me up in a room with two older girls named Liza and Natasha. Liza was small like me, with a sparse ponytail and long blunt bangs. Natasha was a chubby redhead. Likely prediabetic, I noted. They sat on their beds and watched me unpack the purple Beauty and the Beast backpack Papa had sent me from Alaska. I'd also brought a pink American sweatshirt, a box of Mr. Sketch fruit-smelling markers, and two books: *Robinson Crusoe* in Russian and *The Little Mermaid* picture book in English, which I was studying back home at the English Lyceum.

"Your grandma's so fat," Natasha said when Baba Olya had left. "Where does she work? The cake factory?"

Liza nodded, the corner of her lip twisted up.

Oh, yes. It was a sad and medically troubling truth. Baba Olya was so overweight, she could no longer work as a dentist and now dedicated all her time to running the Polyclinika. That's why, when the time had come for my annual dental exam two weeks ago, instead of going to her, I was escorted straight into the chair of the new dentist. Dr. Pasha. He was very young, too young to already be a doctor. Also, he looked like the American actor Kevin Costner.

I liked showing off my "textbook teeth" at the dental wing, which was the loudest and most exciting place in the whole Polyclinika. (I loved the bed chairs, with drills and vacuums attached to cords like tentacles with claws. I loved the orchestra of drilling and buzzing, and the endless supply of snow-white cotton rolls in the tall glass jars.) This time, however, the exam was dreadful. First, the office was stuffed with howling children in various states of dental distress. I couldn't believe I'd been scheduled for the "Happy Teeth Day" again, as though I were still a child. I was already ten years old. And second, the young Dr. Pasha had found a cavity (on tooth number 29)—the first cavity in my life.

"She is chief doctor of Polyclinika Number Twenty-Five," I said to my roommates, wishing Baba Olya had worn her doctor's overcoat.

The girls giggled. "She doesn't look like a doctor. Too fat," Natasha said.

"Never heard of it," Liza said.

"It's by the Komsomolskaya bus station," I said. "And you don't have to *look* like a doctor."

"*Foo*. It's dumpy up there."

"It is not dumpy. They have good doctors," I said, then remembered with a shiver the way Dr. Pasha took off his special glasses, the ones with a miniature telescope attached to one lens (which I was dying to try on), and announced to the entire office: "What do you know, Sophia Anatolyevna! A dentist's granddaughter and with a cavity." And Baba Olya said, in her voice for men, "Here's your chance to prove yourself, Pavel Dmitrievich. One cavity—one chance."

"Then why are you here?" Liza said.

She had a point. While I was deciding on my answer, she pulled her knees up to her chest and started rocking side to side. "Do you throw up every month? Ooooh, I like that special time of the month when I go *bah*—"

Natasha jumped off her bed and ran at me with her mouth open. I covered my face with my hands. She returned to her bed, laughing.

"You throw up all the time?" I said. "I know how you feel."

"It's because she eats garbage." Natasha stuck her finger down her throat.

"Shut up," Liza yelled.

"Only stray dogs would eat the macaroni your mama cooks."

"What macaroni?" I said. If these were the kinds of roommates poor Alina had to cope with, I could understand why she wasn't the biggest fan of the Big Hospital. These girls would only aggravate her headache.

"Your fat grandma should ask Yeltsin," Natasha said.

I tried to stay focused. As a doctor I'd have to deal with hysterical patients often.

"Is the pain sharp, dull, cramp-like, knife-like, twisting, or piercing? And where did you first feel the pain?" I asked as calmly as I could. I'd read the diagnostics chapter in Baba Olya's old pathology textbook just the other week. "Oh, oh, and does vomiting alleviate the pain? Or, you know, vomiting . . . is just vomiting? Unpleasant."

Natasha looked at me like I was the crazy one. "Axe-like and saw-like," she said impassively. "Also knife-like."

"Oh, knife-like?!" I cried out. "That means gastritis! Or it could mean an ulcer. Or gallbladder stones!"

I had almost asked her whether she had blood in her stool when I realized I probably sounded too excited for her real illness. Like Dr. Pasha announcing my cavity.

It was painful to think back to the dental appointment, but I couldn't stop myself. I kept rewinding it in my head over and over. As Dr. Pasha had stuffed my mouth with cotton balls, I had tried to remember what I had for breakfast. *Chyort!* Oatmeal. I was about to clean my teeth with my finger when he stabbed my gum with a needle, a little unsympathetically.

"Lee-ghno-kaeen?" I had mumbled through the cotton balls. I knew of several types of dental anesthesia and wanted to know which one he planned to use.

Dr. Pasha chuckled. "Open wide!" It felt icky to have so much rubber in my mouth. Baba Olya said it was the new technique taught in medical schools, but the older doctors, including Baba Olya, couldn't feel the teeth properly in rubber gloves. They needed live contact. Dr. Pasha dressed differently, too: instead of the white coat and cap, he wore green scrubs, a white T-shirt, and a red bandana.

"You know what's unpleasant?" Natasha said. She eyed my backpack. "You. Where'd you get all those things anyway?"

"From my father. He lives in America," I said and immediately regretted it. I was not allowed to tell anyone about America. Or that I was from Magadan. People could think we were rich and rob us.

"And he left you in some dumpy Polyclinika Number Twenty-six."

"Twenty-five. When I finish—"

"Oh, sure—"

Our consultation was interrupted by Dr. Osip, who walked into the room with a young nurse.

"Hello, girls. Sonechka." He brushed Liza and Natasha with a quick acknowledgment and concentrated his warm, grandfatherly smile on me. "This is Nurse Larissa. She'll take care of you during your stay."

The girls stared at Nurse Larissa. Nurse Larissa stared into space. Her features were exotic: wide-spaced, almost Asian eyes, a beaklike nose, a small mouth. A horseshoe pendant hung between her clavicles. When Dr. Osip left, she gave me a cotton gown.

"I have to go to the bathroom," I said and ran out.

The gown was diaphanous, like dead skin peeling after a sunburn. How many truly sick children had worn it before me? I bunched up a piece of the fabric and pressed the knot to my chest, praying for the health of all the people on earth—especially Alina—and to become a good doctor. Then I yanked off my yellow sundress, folded it over the cracked sink, and changed into the gown.

Back in the room, Nurse Larissa lay on my bed, her pale legs dangling off the side, her face wedged into my pillow. I don't know why, but seeing her like this made me paranoid that all the young medics in town were friends, including Nurse Larissa and Dr. Pasha. I imagined them laughing together about my snot attack during the dental exam, and about my spying on Dr. Pasha after. Yes, I had watched him, a little, but for a totally normal reason.

He often brought branches of lilacs to the receptionists. Hiding behind the shelves of *medcartas,* I listened to them talk about how lucky Dr. Pasha's wife was, although, they said, she was "neither fish nor meat." I wasn't sure what that meant. Dr. Pasha often had lunch with the gynecologist, Anna Vasilievna. According to the receptionists' gossip, she had left her husband for a younger lover and had two illegitimate children with him before kicking him out. Tall, with a long, black ponytail and green eyes underlined with green, she stood out among the other women like an Amazon warrior.

Doctor Pasha left the Polyclinika at five fifteen every day and caught bus number 67.

I watched him because I was waiting for the right moment to show him that I did know a lot about medicine. Whenever he walked by the reception, I pulled out a *medcarta* at random and stared at the pages—they were stained with yellow rings and smelled of iodine—pretending to understand the doctors' jumbled notes. I walked underneath the dental office's windows on my way to house calls with Dr. Borisovna and always carried with me one of Dr. Vera's special sticks. I often helped her with eye exams by pointing at the letters on the chart. I am pretty sure he'd seen me at least once.

Nurse Larissa sat up and looked around. "Time to sail," she said wearily, and we left.

The ceilings were three times higher in the Big Hospital than in the Polyclinika, and it smelled of laundry detergent. Cartoon murals covered the hallway walls. Goldfish, woven from old IV tubes, hung from window frames, afternoon sunlight streaming through their translucent fins. We passed several rooms, where older children watched TV and younger children drew and played with toys. So far, I noted with disappointment, the Big Hospital seemed like playtime at a kindergarten.

"So, why did you decide to become a nurse and not a doctor?" I said.

Nurse Larissa seemed not to hear me; she was biting the nails on her right hand, then left hand, then right again. She stopped abruptly in front of an office door. "First station: cardiology."

While I lay on a cot, connected to the EKG machine, the cardiologist sat with Nurse Larissa and held her hands. They whispered, and again I became suspicious that they were discussing Dr. Pasha and me. Afterward, Nurse Larissa and I went to see the neurologist and the radiologist. All the doctors asked after Baba Olya, and no one showed serious concern about my stomach. Was swallowing a probe for gastric juice analysis on the schedule? It was unpleasant, I'd read, but essential for someone with my abdominal complaints.

I shivered in the hospital gown, regretting that I'd left my warm American sweatshirt back in the room. Nurse Larissa floated next to me in a daze. Several times she almost crashed into other doctors and children. When she tripped on the stairs, it occurred to me that I should've just broken my leg. At least then I would have been able to observe how they laid the cast instead of getting all these silly X-rays. Although, if the bones grew back crooked, like Papa's after his skiing accident, it would ruin my ballroom dancing. And I was just starting to get good.

There was no sign of Alina anywhere.

"So, what's wrong with you?" Nurse Larissa said as we entered yet another examination room. I couldn't diagnose her tone.

"That's what they're trying to find out."

I was about to start on the stomachache and the throwing up when she said, "I can tell it's nothing serious. Just a mild case of inanemia curiosa."

"What?" Iminoglycinuria? Anorexia nervosa? I'd never heard of that one.

"I said, you probably have a mild case of anemia. Happens with kids often enough," she said.

There it was, "with kids" again. When will people learn to tell the difference? "How do you know?" I said.

"It's in the eyes."

My stomach went cold.

"Doctors can tell," she said.

But she wasn't a doctor. Though, if she was right, could Baba Olya and Dr. Osip tell I'd been faking?

On the other hand, mind reading would be an awesome power to have as a doctor, if it was true. It could be true. It would be particularly useful for the kind of specialty I wanted to do—trauma surgery or emergency medicine. Something dangerous and heroic. Which wasn't my answer when Dr. Pasha had asked me after he was done with my teeth.

"A dentist," I had said, wiping my drooling mouth. I guess I was startled he asked me at all, after he had spent the whole exam staring at my snotty nose and smirking.

"I will be waiting for you, Sophia Anatolyevna. I have no doubt you'll make a fantastic dentist. With teeth like yours! We will work together at the Polyclinika, eh?"

"But I had a—"

"Ah, don't even, Pavel Dmitrievich," Baba Olya said. She'd been observing his work the entire time and possibly grading him. "Let me warn you, children grow up fast."

"Children grow up, yet you stay young, Olga Nestorovna," Dr. Pasha said and flashed her a smile. His teeth were as textbook as mine—or, as mine used to be.

"Okay, let's take your blood," Nurse Larissa said. "Sit down." She wasn't wearing rubber gloves.

She tied my upper arm with a rubber band, soaked a cotton ball in alcohol, and disinfected a spot on my anterior forearm. I closed my eyes and braced myself for the prick. After a short while, I heard sobbing and opened my eyes. The syringe was on the desk, its needle resting against a grimy red telephone.

For a long time I didn't know what to say, so I stared at her face. Nurse Larissa had an honest, ugly cry, not like in the movies where the actress's tears ran down expressive, curvy paths on the cheeks. The stay at the Big Hospital was turning into a real practicum. I searched her face for symptoms that would give me a clue to the root of her distress. Guttural wails broke so sharply out of her chest—as though someone were flicking her throat—I became nervous she would choke on her own sobs.

I found a roll of bandage in a cabinet and gave Nurse Larissa a length. She continued to cry. I took the hand of hers that was holding the bandage and brought it up to her face, covertly measuring her pulse. Her hand was hot.

"Are you sick?" I said. "Your heart rate is elevated. I think you're also running a fever."

Nurse Larissa looked at me through her tears as if I were an alien. "*Da,* they weren't kidding about you. I am fine, Sonya."

"You can tell me. I can keep confidentiality."

"You can, can you? Well, that's a relief," she said, I think sarcastically. She had stopped crying. "It's not about me."

"Did your boyfriend leave you?"

"No."

"Then what?"

She wiped her face with the bandage. "My friend died."

"Was she sick?" I said. I was acutely aware of the cardio-vascular dangers of grief. My other grandma, Baba Mila, had died of cancer of the bladder when I was eight. Also my cousin died, of ventricular septal defect. She was a year old. I was four, and I cried all day, though I barely remembered what the baby had looked like. I had only seen her once. I was in Magadan and they were in Ukraine, and even with all that distance between us I had felt the loud heart murmurs from my sadness. I would have had a heart attack if we were closer.

"She wasn't sick. She was a nurse here, too."

"A car accident?"

"A fire. In her apartment." Nurse Larissa fumbled with the phone's dial.

"Did she suffocate?"

We sat in silence. I noticed an ornate cuckoo clock on the wall. Somebody must've brought it from home, somebody who'd spent a lot of time in this office.

"Or burn alive?"

She gave me a hard look. "Yes, she burned alive."

"Honestly? That's terrible," I said. I wanted to show her real sympathy. To do it right, I first had to feel what she felt. But I couldn't. I didn't know anyone who had died in a fire.

"You're a bit weird, you know that, Sonya?"

"Why?"

"You have morbid interests," Nurse Larissa said more softly. "Ask too many questions."

"No, no, no. I want to be a doctor so I have to know everything. Are you part Mongolian?"

"You know the proverb 'He who knows too much, doesn't sleep well'?"

"Yes, I know, but I don't believe in it."

She chuckled. "Proverbs are not for believing. They just are." Her eyes were two small slits.

I took Nurse Larissa's hands, like the cardiologist had done, and whispered, "What happened?"

"Tatar."

"What?"

"I'm part Tatar, Sonya . . . My friend had this boyfriend, a criminal. Half a year ago she decided to leave him, after a fight." Nurse Larissa's voice became husky. "He and his gang set fire to her apartment and barricaded the door. Maybe she knew too much, or he was just angry."

"He killed her? But why?" I said.

"I told you why." She looked at the cuckoo clock and waited several seconds. "The neighbors were afraid to call the police. They could hear her screaming. Can you imagine?"

I tried imagining. I tried hard and just couldn't. The only thing I'd heard that might be close to a scream like that was in Michael Jackson's "Thriller." "I would've called the police," I said.

"What gets me the most is that it happened in this shitty nowhere town. This is not Moscow. Things like that happen there every day."

I patted Nurse Larissa's arm, though I didn't like her calling Baba Olya's Syktyvkar shitty. "I think you have post-traumatic stress disorder. People get it after war, too. You need to go to a sanatorium on the sea for a whole summer and you'll feel better. Do you have some *valerianka* to take for calmness?"

Again, Nurse Larissa narrowed her swollen Tatar eyes at me. Her nose was still red from crying. "Not a bad idea, Dr. Sonya." I felt uncontrollably excited when she called me that. She combed through the desk drawers and the supply cabinets. "Don't have it here." Then she found a metal cup, poured some ethyl alcohol in it, and added water from the sink in the corner.

"Never do this." She poured the mixture down her throat. Her face lemon-squished and so did mine. "Let's go. I have to report for my rounds."

"Where?"

"Infectious diseases."

"Oh." Wasn't I sick enough to get admitted there?

We made several wrong turns and detours before reaching my room. The Big Hospital was a real labyrinth, or maybe Nurse Larissa was now intoxicated. I held her hand just in case. Before letting her go, I asked whether she'd heard of a patient named Alina being treated at the hospital for migraines this summer, and Nurse Larissa said no, no one by that name.

The room was empty when I returned. I climbed into bed and opened *Robinson Crusoe*. How would *I* escape from a burning apartment? I could break the windows in Baba Olya's glassed-in balcony using one of the flowerpots, then tie the clotheslines together to make a ladder. I thought about Nurse Larissa's friend, about the flames and the screams. I imagined her pushing against the door so hard she broke her nails, but my tears were still not coming.

The girls came back before dinner. Natasha pulled out a box of Bird's Milk candies from under her bed and offered some to me. Only up close did I notice how dull and yellow her sclera was, like eggplant flesh.

"I'm not supposed to eat candy because of my stomach," I said. I liked Bird's Milk, but I had to maintain my cover.

"*Cho,* mad at us or something?" Liza said.

"No."

"Forget about it already. We were kidding before, right?" Natasha said.

"Yeah. You're too young to get the joke."

"At least I don't pretend to throw up," I lied—in the name of medicine.

"Come to the cafeteria with us. Or are you gonna eat your stinky markers?"

I tried to concentrate on my book; the letters trembled on the page. "My grandma's bringing me a homemade dinner. She has a car with a driver, and her friends at the Ministry of Health give her smoked sturgeon and black caviar for free. She has eleven Lenin honorary awards, and I'm moving to America in the fall to live with my father."

As soon as those words escaped my mouth, I heard Baba Olya's reproachful voice in my head: a doctor must walk a kilometer in her patient's shoes.

"Hope you choke on your caviar and the little fishes hatch in your stomach and eat you from inside out."

They banged the door hard when they left.

I put on my sweatshirt, which hadn't been washed yet, and inhaled the bright, clean smell of America. I hadn't noticed earlier how hideous the sickroom was—sinusitis-yellow walls, a constellation of brown spots splattered in the ceiling's far corner like bacterial growth in a petri dish. The paint on the heating pipe had peeled in so many places that the pipe looked like a wet cat's tail. Outside, the hospital park was sinking into darkness. Patients and nurses in white flashed ghost-like between the trees.

I had seen a ghost once, the ghost of Baba Mila. On the fortieth day after she died, when her soul finished visiting all the places she had loved on earth one last time, I saw her back in Magadan, standing behind our living room curtains. I wasn't scared. In her last months, when she didn't leave the bed, Deda Misha fed her soup and pureed apples, and gave her birch juice to drink. I liked birch juice, too, but I held back from drinking it for fear there wouldn't be enough left for Baba Mila. On some days, some very hot days, I couldn't resist. I didn't understand anything about medicine back then. The day I saw Baba Mila's ghost, I had whispered "I am sorry" and promised her I would become a doctor.

I turned on the night lamp on the shelf next to my bed, waited for a few minutes, and put my finger on the lightbulb. I closed my eyes and let it burn. One. Two. Three. Four. I wanted to scream. How long did it take Nurse Larissa's friend to feel her skin begin to peel off? How long did it take her to die?

Suddenly, I remembered what Natasha said about the markers. I pulled away my finger. The tip was red, and my first thought was: I will never play piano again. I could be free! But of course I couldn't, of course Mama would make me practice just the same. I opened the box of Mr. Sketch. Purple-Grape, Orange-Orange, and Blue-Blueberry were missing their caps. I looked under all three beds and every nightstand. The scent of Orange-Orange was already fading. Why, why did I bring the markers when I knew I'd be too busy with patients?

Soon Baba Olya brought me dinner—barley soup, hard-boiled eggs, and bread. Nothing new had happened at the Polyclinika, she reported. Thank God. She said everyone missed me and sent hellos. I wondered whether that included Dr. Pasha, whether he even knew that I was in the hospital.

"What are you having for dinner, Babushka?"

Baba Olya knew as well as I did that aside from her already rampant hypertension, her obesity could cause everything from diabetes to cancer.

"Chicken and rice, Sonechka," she said. I didn't believe her.

"Just without the skin, please." It was painful to watch her eat, even as she reminded me that she and her sisters had a hungry childhood because of the war, and it was immoral not to eat well when food was available and one could afford to.

After I ate, we went to the lounge to watch the evening installment of *Felicidade*.

"Is it true that one of the nurses here burned alive? Her boyfriend started the fire because he's a gangster?" I asked Baba Olya during a commercial break.

"Who told you this?"

Maybe the fire was a secret because the secret police were investigating the gangster ring. I didn't want to give away Nurse Larissa. "I don't remember. Is it true?"

The shadow from Baba Olya's painted lashes made her dark blue eyes look violet. I'd always wished my eyes were like hers. "Yes. It's such a pity. She was a beautiful girl."

"Why do you say this, Baba? What's the difference if she was beautiful or ugly? Are you saying she deserved it or didn't deserve it?"

"I'm not saying either way, Sonya." She held me tight against her warm side as though I were a fractured limb and she a splint. "No one deserves to die in a fire. But you, you should always be careful around people. Not everyone wishes you well for free. Most people are petty, unkind, jealous. Especially men. Choose well which men you trust. And better yet, don't trust any."

I hated when Baba Olya talked like that about men. Like they were carriers of some deadly virus. It made me feel bad for Papa and his papa, Deda Misha.

"By the way, how are you feeling?" Baba Olya said.

"Good."

"Stomach?"

"Oh." My stomach felt like a locked elevator with all of them inside—Natasha, Liza, Dr. Pasha, Nurse Larissa, and her dead friend—plummeting down through the earth. "Nauseous." If I thought about them enough, I could probably make myself sick. For real this time.

Later, when Baba Olya tucked me into bed, I noticed Liza and Natasha glaring at her crisp white doctor's coat. I felt safe in the proximity of her warm, powdered neck as she kissed me good night, proud to be her granddaughter, though so far I was nothing of interest myself. Not even to the doctors.

"Sweet dreams, girls," Baba Olya said and turned off the lights.

About a half hour after she left, Natasha and Liza began whispering in the dark. One of them turned on the lights. I kept my eyes closed. Somebody yanked my hair.

"Get up, stinky." Natasha was pulling me out of bed.

I scrambled out.

"Go stand by the wall," Liza commanded from her bed and wrapped the blanket tighter around herself.

"What happened?" I said. The wall was icy cold.

Natasha marched to my nightstand and took out the Mr. Sketch box. She examined the markers for a while, sniffing them like a babushka at a fish market. The night snuck in through the windowpane cracks and poked me with its chilly fingers. Natasha settled on Pink-Melon, Magenta-Raspberry, Yellow-Lemon, and Dark-Green-Apple.

She drew feverishly, virulently, shifting my gown around for better reach. Red contusions appeared on my arms and chest, pink scars veined my legs. My thighs and shoulders were covered with lemon liver spots. Dark green flecks, resembling *zelyonka*—the green iodine used to treat chicken pox—dotted my whole body. On my forehead she drew a raspberry medical cross.

"That's better." Natasha looked me over with satisfaction. "At least now you don't reek so much." She opened the window, threw out the caps, and turned off the lights.

"And remember, it'll hurt to lie down because of your rash and burns. So you better be standing there in the morning," one of them added.

And I stood. My sinuses were stuffed, my skin goose-bumped. I was a little hungry, too. Part of me wanted to cry, yet another part realized that, in a way, I'd gotten what I'd asked for: I was finally a true patient. I now deserved to be in the Big Hospital.

How late was it? Baba Olya would be reading a book in bed, her white fluffy cat, Kelly, purring next to her. I missed my bed, set up in the glassed-in balcony among the cucumber and tomato pots. I liked so many things about Baba Olya's apartment. The vanity dressing table in her bedroom with a multitude of little boxes in the drawers, each containing gold jewelry and treasures she'd collected on her travels. Also the medical instruments she used for everything. She raked the soil in the pots with curved dental picks, decorated cakes (which she shouldn't have been eating) by pushing the cream through a syringe without a needle, opened letters with a scalpel, and plucked her eyebrows with a pair of surgical pincers. The first thing I always did when I arrived for the summer was to comb the apartment for new medical tools in whatever novel use they had found. This year, her bedroom curtains were held back with towel clamps. I suddenly missed all of it.

What time was it in Alaska? I'd heard that in the summer the sun never set there, and moose roamed the streets. I imagined Papa lying in bed on a daylight night, unable to fall asleep and thinking of me. I thought of Mama, too, alone in rainy Magadan and without hot water, playing piano in the empty arts college.

I was about to climb back under the covers when a sharp moan came from Liza's bed. I held my breath. Another moan.

Liza thrashed on her side and curled into a ball. I waited. Then Natasha moaned.

I tiptoed to Liza's bed and bent to her: her breath smelled like spoiled peaches. Was she in pain or pretending? Then I saw a dark liquid spreading all over her sheets. I turned on the lights. The sheets were streaked with red and pink. Blood! I saw clumps of blood cells here and there, congregating in little pools.

"Are you okay?" I said. I tried to lift the sheet to look for a possible wound, but Liza was wrapped in a tight ball, her eyes shut, her knees clutched to her stomach. I could not move or unclasp her.

She cried out again, and I jumped back. Somewhere a door banged. Light footsteps tapped by our room. Maybe it was Nurse Larissa, or someone else who would know what to do.

I opened the door. A figure in white stood by the window at the end of the dark, empty hallway.

"Nurse Larissa," I yelled.

Without turning around, the figure disappeared through the side door. I ran barefoot on the cold floor. Bed creaks and coughs emanated from other sickrooms. The TV in the empty nurses' station reported the news in angry monotone.

Where were all the nurses, the doctors? The hospital seemed abandoned.

Another bang, this time from above. I darted through the side door and up the stairs to a deserted hallway with stacks of chairs lining the walls. No sign of Nurse Larissa. I ran back down. The door I'd come through moments ago was locked.

I hurried back up the stairs and farther down this particularly freezing hallway. There were no nurses' stations here, and the windows in the doors were painted over with white. This was very odd. I'd imagined the hospital would be bustling with activity even at night. Especially at night. I opened one of the doors. In the dark room I thought I saw high metal shelves with large plastic bags. And inside those bags something white—bodies?

I banged the door and took off. I ripped through empty hallways, up and down stairs and around corners, afraid to look back, half believing that rotting bodies were chasing after me. I ran ran ran. I rubbed my burned finger and ran faster. I had to save Liza before it was too late.

I burst through yet another door and found myself in a brightly lit, noisy reception area. A doctor and a nurse stood talking in the hallway. Somewhere down a concealed hallway a baby was crying. On one of the chairs by the open window sat Dr. Pasha, dressed in jeans and a blue plaid shirt. No red bandana.

I knew I had no history of sleep-onset hallucinations, yet I had to be dreaming.

Dr. Pasha was hunched over, his head in his hands. First, I thought he might be sleeping; then he began to tap his foot. I came up to him and touched his curly hair. It was much coarser than I'd imagined.

"Sonya?" He looked at me with irritation, but he didn't seem surprised to see me. I started to back away.

"Are those marker stains?" Amusement loosened his face.

"Pavel Dmitrievch, please come with me. A girl in my room is bleeding. At the other end of the hospital. There's nobody there. No doctors, no nurses. We have to call someone. She's having gastritis. Or ulcers." I thought for a moment, then added, "Or gallbladder stones."

"Cover yourself or you'll catch a cold. A real cold." He picked up his jacket from the next chair and threw it at me.

"We must run, please. There was blood on her sheets, lots and lots of blood!"

"That does sound serious, Sophia Anatolyevna." Dr. Pasha grabbed my arm and twisted it back and forth to get a better look at the red marker contusions. "What are you doing here anyway?"

"Oh, well, I'm here for some diagnostic tests, for my stomach, but Liza—"

"I know that part."

"What part?"

"Your grandma told us—your mushroom recipe was very original, I must say—but drawing the cross and the rash is overdoing it a bit, baby."

So everybody knew . . . And everybody had played along. I could never go back to the Polyclinika now. I wiped my eyes with the backs of my hands.

"The things we do to get attention. The stupid things I did as a boy, still do."

"Dr. Pasha, you don't understand," I said in a shaky voice. I wished for instant death or at least humiliation-induced coma. "You have to help me find someone for Liza. We don't have time to lose. She'll bleed to death!"

"I'm too busy to play your and your friends' idiot games."

"This is not a game!" I hollered and tried to pull him off the chair.

"Sonya, are you insane? Don't scream here. This is a maternity ward. My son was just born."

A son. Blood beat against my eardrums.

"Congratulations," I said.

"Well, a big thank-you."

What if he was right, I thought, and Liza was trying to fool me. Maybe it wasn't blood but tomato juice—something I would have probably used for blood. No, a good doctor couldn't think like that.

"Do you know about the get-up test?" Dr. Pasha said.

The what?

"I think so," I lied.

"A pregnant woman sits down on the floor and, depending on which arm she instinctively uses first to help herself up, that's how you know the gender of the baby," he said with a dead-serious expression. "Right arm—girl, left arm—boy."

"Really?" I hadn't spent much time in the gynecology office. Almost anything was possible in medicine.

"Really. The test is ninety percent accurate, as long as the pregnant woman doesn't eat any mushrooms beforehand."

"I didn't eat the mushrooms to—" I burst out sobbing. I let it all go. I fell on my knees in front of Dr. Pasha. "Pavel Dmitrievich, please help me find a doctor. Please. I am not lying, I am not pretending this time."

He snapped me on my forehead cross and smelled his fingers. "*Raspberry—berry, you beckoned us,*" he sang out in a surprisingly squeaky voice. "Promise me you'll never grow up, Sonya."

I got up from my knees and yanked Dr. Pasha's hand with all my might.

"What are you doing? I told you, I'm waiting for the baby." He looked terrified. And terrifying, too. I knew that he wouldn't help. I tried to free my hand, but now he wouldn't let go.

"There's your baby!" I pointed toward the double doors with my free hand. As he slackened his clammy grip, I ran out of the reception room. The darkness swallowed me back like a swamp.

Again I stumbled through empty hallways, up and down stairs, looking for somebody, anybody. I was so tired. The hospital was endless, sprouting and shedding new hallways and stairs. Maybe I was going psychotic. Maybe I had hallucinated them all—Natasha, Liza, and this Dr. Pasha. I wished I could talk to Alina; she knew all about hallucinations.

At last, I arrived in a hallway that wasn't so dark. I looked into one of the rooms: six patients with dark faces snored sonorously. They were alive—that was a good sign. I lay down on a cold faux-leather bench in the hallway and pulled Dr. Pasha's jacket over my head. I closed my eyes. It was all over now. My medical career was ruined. Liza was probably dead. Baba Olya had betrayed me. I wanted to be sick with something curable only in America, then Papa would have no choice but to take me with him right away, and everyone would be helpless and sorry. I lay there, in tears, not knowing which plague to wish upon myself. I scoured my body for pain—after all I had gone through today, it had to be somewhere . . . I couldn't be the same. Something was pressing against my stomach, I think. I think I was already sleeping.

Kruchina

1998

~

Five nights before her scheduled return flight from Fairbanks, Alaska, to Magadan, Masha stood by the door of her granddaughter's bedroom. She checked one more time to make sure no one was around and then she knocked.

"What?" Katya yelled in English. Masha knew that word well.

She came in and closed the door. The overheated room was half the size of Masha's entire apartment in Magadan. Katya, heartbreakingly scrawny in her blue parachutelike nightgown, was lying on her bed in a jumble of thick math books, crumpled pieces of paper, and candy wrappers. She raised her head and looked at Masha through the curtain of her sparse brown bangs, annoyed.

"Katen'ka, I need your help," Masha said. Katya stuck a

yellow pencil into her mouth and chewed. "Please, sing one song with me at the green card party. For your mama." Masha sat down on the side of the bed, and Katya's trash and books slid toward her.

"Baba, you're ruining everything," Katya yelled.

"Shhh." Masha picked up the candy wrappers and stuffed them into the pocket of the apron she wore over her flower-patterned housedress. "Please."

"I can't."

"Katya, please speak Russian. You know I don't understand." Masha could read the English alphabet and look up words in a dictionary, but when listening she couldn't catch much beyond "hello," "good-bye," "please," and "thank you." And "what."

"I hate singing. I'm only good at math." Katya took Masha's hot, plump hand and massaged it with her icicle fingers. It was in these private, transient moments that Katya shed the mask of American coolness, which she worked so hard to maintain in front of her stepsister, Brittny. She smiled archly. "Maybe if Brittny sang with us, too?"

"Katya, don't joke. She's *Americanka*, how can she sing with us? She doesn't speak Russian."

"I'm *Americanka*, too." Katya dropped Masha's hand and pulled out a lollipop from the pillowy recess. Masha could never understand why Americans had to have so many pillows on their beds and couches. Katya unwrapped the lollipop and looked impatiently at her opened math books.

"You're a different kind, Katya. You live in two worlds.

Imagine, each foot standing on a globe beach ball. Remember, like we had in Yalta?"

"I'm not five years old, Ba."

"One day, Katya, you'll realize that there is no bigger blessing in life than an opportunity to help someone, especially someone whose blood runs through your own veins."

"Gross," Katya said in English and rolled her eyes.

Masha looked at Katya's thin neck sticking out of the collar of her nightgown, the slingshot fork of her clavicle and ropy shoulder, the pollen sprinkling of freckles, like her mother's. "Do you love your mama?" she said.

Katya frowned and sat up. "Why?"

"If you love her and want to show gratitude for all she's done for you, sing with me."

Katya narrowed her dark eyes.

"It will make her happy," Masha said.

"She's fine already."

"Katen'ka, please. I would be embarrassed to sing by myself. You know I don't sing well. What if I paid you?"

A flicker of innocent superiority flashed in Katya's eyes. "Okay, Baba, okay, I'll sing with you. I don't know why we have to sing at all. People don't sing at American parties. But I'll try; we'll be embarrassed together."

"Everyone will be too drunk to notice," Masha said, and Katya threw back her head and laughed, the white lollipop stick bobbing in her throat. Masha lunged toward her and pulled out the candy.

"*Bozhe moi*, Katya, you'll choke!" She broke out in a sweat from even this small exertion. Her housedress had ridden up her stocky thighs, and her heart was pounding.

ও্ঠ

Masha had come to America for three weeks to visit her daughter, Sveta, for the first time. Sveta had married Brian two years earlier through a special agency and moved with now eleven-year-old Katya to Fairbanks, which in the winter turned out to be as frostbite-cold and snowy as their own Magadan.

The marriage had been Masha's idea. She had followed the lead of a retired colleague who had married off her divorced and just as hardworking and beautiful daughter (there were so many of them!) to an American, thus, as she'd put it, fulfilling her role as a mother. Masha, too, wanted to be a good mother.

"You must get in line for luck, Svetochka. How else?" she had said to her daughter. "Under the stationary stone water doesn't flow." Sveta's boyfriends after the divorce were all cheaters, alcoholics, men who disappeared for days, and the one who found it funny, when Sveta asked him something important, to reply "Yes, dear, you should buy yourself that little hat."

Sveta crossed her arms. Her cobalt eye shadow and frosted hair made her look older than thirty-seven.

"Give me one reason why you don't want to try." Masha felt the familiar strain of her heart muscle in the starting blocks before a race. She could see her daughter's success, while Sveta herself was still far from considering it.

"I am not a prostitute, for a start," Sveta said. Her lipstick had seeped into the groove of a small scar above her lip.

"No one's selling anyone. You'll try to find someone decent, who wants the same as you—a companion and to make a family," Masha said. "You can find a job at the hospital and actually get paid for it. I heard the doctors have a very good salary over there."

With A-student diligence, Masha studied the success stories in the pamphlets and translated with a dictionary the letters from potential suitors. They found that decent person in Brian, a high school history teacher—an employed nonalcoholic with no criminal record. What more could one ask for? After months of correspondence and a few linguistically trying phone conversations, Brian traveled to Magadan to propose and to explore nearby Gulag ruins. He was a Russian history buff.

"And you? How are you going to be here, all alone?" Sveta said, when she was almost convinced.

"You can send for me when you're a citizen, Svetochka. They have what is called 'reunification of the family.' You don't worry for now. I'll finally have time to read all of our World Literature series and organize those boxes of photographs," Masha had said, already feeling the pleasurable pain of a lucrative sacrifice.

❧

As Masha was acclimating to the cluttered, overheated house in Fairbanks, an inkling of unsettlement lodged into her, and the more she tried to tease it out, the deeper it burrowed, like a fractured splinter.

She observed Sveta's new family. There was Brittny—with the stylishly misspelled name (Masha was told)—Brian's fourteen-year-old daughter, who was so developed, blond, and luminescent in her health that it hurt Masha's eyes to look at her next to Katya. Her own granddaughter was still a closed bud of a girl. Her skin yellowish from a sickly early childhood, her hair mousy. Her cunning, olive-dark eyes were her liveliest feature—the sole inheritance from a father she didn't remember.

Yet Masha considered a motherless fate more tragic. She sympathized with Brittny, who had lost her mother to cancer at five, and tried to surround the girl with wordless care. In return Brittny, strawberry-lipped and breathless, looked at Masha with amused condescension. She stepped around her as though Masha were a stranger who had fallen on a busy sidewalk and spilled the embarrassing contents of her bag.

Then there was Brian. Though his belly had extended several centimeters forward and his graying hairline had retreated several centimeters back, he looked much the same as when Masha first met him: tall and solid, with bright blue eyes, like Brittny's, straw-colored brows and mustache, and ruddy dimpled cheeks. The perfect American. Masha quickly remembered his irritating habit of pulling on his nose when he spoke.

Sveta and Brian treated each other as though the other were a sick, sensitive child. Brian discouraged Sveta from doing any housekeeping, although Sveta cleaned houses part-time with Lizochka, the Russian wife of one of Brian's teacher friends. Several times Masha saw Brian turn off the faucet when Sveta was about to wash the dishes. He snuck up on her, a superhero in a tucked-in flannel shirt and sweatpants, when she was folding clothes in the laundry room. He tore anything weighing more than three kilos out of her hands. He allowed Sveta to cook Russian food only; the rest he made or brought home himself. He closed her textbooks—Sveta was studying to confirm her medical degree—walked her over to the squashy couch in the living room, and massaged her shoulders and feet.

Sveta played her part of damsel-in-domestic-distress with gusto. She shut her medical textbooks, sighing every time as if this was the relief she'd been secretly hoping for, only to continue her studies into the night, long after Brian had gone to sleep. In fact, she accomplished most of what was needed to run the household while he was at work or sleeping. She packed Russian-style sandwiches for lunch, with butter and kielbasa. She laundered, ironed, folded, and rolled things up. She cleaned. She even started making special low-sodium meals for Masha's high blood pressure, until Masha convinced her to stop fussing and took over the kitchen.

It was the spectacle of their selective, almost aggressive care that made Masha suspicious of its sincerity and, by extension, the sincerity of the whole marriage. Of course, it was preposterous to think of the situation in these terms. Sveta's marriage to Brian was never meant to be entirely sincere.

Yet, all the advantages of America now paled in comparison with the look in Sveta's eyes: half the time glazed, and the

other half tense and calculating. Nothing like the bored con-
tentedness Masha had hoped for.

One night in the second week of her stay, Masha had
made tea and sat Sveta down at the kitchen table. Brian was at
his favorite café, grading midterm papers.

"Svetochka, what is this circus you and Brian are putting
up? You can tell me what is happening. I'm your mother, I'll
understand everything."

Sveta looked betrayed, as though Masha were a teacher
who had intercepted a love note and read it to the class. Then
she smiled toothily—the American way—and said, "You
mean the dishes? Brian thinks a woman like me shouldn't
have to do housework."

Sveta had gained some weight since Masha last saw her.
Sveta's face had softened, and the wrinkles around her eyes
and mouth had filled out. She wore less makeup now, usually
just lip gloss, and let her golden brown hair grow long and
natural. Looking at her daughter, dressed in loose blue jeans
and a T-shirt, and with her hair in a ponytail, Masha had an
irksome sensation that she had been transported to the past,
to Sveta's medical school years, but now the role of Sveta was
played by an older, skillfully deceptive actress.

"I thought such men existed only in fairy tales," Masha
joked. "Besides, you work as a housecleaner—"

"That's different, Mama. I know what you're thinking: if
he's such a knight, why does he procrastinate over doing the
housework himself? He also could be more strict with making
the girls do their chores." Sveta rubbed her fingers. "Right
now is the time for the girls to concentrate on their education.

There will always be dirty dishes and smelly socks, whereas the young mind won't absorb knowledge like a sponge forever."

This seemed to Masha a Potemkin speech, prepared especially for her visit.

"If there is another car, why does he drive you to the store for tampons? You were a professional in Russia. You saved lives."

"He's trying to help the only way he knows how. I can save a lot more lives if I keep off the icy roads. Besides, I didn't save lives, you know that. With all the shortages at the hospital—no supplies, power outages—it was mostly the talking cure." Sveta giggled, but it felt mechanical. When she belittled her own achievements, she stripped away at the coating of pride that kept Masha going through the most difficult and lonely times of their separation.

"Everything is somehow not right," Masha said, staring at her daughter's fingers. They had retained their original childish shape, now even more pronounced because of Sveta's weight gain: plump bases tapering toward the tips, dimples on her knuckles. Masha wanted to shake her. "Do you want me to talk to him? I've been learning English. Maybe I can—"

"Mamochka, don't." Sveta folded her hands under her chin. "Everything is good. He's been very nice to us. He never even raises his voice. If you like to slide, you must like to pull the sled, as they say."

"He doesn't have the right to interfere with your studying. You didn't come here to die a housecleaner."

"He doesn't. I am lucky to stand a chance of translating my profession. Lizochka used to be a chemical engineer, but she can't work now the way she worked in the Union. It's all different here. If everything goes according to plan, we'll send Katya to a special boarding school for math and science. And if she does well, she might get a scholarship to one of the best colleges, like Harvard or Princeton. Scholarship means studying for free. Good education is very expensive here. From Magadan to Princeton, can you imagine?" Sveta's face finally brightened and relaxed.

Masha nodded and got up from the table. She tore off a paper towel, softened it in her hands, and blew her nose.

"*Nu,* if you're happy, I'm happy." She wondered how many times she would have to repeat it to herself to make both parts feel true.

"Come." Sveta took Masha's hand. "I want to show you something."

She led Masha to the master bedroom, on the second floor, next to Katya's bedroom. The room was hot and smelled of vanilla. Masha began to perspire. Sveta got out a key from the back of a desk drawer and unlocked the double doors of a tall oak cabinet.

"Brian's treasures," she said and opened the creaky door.

Books about the Soviet Union occupied the top shelves. Reproductions of campaign posters for five-year plans and movie playbills were pinned to the back of the middle section. Several more stood rolled up on the bottom. Plastic boxes with pins and military patches, commander watches, and several generations of Soviet and Russian money filled the middle shelves.

Next to a crowd of traditional *matryoshkas* and *matryosh-*

kas with faces of Russian politicians and American sports stars, Masha noticed a box from the porcelain tea set that she and Sveta had bought together in Magadan.

"*Docha,* why is our tea set locked up in this cabinet? You don't want to use it?"

"I thought it was too nice for every day. I'm saving it. Maybe to give Katya for her wedding."

"The future is an interesting thing. During the Soviet years we sacrificed for the future—"

"Mama, don't start on that."

Sveta squatted down and pulled out a cardboard box from the bottom of the cabinet.

"Fragile," she translated the word handwritten on the top. She lifted the cover to reveal a drab olive-colored backpack with a faint red cross etched on the flap.

Sveta sat down cross-legged on the floor, and Masha settled next to her, her knee joints cracking. She was still surprised at how quickly she'd gained weight after she was laid off from the Aviation Administration, despite the general hunger of the post-Soviet years; how fast she'd developed high blood pressure.

"One of the original first-aid bags made for the Red Army combat medics in World War Two. Some medicines and instruments are still inside," Sveta said.

"Great Patriotic War."

"Yes. Same war. This is Brian's favorite piece. Two hundred dollars for such a museum exhibit, can you believe it?"

Two hundred dollars. That was more than Masha's monthly pension.

Sveta opened the buckles and pulled out several packs of gauze bandages wrapped in brown paper, a tourniquet, a brown bottle of iodine with a dropper, and a small syringe, its needle still intact. She neatly laid out the contents on the floor. Everything looked brand-new. There wasn't a single spot on the gauze, nor a speck of rust on the glittering syringe stopper.

"Sometimes, when I'm alone, I look through these things over and over, I don't know why. The longer I am away from Russia, the more surreal it all seems. Most of all, my childhood. Everything else I don't mind forgetting."

Masha picked up a book about Stakhanovites and brought it up to her nose. It smelled of salt and rust, like the window heater in the library where she had studied for exams almost forty years ago.

"You can return anytime, if you've changed your mind. We'll make something up. We'll help each other," Masha said, looking up at the colorful army of grinning *matryoshkas.*

"That wouldn't help." Sveta laughed. "Nostalgia goes down better with vodka."

Masha waited for Sveta to tell her what *would* help. She considered raising the question of "family reunification." The term seemed absurdly grandiose and brought to mind exhausted soldiers in bloodstained fatigues rushing off the trains into the arms of their mothers, wives, and daughters. Masha yearned for a simpler kind of daily reunion: to cook a good breakfast for her girls in the morning, to bring Sveta tea with raspberry jam and a blanket when she studied, to braid Katya's wispy hair and sprinkle it with bright barrettes. To be privy to all their moods, good and bad.

It would take Sveta another three years to become a citizen, and only then would she be eligible to apply for the reunification. By then Masha would be truly old and sick, a burden. And what if Sveta failed to reestablish her medical career? Brian didn't seem to want Masha in the house any longer than necessary. He treated her with measured, ceremonial complaisance.

"Svetochka, remember how one winter when you were seven, you took off your boots outside when I wasn't looking and jumped barefoot in icy puddles? You wanted to catch a cold so that we could stay home together and watch figure skating."

Sveta smiled. She seemed relieved to change the topic.

"Instead you caught pneumonia, and we ended up at the hospital. Only one TV, in that horribly drafty common room, and of course we never watched it. Instead we read your favorite fairy tales and made up our own."

"I remember." Sveta picked up the syringe and rolled it between her fingers.

"You know, once, back in the early eighties, the gossip reached us at the Aviation Administration about a young engineer at the airport who had injected milk into his veins to trigger high fever. He wanted to stir up pity in the girl who had left him for another guy at the March eighth dance. He spent a week in bed, hoping she'd come back."

"Did she?"

"No."

"Hmm. Anyway, that can't be right, Mama." Sveta sat up straighter. "A milk injection into the vein could cause an embolism or sepsis. Blood poisoning. It's much more serious than spending a week in bed. He'd need antibiotics, intravenous fluids, possibly a transfusion or dialysis. Could be fatal. Are you sure that's what your lovesick engineer did?"

Sveta was so smart and lively, talking like this, even more beautiful than before. "You don't think Brian's obsession with Russian things is bizarre?" Masha said.

The look in Sveta's eyes was both harsh and amused, as if she'd been waiting for Masha to say something yet was disappointed that she finally had. Masha thought Sveta would go on about America, how everything was a business deal here, and how what Masha now felt was buyer's remorse.

"If he collected stamps or first editions, that would be fine. But historical artifacts—that's somehow strange. Why?" Sveta said, putting the bandages and the syringe back into the medic bag. "He's a history teacher, for God's sake. And he loves our history the most."

Later that night Masha came up with the idea of singing a song called "Kruchina" at the party in honor of Sveta and Katya receiving their green cards.

❧

The green card party was held two days before Masha's scheduled flight back home. She and Sveta stayed up well past midnight the night before, making the dumplings and cutting up piles of ingredients for three different kinds of salads: Olivier, herring and potato, and cucumber. They got up at seven to make stuffed cabbage and a giant pot of borsch. Then Masha put the finishing touches on the eight-tiered cake Napoleon, Sveta's favorite, and placed two bottles of champagne into the fridge to chill, worrying that just two wouldn't be enough.

While Masha and Sveta cooked, Brian, who had been beaming like a birthday boy since morning, recruited Katya and Brittny for the cleaning detail. Katya refused at first, citing again the impending math decathlon. But when she saw Brittny grudgingly twist her T-shirt into a knot above her belly button, crank up the radio, and attack the carpet with a vacuum, Katya tied up her T-shirt, too, and dusted, shaking her tiny backside in time with the beat.

By five o'clock the table was set, the house decorated with red, white, and blue, and each member of the family was dressed as if for completely different occasions. Brian wore his work outfit—khaki pants and a navy corduroy shirt, clandestinely pressed by Sveta the night before. He had pomaded and combed back his hair. He looked trustworthy.

Sveta had plaited her hair into a thick braid and put on makeup for the first time since Masha's arrival. She wore jeans, a sweater, and a black Russian shawl with bright traditional designs. The girls, too, wore jeans and turtleneck sweaters.

Masha discovered just how overdressed she was when she came upstairs from the basement, where they had set up her bed. She was in her staple party outfit—an old maroon velvet suit and a silk yellow blouse with a bow tie. Now, with her heavy makeup and a low bun of hennaed hair, she felt like a matron about to receive some Soviet medal she didn't deserve.

By six o'clock Brian's friends arrived with giant bags of chips, tubs of dip, trays of carrots, beer, wine, and a bucket of fried chicken, the smell of which quickly permeated the entire house.

Lizochka, Sveta's housecleaning partner, brought two bottles of vodka. Her high-busted peasant girl's body was stuffed into a floor-length green dress and accessorized with three strands of faux pearls and a gold Orthodox cross. The American guests blended into one androgynous crowd of khakis and sweaters. Masha forgot their names soon after the introductions.

The guests took to the Russian food first, asking Sveta questions and pointing into the bowls. Masha couldn't pick out a single English word she knew. She was unhappy with the results of her cooking: with American ingredients, all the dishes came out either too bland or too salty or too sweet. She poured herself a glass of vodka while Sveta wasn't looking. It was bad for her blood pressure.

Miladze, a Georgian-Russian singer whose one CD Brian proudly owned, wailed sad songs about lost love in his breaking falsetto. Brian sat next to Sveta, monitoring her every move and fingering the fringe of her Russian shawl. She pulled up his sleeve seconds before he was about to drag it through a glop of sour cream that was melting into the scarlet borsch, and went right on translating the questions about the Soviet Union and the Cold War some of Brian's friends had for Masha. They peered at Masha as though searching for signs of something alien and tragic. She smiled politely and answered for a while, then took her vodka glass to the armchair by the window.

Soon, the guests tired of the Russian food and moved

on to the fried chicken. From time to time the men stole glances at the muted American football game on TV. Masha noticed Brittny sneaking some vodka into her apple juice. Katya pecked at her food, then attempted a wiggly dance to Miladze, but after an eye roll from Brittny, she quit and went to sit on her mother's lap.

The house was hotter than ever. Blood pumped in and out of Masha's head. All the noise had congealed into a thick mass of linguistic DNA, and she couldn't catch a word in either English or Russian. She sat isolated by incomprehension, a fish in a tank.

People were grouped in threes or fours now, their mouths in constant motion: chewing, swallowing, talking. The expressions were strained, thinking hard about what to say next. A few times Masha noticed a yawn, stifled hastily by a doughy hand. It was nothing like the parties they used to have in Russia, when everyone sang songs and fell asleep on the floor. What had they talked about back then? What had they laughed about? She couldn't remember, but she was angry at these people. They'd come out of obligation, and now not only did they take up priceless time she could be spending with Sveta and Katya, they also got the wrong idea about Russian cuisine.

Through the window the winter looked like an impressionist painting, blue and streaked with shadow, the edges of houses and cars blurred by the snowstorm. The trees stood hunched under heaps of snow. They reminded Masha of her elderly friends back home. She imagined them gossiping about her and her girls now, while they dawdled by the porch of her dilapidated *khrushchyovka*, spitting shells from toasted sunflower seeds into the gray snow. These same friends would vie for American souvenirs when she returned home.

৭৯

After Sveta and Katya had fluttered away to America, Masha's days took on the calm rhythm she had dreamt of since her early motherhood years. Back then, she had felt utterly alone in the world, despite being surrounded by people who constantly wanted something from her: Svetochka, coworkers, girlfriends—single or tormented by screaming children and indolent husbands—and her elderly parents, who called precisely ten minutes after she'd fallen asleep. Now she could sleep for as long as she wanted.

Most mornings Masha snapped to wakefulness before sunrise. She often had nightmares about Sveta and Katya's new lives, fueled by the influx of American movies into Russia. The dreams ranged from nonsensical domestic disasters out of *Home Alone* to full-blown *Terminator*-style apocalypses. She promptly turned on the TV and watched the latest Mexican or Brazilian soap opera, then the news. Daily reports of the development of yet another economic crisis and the attendant social miseries were comforting: it meant that sending the girls away was the right decision.

To escape the oppressiveness of her small apartment, Masha went for long walks. She passed the Palace of ProfUnions, the recently unveiled war memorial, School #15—now the English Lyceum—where both Svetochka and Katya had studied. In the winter, Masha still caught glimpses of them among the squealing students riding their backpacks down the iced porch steps.

A few blocks up was the Children's World store, where the girls had cried rivers from both happiness and disappointment.

Their music school was a squat wooden building from the forties, its floors sagging from the weight of all those pianos. And there was the small park with wooden benches and a greenish bust of Berzin, leprous from decades of spiteful weather and pigeon droppings. How much ice cream had been licked there, how many chocolate potatoes eaten, kilos of sunflower seeds crunched? On that curb by the third bench from the left, little Sveta fell and tore open her lip, and behind that garbage can Katya hid from Sveta and Masha. It seemed that everything had happened on a single, maddeningly short day.

In the evenings Masha took the bus to the town hospital, where she now worked as a part-time cleaner, and where Sveta had once been the attending emergency room physician. More and more Masha came across her former colleagues from the Aviation Administration installed there. Some looked comfortable roaming the hallways in their favorite robes or snuggled in beds, surrounded by books and parcels from visitors; others lay in semiconsciousness with their mouths half open, already oblivious to the switches between day and night. She cleaned the floors in the patient rooms and the hallways, she cleaned the radiators, the windows, the stairs. Blood knocked on the back of her skull like a chime: soon it would be her time. She hummed "Kruchina" under her breath.

Kruchina was an archaic word for grief, found mostly in the old folk songs and poems. *Kruchina* grief was not regular sadness or disappointment with everyday troubles, but rather the existential sorrow about a woman's lot that never goes away, not even at the happiest of moments.

Masha remembered this song from one of the movies of her youth, when all the movies and books were about the war and patriotism, about the great sacrifice for the future. German soldiers were burning a Russian village. The children screamed, the helpless grandmas and grandpas shrieked, the animals and fowl scattered for their lives. A young German soldier broke into the last *izba* standing and found two women huddled on a bench. Except for a single candle, the house was dark and it was hard to see what was in the shadowy corner: a trunk or a cradle.

Before the soldiers could reload their guns, the women began to sing "Kruchina." In the middle of this chaos, time stopped. The soldiers listened as the voices washed over their round helmets and tense shoulders, crept into their machine guns, and spread through their stiffened veins and cold stomachs, like mother's milk.

Sveta might not have even seen the movie, but she and Masha always sang "Kruchina" when their hearts, one or both, were in the wrong place.

৵

Somebody's heavy hand patted Masha's shoulder. She started.

"*Nu*, where you going to hide when it's time to go back?" Lizochka whispered in a soggy, commiserative tone. She plopped into an armchair next to Masha. "You know, when I was a child and misbehaved, my mother always said she'd send me to Magadan."

Masha was irritated at being disturbed.

"Svetochka got lucky, with a grown child and all. Do you know how rarely the immigration goes smoothly?"

Masha shook her head, although, of course, she knew. She looked toward the table, where Brian was clearing the dishes. "We tried not to think of the complications."

"And look at her now. Don't you dare pay any attention to the dirty looks."

"Nobody throws dirty looks at me," Masha lied again.

"So, how did she choose him?"

Masha sighed.

"He had the right persistence. Translated his letters into Russian. Sent flowers, money for Sveta's English lessons. And—very important—he looked like in the photos, not much fatter or older."

"*A-ga*. He probably studied with a life coach—everyone has one here. He didn't make the mistake of sending a gift that required taxes to be paid at the post office, like my Roger. We can't all afford to receive such packages."

"Well, he's a history teacher," Masha said, surprised to feel a tinge of pride.

There was laughter at the table. Lizochka threw back her head in a snorty giggle.

"Americans, they're funny. Humor is different, you have to get used to it."

Masha was about to ask her to translate the joke, then changed her mind.

"Does Sveta ever complain to you about anything?" she said.

Lizochka gripped Masha's hands. "No, never. She knows better than to look a gift horse in the mouth."

Masha nodded, suddenly tipsy.

"Worry about yourself, Mashen'ka. Sveta's going to be fine," Lizochka said. "Time to check on my Roger before he starts making his bed under the table. Don't want him saying it's my Russian drinking influence." She pecked Masha on the forehead and waddled back to the table. Masha didn't even see that Americans were drinking that much.

Miladze stopped, mid-wail. Brian was standing by the stereo with a glass of champagne. Lizochka quickly returned with a glass of champagne for Masha.

"I'll translate for you," Lizochka said, gesticulating "no need to thank me." "Brian is very eloquent. He'll say something nice about you, too, you'll see."

Brian raised his glass.

"*Tak*, he's starting . . . I'll do my best here but I'm not signing any papers. You know, Americans, they never sign anything without a lawyer. Now he's saying he'd like to congratulate Sveta and Katya on their new green cards, though they're still conditional. Soon, they'll become real citizens and their old friends back in Russia will be green with jealousy." Lizochka laughed with the rest of the guests, her breath hot and sour.

Brian talked on, conducting with his champagne glass and, from time to time, checking the length of his nose. It seemed to Masha that Lizochka was translating much too slowly, leaving out crucial information. "Something about shame and the government. He feels he has known your daughter all his life. Something about how he almost died when he came to

Magadan. *Oi*, I hope he's not talking about that Gulag hike he and Roger went on. Okay, okay—oh, that is very romantic. He's saying that he has finally found the love of his life, Sveta, and Katya, a wonderful second daughter and sister for Brittny."

Sveta smiled and nodded to everyone at the table. She patted Katya's knee. Katya, who had been resting her head on Sveta's shoulder, eyes closed, wiggled her leg, and Sveta's hand slid off.

"He's saying that we all know how much he loves Russia. His boys at school collect Lenin pins and Komsomol banners, and watch documentaries." Lizochka paused and furrowed her painted eyebrows.

"What? What is he saying?" Masha poked Lizochka's thigh. She felt, absurdly, that her life depended on this speech by this strange man, who was, thanks largely to her, her daughter's husband.

"It's hard to understand. Something about a circle, and we, well them, being a part of the real history. They can look into your, our, our eyes, the eyes of the people who had been through it all, who had once been strangers on television and in newspapers, the enemy, and see for ourselves, themselves, that you, no we, are just like us. Them. I don't know what the devil he's talking about . . ."

Masha latched on to the one word she understood—"dream." She'd used it over and over in the correspondence with Sveta's potential suitors. Everyone emptied their glasses and applauded. Brian's eyes were phosphorescent with alcohol and pride.

Sveta dabbed the inner corners of her eyes and smiled at

Masha from across the room. Masha wanted to go to the table and sit with her daughter, to hold her plump, childlike hand, but she couldn't bear another question about toilet paper rationing or surviving on a diet of cabbage and potatoes.

Perhaps Lizochka was right, and Sveta was going to be fine with Brian. As long as neither of them ad-libbed. He was not unkind. Perhaps Sveta did harbor that mutant feeling some women were capable of: grateful love. And its fraternal twin—separate happiness.

Brian bent down and tried to draw Sveta's face out from its hiding place in the crook of Katya's neck. Sveta looked up and, as he went in for a celebratory kiss, instinctively offered him her cheek. The confirmation of this banal domestic tragedy—getting exactly what you expected and not one gram more—stung Masha doubly, for herself and for Sveta. She wanted to stomp her feet, throw a tantrum, like a girl.

She saw Brian approaching her. The broken capillaries under his skin made it look like rotten watermelon flesh. And that repulsive yellow mustache.

"Babushka, it's time for our surprise," Katya sing-songed in Russian. Her voice was thin and loud, ideal for folk melodies.

"No, no," Masha said. How to say "different plan" in English? "Katya, stop. I think, *ne nado, nezachem* all this," she whispered, but Sveta had already heard them.

Brian announced something to the guests. They perked up. Lizochka went up to the table and downed another shot of vodka.

"And then cake Napoleon, right?" Katya squealed and plopped down on the chair next to Masha's. "Ooooh. Warm."

"Mama, what's happening?" Sveta said in Russian.

Masha stood up. The world darkened.

"Babooshka, *mee zhdat'*," Brian said in his broken Russian.

"Mama, are you feeling all right?"

"Grandma, c'mon, I want to eat the cake!"

"*Apladismenty*!" Lizochka cried out and began clapping. Everyone followed suit. Masha sat back down.

"Oh, dedicated to Mama," Katya said; this Masha understood.

Katya began to sing, and Masha had to join.

That is not the wind bending the branch,
That is not the bugle grass humming.

Their voices poured out clear and a little off-key, mew-like on the high notes. They breathed at the wrong places. Katya was singing with so many "ah"s, so many "ah"s didn't exist in the modern Russian language. Masha didn't dare look at her daughter. Instead she focused on a constellation of red spots on the carpet.

That is my heart moaning,
Trembling like an aspen leaf.

Katya's voice stuttered.

Kruchina haas exhoh-oh-ohsted meee . . .

She was choking on giggles now. Masha scanned the room and easily located the source of trouble: Brittny was wiggling her hands in fake sign language.

Treacherrrous snake . . .
Burn, buuuurn, my k-kindle . . .

Brian jumped up from his seat and, without uttering a single word, slapped his daughter on her beautiful pink cheek.

Brittny screamed at him and flew up the stairs. Moments later, a door thundered shut. Katya ran up to Sveta and they draped their arms tightly around each other and closed their eyes as the wave of deafening pop music crashed on the frozen room from the second floor.

Masha grabbed a few empty plates from the table and escaped to the kitchen. She felt nauseous and hot, her body swimming. She took the cake Napoleon out of the fridge and cut it, then licked the frosting off the knife blade—a bad omen in Russia that meant you will become mean. She didn't care; she already was mean. She hoped that Sveta would come into the kitchen and forgive her, let her save them, all three.

For a wild instant, Masha considered going up to the master bedroom, getting out the ancient syringe, and injecting herself with milk. If she ended up at the hospital, she would spend a few more days with her girls. And if she died— well, that would be an interesting little twist of her fate.

It was so hot in the house, always so stuffy and hot. She needed fresh air. She opened the hallway closet, where the guests' coats had fallen from the hangers, and sat down on the soft pile to rest for a second. Her head was spinning. The coats smelled of cigarettes, stale bedsheets, and dogs—of long, boring, happy lives.

Our Upstairs Neighbor

1997

~

Sonya sat in the first row of the balcony and stared at the theater curtain, seeing nothing but a blur of red. The eye incident happened almost a week ago, but she was still thinking about what she should have said to Max, reevaluating the timing of her sighs and awkward giggles. Her friends had seen him so close to her face—they didn't know she'd almost lost an eye—and concluded that they had been kissing. Max looked like he wanted to, maybe, and she had felt as though a giant envelope were opening up inside her chest. He had such kind eyes, for a boy. But.

She couldn't wait for the concert to begin so that she would have something else to think about before her head burst.

This wasn't a concert, exactly, but a celebration of the

ninetieth birthday of the renowned Soviet tenor Vadim Makin. Several famous singers and TV personalities had flown into Magadan from St. Petersburg and Moscow for the occasion, which was all the teachers at the arts college had talked about for the last month. Sonya was a student in the gifted section there. Her mother was the accompanist in tonight's program, and Sonya was excited to see her onstage, next to this Makin, though she'd only heard of him a month ago. Maybe her mother would also play for someone Sonya would recognized from TV.

Sonya watched the auditorium fill until only a small island in front of the stage was still empty. This was the VIP section for the guests from the capitals. Max was not someone who would voluntarily attend an event like this, probably, yet she still looked out for his tall figure. Couldn't he be pulled into the theater if she thought about him hard enough?

Though they had been officially going together for almost two months, the ten minutes leading up to the eye incident was the longest time they'd spent one-on-one. The power had gone out at the school and second-shift grades were let out early. Instead of going home, several of them from ninth A and ninth C lingered at an abandoned construction site behind the soccer field. They played hide-and-seek among the concrete beams, tripping over metal rods and halfheartedly shouting the latest obscenities into the darkness. By accident or conspiracy, as the others were hiding, Sonya and Max found themselves sitting on two perpendicular slabs of cold concrete, all alone.

Here he was, so near. Sonya was barely breathing. He

smiled, and she smiled. She was afraid. He was the captain of the basketball team and the tallest boy in all the ninth grade sections. His nose was large and his eyes slightly close-set, but he was very cute. He wore a neon yellow pom-pom hat, the hat she watched come out of the apartment building across from hers to take out the trash every evening. The hat she followed to school every morning, hanging back at a safe distance. In the evenings, she turned off the light in her room and stared at Max's windows. If the lights in his room lit up before she counted to ten, he loved her. If his silhouette appeared in the kitchen, she loved him.

On those concrete slabs they were shy and tongue-tied. Sonya still couldn't tell whether his eyes were brown or moss green. She had no siblings, she said when he asked. And yes, her father would be returning to America soon. His older brother was in the army, Max said; he himself wanted to be an engineer. His mother was already saving for the bribes to get him out of the mandatory two-year military service. Why? she asked. Terrible things happen to young men in the army. She didn't ask for elaboration. He picked up some of last night's snow and balled it up. What about his father? His father lived in another town with another family. She wondered what he thought of her family: he must have seen both her father and Oleg, her mother's boyfriend, at the school.

Max threw the snowball and it hit Sonya smack in the left eye. The darkness around her became more solid, then flashed with yellow triangles. I will be blind, she thought. Tears ran down her face, out of surprise and pain and embarrassment. Max rushed over to her. "I didn't mean to, it was a joke. I am so sorry. Does it hurt bad?" The pain began to recede and Sonya forced herself to smile. "I sure have excellent aim," he said, dabbing her tears with his hat's pompom. She laughed. She realized that he was holding her hand. And then everybody else appeared, stumbling and giggling, tired of waiting to be found.

❧

Almost half an hour after the concert was supposed to start, the celebrity guests walked in—some men in suits and some in torn jeans and half-unbuttoned shirts with billowing sleeves. A group of beautiful young women in high heels tottered after them. Somebody started clapping and the rest of the audience joined in. The celebrities gave half bows from their chairs.

As the lights went down Sonya edged toward the balcony railing. The curtain rolled up to reveal a red throne in the corner of the stage; she remembered it from an operetta earlier in the season. It was empty. In the back, suspended by two wires, hung a huge black-and-white portrait of a handsome young man. Makin a long time ago, she assumed. Sergey Yakovlevich Frenkel, the theater director, strode out to the microphone in the middle of the stage. He was a massive man with red hair and an even redder beard. The applause petered out.

"Dear Magadanians and guests," he thundered. "Thank you for coming to our historic celebration. I've just gotten word that Vadim Andreevich Makin is running a little late, so while we wait, and for the entertainment of our esteemed guests, please enjoy a performance by the youngest members of Magadan's music community—the choir of the Children's Music School Number One."

A group of thirty children shuffled onto the stage. Sonya knew several of them as former students of her piano teacher, Faina Grigorievna. She had kicked them out for lack of talent. Sonya had studied with Faina Grigorievna since she was seven, half of her life. Her mother didn't allow her to quit and her father always said: "What doesn't kill you makes you stronger." Music School #1, on the other hand, accepted everyone, except the completely tone-deaf. According to some people at the arts college. The choir was dreadful. Sonya sank into her chair and watched the side curtains for any movement. She couldn't believe this Makin would be late for his own concert.

After the choir finished its last song, two of the children brought out a large wreath of flowers and leaned it against Makin's throne. Sonya would count to ten, she decided, and on ten Makin must appear. She counted to ten—no Makin. She counted again.

The theater director came out. He looked at the looming portrait.

"Dear comrades, unfortunately Vadim Andreevich is not here yet, but we cannot delay our show any longer. A special thank-you to our guests for making the journey all the way to our forgotten Arctic corner. Now we will celebrate the life of our dear Vadim Andreevich how he deserved to be celebrated a long time ago. Better late than never, yes, friends? *Nu*, of course, yes!"

The audience clapped. Sonya clapped, too—what else was

there to do? Oleg had told her that Makin lived just across from the theater, on Port Street. So it couldn't have been the distance. Or the weather: Magadan had known much fiercer winds.

The lights came up, then down again. Then Yakov Gutman came onstage with a cloth bag. Sonya had seen him many times on TV, but she hadn't known that he was the most decorated singer in the history of both the USSR and the Russian Federation, as the theater director had remarked in his introduction. She'd always wondered whether his signature hairstyle—cut at sharp angles around his forehead—was a wig.

"I will now read passages from several telegrams and birthday cards received from Vadim Makin's old stage friends and fans." He pulled out a piece of cardboard paper from the bag. "'My dearheart Vadimushka,'" Gutman addressed the throne in his distinct oily baritone, "writes Izabella Yurieva. You, of course, all know Yurieva, the legend of the Russian romance song. 'So many years have passed,' she writes, 'so many lives we've lived, and we survived them all. Youth is in the soul, Vadimushka, keep singing.'"

The audience clapped, some whistled. Gutman put his finger to his lips and pulled out another piece of cardboard from the bag. "And this is a telegram from Yegor Tarasov, Junior Lieutenant, Veteran of the Great Patriotic War, residing in Rostov-on-Don. 'When you sang,' he writes, 'hope was planted in our hearts and through all the noise and confetti, your angelic voice hewed a window to the essential, to the truth. You are not forgotten, Vadim Andreevich. Happy birthday.'" Gutman shook his head. "He is a poet, this comrade veteran, isn't he? We should get our veterans to write our modern pop lyrics, eh?"

The audience laughed in approval. After the reading of postcards, a line formed at the base of the stage. People came up to Makin's throne and piled on flowers, envelopes, and other gifts.

The theater director, Frenkel, lumbered on stage with a red folder. "We will now present a dramatic sketch about Makin's life called 'The World Spins Around the Song,'" he said. "Unfortunately, our respected Vadim Andreevich is still en route, but don't despair, we have plenty of our own Makins waiting right here in the wings."

Sonya was starting to feel cold and hungry. Her mother had insisted she wear her piano recital outfit—a brown corduroy dress with a three-tiered skirt that she couldn't wait to grow out of. She wouldn't want Max to see her like this. Despite herself, she searched for him in the audience again.

The theater director leaned on Makin's throne and opened the red folder.

"Act One. It's the dawn of the twentieth century . . ." He outlined some mountains in the air. "Revolutionary tremors are already quaking Russia, but certain families will be able to enjoy their privileged lifestyle a little longer." Two boys from the Music School #1 Choir wheeled on an elaborately painted set piece of the St. Petersburg skyline. "Among such families is Makin's: his father is a wealthy merchant, his mother—a beautiful gypsy, the great-niece of a famous gypsy singer, Varvara Vasilieva. Makin has seven sisters."

An actress dressed in a gypsy costume and seven girls

from the choir came out onstage to the sounds of "Gypsy Walks," a song about the call of the gypsy star and following your true love over the edge of the earth. The girls knocked their feet against their ankles and squatted halfway in abysmal imitation of the gypsy dance. There were better dancers in Magadan and a much better children's choir, the one at the arts college, Sonya thought with disappointment. Makin's mother sat down at the piano, and the girls formed a circle around her. Then, a red-haired boy ran onto the stage and yelled into the ceiling, "Mama, I want to sing, too! I want to be a star!" Sonya almost fell off her chair. It was the director's son, Zahar, Sonya's classmate. A dedicated prankster. He looked nothing like Makin's noble portrait, but the audience was rolling with laughter.

More people came out on stage, and the music-school boys brought out a fireplace with an electric fire and chairs.

"Makin's father hosts cultural evenings in their opulent home on the Neva embankment and invites all kinds of historical personages, for example the young poet Vladimir Mayakovsky." He pointed at an actor named Ruslan Belyaev, who played all the leads in the theater's operettas. Belyaev was reciting: ". . . 'Upon the scales of tinny fishes new lips summoned, though yet mute. But could you play right to the finish a nocturne on a drainpipe flute?' "

The audience clapped and laughed.

"Then came the revolutions." Four girls in red leotards danced to Prokofiev's *Romeo and Juliet*. "Makin dreamed of the sea since childhood, but he is expelled from the navy academy because of his bourgeois father." The gymnasts tore off

Zahar/Makin's sailor cap and banished him off the stage, lashing him with their red ribbons.

The theater director talked about how Makin worked as a cargo loader at the port, put up handbills, and at night played tangos and fox-trots for the silent movies. How he was discovered singing at the Port Workers' Club. Zahar/Makin acted all of this out, exclaiming, "I want to sing for the people!" Then he was replaced by a short, bald actor, who usually played fumbling villains. Makin recorded hundreds of songs and performed in private concerts for Stalin (Belyaev with a mustache). When the war started, he volunteered to travel to the front lines to perform for the soldiers, who hoisted terrified Makin over their heads and disappeared into the side curtains.

"He inspired our country to defeat fascism—for words, if they are true, can be a weapon as formidable as tanks or rockets!"

The lights lowered and began to flash with red. "Act Two. In 1942, Vadim Makin falls out of favor with Stalin and, along with hundreds of thousands of others, is sent to the labor camps." Makin appeared stage right, still dangling precariously over the soldiers' shoulders, and then was carried off stage left. The last soldier was dragging behind him a length of barbed wire.

"Luckily for us, Makin ends up here, in Magadan. When he is released, he makes Magadan his home. And that is Act Three," the director concluded triumphantly.

Actors dressed as reindeer pulled a big sled onto the stage.

"I want to sing for the people!" Makin shouted from his

burrow inside the sled, and waved a toy cat at the audience. A cat? Maybe it was for the better that the real Makin wouldn't see the play, Sonya thought.

The red curtain fell and the lights went up to the sound of mad applause. The director announced he'd gotten word that Makin would arrive by the start of the second part of the concert. The celebrities had already disappeared from the audience.

"He is all right, Sonechka, don't worry. Yakov Gutman himself spent an hour trying to persuade him to come," Sonya's mother said when Sonya saw her during the intermission. Her long red hair was done up in an old-fashioned updo. She looked tired. "Makin said he had nothing appropriate to wear."

"Nothing to wear?"

"Somebody from Moscow even offered him his tuxedo. Makin refused. He said he hadn't taken off his felt boots in five years, and a tuxedo didn't go with felt boots."

"Was he joking?"

Sonya wanted to ask Oleg if he knew anything, but he was busy interviewing some elderly people for his TV segment on Makin.

A third of the audience didn't return after the intermission. Makin didn't appear either.

In the fourth hour of the concert, the pop stars from Moscow sang Makin's songs with lots of bass, synthesizers, and guitar riffs. Then recordings of Makin were played from a record player that somebody had put on the red throne. Sonya was shocked to finally hear Makin's real voice. Through the crackle of years it came out strong and silvery, and so fervent—like he was confessing to a person who already knew everything and agreed, not a whole world of strangers. She felt her face get red. The accompaniment was simple, just piano or guitar.

The director announced that Makin would be joining the celebration in half an hour. Sonya put her head on the wide balcony railing. It was draped in scarlet velvet and smelled like the last century. She must have dozed off because when she opened her eyes Belyaev was singing to Makin's empty throne, one arm hugging its back: *"Write to me, I beg of you. Write to me, if just a single line."* Sonya's mother was on stage, hunched over the piano keys.

At the construction site Sonya had told Max that she wanted to be a doctor, her childhood ambition, largely because he said he wanted to be an engineer—a respectable, practical profession. In truth, these days she dreamed of doing something artistic: acting in films, or, better yet, making films. But she said "doctor" because she thought everyone considered her too serious, too good of a student. Max would laugh. And then she had cried when the snowball hit her in the eye. If she had been brave enough to say "actress," she could've at least pretended the crying was on cue, a demonstration of her skill.

The lights went up. Sonya couldn't believe it was finally over. She got her coat, put on woolen leggings over her tights, and leaned against a column in the foyer downstairs to wait for her mother and Oleg. She didn't feel the usual post-theater headiness (like her first taste of rum mixed with milk at her grandmother's), when just walking around under the influence of the performance felt exhilarating, romantic. Though the concert had lasted almost six hours, the evening still felt unfinished. Her stomach ached from hunger. She spotted some people from the arts college in the almost empty foyer. The rest were pensioners, bundling up in slow motion.

"All set, cabaret-beauty?" Sonya recognized Oleg by his nasal voice before she turned around. He was stuffed into all black: tight jeans and a short leather jacket stretched over slouched shoulders. Even though he was slim (except for his potato nose), his clothes always looked too small. She didn't like it when he called her cabaret-beauty. She wasn't supposed to like Oleg at all. When her father had returned from Alaska last year, her mother packed her things, packed Oleg's things, too—he'd been living with them in their old apartment for almost a year—and moved to Oleg's minuscule room in a *kommunalka* apartment on the edge of town. A long time before that, her father had promised that the three of them—Papa, Mama, and Sonya—would move to America. Now Sonya shuttled between her mother and father like a silent messenger, afraid to ask whether they would be exiled in Magadan forever.

Since she was now going with Max, she probably wasn't supposed to still want to go to America.

"Why didn't Makin come?" Sonya asked Oleg.

"Yes, he embarrassed us in front of the Moscow guests. You know I saw him last night?"

"Last night?"

"My cameraman and I were the only local media allowed to the opening party. They built a whole museum dedicated to Makin in the three-bedroom apartment next door to his place, which, by the way, the city bought him for his birthday. Organized a special 'retro corner' with an antique gramophone, his old concert posters and photographs. Very elegant. There's even a one-of-a-kind cherry-red grand piano that they transported from St. Petersburg and installed through his fifth-floor window with a crane. In that crazy wind! I got it all on film." Oleg scanned the foyer. "Your mother is taking her time, as usual."

They sat down on a bench next to the coat check.

"Gutman banged on the piano so hard, Makin's old rubber cat fell on the floor. The same cat who'd seen Stalin and Beria, and Churchill in Yalta. You know, when Makin performed, he used to put a rubber cat on the piano."

"A cat? How do you know it was the same one?"

"Makin stood up and sang the last few lines. His voice was weak now, so he overcompensated with passion. Everyone was a little uncomfortable. I managed get a glimpse of his nails."

"There's Mama." Sonya's mother was coming from the back stairs. She had already put on her fur hat and was barely holding on to her frost-proof fur coat, a thing so big and bulky it was known in the family as Little House.

"Our cabaret-beauty," Oleg said. "There was a rumor that Makin had abandoned personal hygiene, and his nails grew so deep into his skin that he had to have surgery. But his nails looked completely normal to me, and he didn't stink. He wore what they said he always wears now: a ratty turtleneck sweater with safety pins on the chest and felt boots."

"Why was he wearing safety pins?" Sonya said. The story was making her sad.

"Protection against evil eye. And Gutman, I guess." Oleg chortled.

"What are you talking about?" Sonya's mother said.

"I haven't even gotten to the good part." Oleg tore Little House out of her arms and opened it up, a little too high for her. She climbed in. "In the middle of yet another round of toasts, an old woman in a housedress and slippers bursts in and starts assaulting the Moscow guests, screaming and flailing—something about Yeltsin's mafiosos. She tried to drag Gutman out the door. To see a grandma curse like that. . ." Oleg shook his head.

"Who was she?" Sonya said. Her mother was looking at Oleg with suspicion, an expression Sonya noticed more and more often lately.

"Maestro didn't explain anything. We caught it all on film, I can let you watch later."

"He is an old man and a giant, giant talent," her mother said.

"So, for him it's forgivable?" Oleg said.

"If he's made mistakes, I'll be the last in line to judge him."

Sonya stared at the way her mother's nostrils flared when she spoke with ardor. In frosty weather, her cheeks became picturesquely red, and her nose stayed small and pale. The opposite always happened to Sonya: her nose reddened and her cheeks' color drained.

"Let's go, philosophers." Oleg ushered them toward the exit.

"I still don't understand why Makin didn't come," Sonya said.

Her mother bent toward her and whispered, "Your grandfather knew Makin when he lived in Magadan, did you know? Ask him before he leaves."

Sonya had almost forgotten about Deda Misha, who was visiting from Kiev. She knew, of course, that he'd lived in Magadan when he was young, but in her mind, she could only picture him as she knew him in the summers during her school breaks, tending his vegetable garden in a short-sleeved plaid shirt.

Oleg strained to push open the theater's heavy doors. "What are you two conspiring about? I think—" he said, and was cut off by the wind.

Sonya turned for one last look at the four figures on the theater roof: a soldier with a machine gun, a *kolkhoznitsa* with a bundle of rye and a sickle, a miner with a hammer, and a huntress with a rifle, gazing into the snowy distance. Legend had it that if a person stared at the statues long enough, they would make a sign revealing the secret location of the Kolyma gold stolen by the escaped Gulag prisoners. She found the two windows Oleg had told her were Makin's. They were dark, but Makin had an unobstructed view.

❧

Oleg waited downstairs while her mother walked Sonya up to the fourth floor of their building. They still had a wooden door, tooled with cracked faux leather and tacks, while all their neighbors had installed heavy metal doors. If they had

had a metal door, Sonya's father liked to joke, would it have prevented her mother from leaving?

"How is Papa?" her mother whispered.

"He talks to Americans on the phone a lot." Sonya realized she could've said anything; she could've even lied. But she didn't know what she wanted to happen now.

"Good." Her mother took off one of her gloves and pressed her red fingers to the keyhole. She stood like this for a moment, as if letting a few fingertip cells sneak into her old home. "Tell Deda Misha I send hello and wish him safe travels for me. And don't forget to ask him about Makin."

Sonya felt terribly sad that her mother would now have to take a long bus ride to Oleg's *kommunalka,* with that cold-tiled communal bathroom and the cockroaches spying from the cracks in the wall. "Bye, Mama." She buried her nose in the wet fur of Little House.

Once her mother disappeared down the first flight of stairs, Sonya rang the bell. After some time Deda Misha opened the door. He wore her father's brown sweater and her mother's pink apron.

"We thought they'd kidnapped you! Come in, come in. Hungry?"

"Hungry, of course."

Sonya's father lay on the couch, watching the news and reading a book called *Business Advice from an American Lawyer.* Sonya kissed him on the forehead. He smelled faintly of sweat, but—it was obvious now—he was so much better and more handsome than Oleg. Her favorite feature of her father's were his pale green eyes, which, like her mother's nostrils, she didn't inherit.

"*Shto*, survived?" he said. A sly smile ruffled his mustache. "Makin didn't even come."

Her father shook his head. "An understandable matter."

"Sonya, come eat!" Deda Misha called from the kitchen.

"Go eat, Sonya," her father said. It was a command veiled by a joking tone. He talked often this way since he got back from America.

"I was about to," Sonya said. "Am I at least allowed to take this stupid dress off? Mama sent hello, by the way."

"Just the hello? What about the money? They must be waiting till he wins the Palme d'Or and Hollywood calls. All right, I'll wait, too. See you in L.A."

Sonya didn't reply; she never knew what to say to her father's digs at Oleg or her mother. When she was with him, her father consumed all of her daughterly attention. She changed into track pants and an old turtleneck sweater, thinking of Makin's safety pins. The New Year's discotheque was just a week away, Sonya remembered with a jolt. She wanted it to be both sooner and later. Max would be there, of course, and he would ask her to dance. Everybody expected from them at least one slow *medlyak*—face-to-face, his arms around her waist, her arms around his neck. She would have to say yes.

In the kitchen, Deda Misha was pouring borsch into bowls. He'd made it Ukrainian style, with squares of lard floating on the scarlet surface. Sonya parted the curtains and rubbed the cold, frost-white window until a clear hole appeared on the glass. All three windows of Max's apartment were dark. Where could he be? The basketball practice had finished hours ago, and he never went to bed early. Maybe at one of his teammates' apartments. She'd heard of wild parties hosted by the girls in the B section; those girls were the most developed and grown-up in all of ninth grade. The booths by the theater would sell anything to anyone, even cheap vodka that made you go blind. And where was Max's mother?

She closed the curtains and held on to the fabric for a second. She had recently decided, after much agonizing, that her first memory was of her mother hemming these curtains—Sonya distinctly remembered the pattern of blue and orange pears—and therefore, all the memories prior belonged to her previous lives.

She sat down at the table and began to fish the pieces of lard out of the borsch. Deda Misha put out a plate with black bread and sat down opposite her. He had thin knees and a formidable belly that was squared on top from the hernia he earned at fourteen, during the war. His white hair was thick and wavy—the best in the family.

"*Tak,* you say our maestro didn't come?" he said and bit into a piece of garlic. He had excellent ivory teeth thanks to fearlessness of raw garlic and onion. "How old is he now, ninety?"

"Yes, ninety. The concert was for his birthday. Deda, tell me about him. Mama said you knew him." Deda Misha's eyes began to shine, so, in spite of herself, she added, "You know, Mama always adds beans to her borsch."

"Your mama knows a lot about many things, just not the important ones. She is still young, we have hope."

Sonya stared at the lard, itching to hit the table hard enough that the plate would flop over on the floor.

"Yes, Makin and I were friends."

Deda Misha had arrived in Magadan full of stories, like a barrel full of pickled cabbage, and he was in a hurry to tell them. He had already gone through most of his childhood and adolescence, proving—Sonya had to concede—that his life at her age had been vastly more dramatic and historical. Deda's mother had carried him out of Ukraine and into Chechnya to escape *holodomor*, the terror famine under Stalin. During the war, he had thrown twenty incendiary bombs off his apartment building with the help of giant metal pincers. He founded a club to grow silkworms and provide fabric for the military parachutes. Her own grandfather, contributing to the victory—it was incredible. She'd never heard of any of this before. He was drafted to help Russian soldiers catch horses, which the Chechens had released into the mountains before Stalin deported them to Kazakhstan and Siberia. He became a Young Pioneer, then a Komsomolets, and then joined the Party.

Sometimes, as Deda Misha talked, Sonya tried to imagine Max in Deda Misha's stories, having his adventures. Max throwing bombs off the roof, Max rounding up the wild Chechen horses like a cowboy. Max was brave, there was no doubt about that. He'd once jumped off a five-story building into a giant snowbank on a dare. Then everybody else jumped after him. Then the police arrived and they ran away, except for Pet'ka, who had broken his leg.

"You could say I'd played a crucial role in Makin's life," Deda Misha said. "I'll give you a garlic clove to gnaw on. It kills the microbes."

"I don't want a garlic clove. Do you know why he didn't come?"

"Pride and stubbornness. He's always been like that, stubborn as a crayfish. Now that he's got the public's attention, he wants to make a point. Eat up, Sonya."

"What point?"

Deda Misha got up and put on a teakettle. Under his big square glasses, his eyes were slightly hooded. They said everyone in the world, and definitely everybody in Russia, had at least one gene from Genghis Khan. What if Deda Misha was Genghis Khan himself in his prior life? In the living room, her father had fallen asleep.

"To understand what happened with Makin, Sonya, I need to first tell you what happened with me, how I left Grozny after the Petroleum Institute and ended up in Magadan. '*Magadan, Magadan, a windy city between two bays*,'" he sang in a soothing baritone. "It's already very late."

"But I want to know about Makin, Deda, and you leave tomorrow. Was he really as famous as they say?"

"Yes, 'okay,' as you Americans say. I will begin from the beginning. First, you have to know I didn't want to leave my mother all alone in Grozny. My father left the family eighteen years before, for another woman—she'd lied that she was pregnant. I went to him, we talked man to man, and I persuaded him to come back and live with Mother. You have to always take care of your parents, Sonya."

"She just forgave him after eighteen years?" Sonya couldn't imagine forcing her parents to be together.

"I don't know if she forgave, but it was better this way, not to be alone. Your baba Mila and I arrived in Magadan in 1951. We took a train from Moscow to Vladivostok, and down to the port of Nahodka. Our ship was a German ocean liner named *Russia,* formerly *Adolf Hitler.* It was illegally seized by the USSR after the war and would have been arrested if it went into international waters. So it sailed to Magadan, Gulag country—the gateway to Hell, people called it then. The ship was very luxurious: plush carpets, mirrors, curved wooden staircases, German words everywhere. They'd managed to remove most of the swastikas."

"You met Makin on the ship?"

The kettle began to whistle. Deda Misha took it off the burner and poured boiling water into the brew pot.

"I will get to Makin, Sonechka. He was already in Magadan. Listen. The closer we got to Magadan, the more horror stories our fellow travelers told us about our future hometown . . ."

Deda Misha talked about how the camps were everywhere, even in the center of Magadan. Sonya hadn't known that. Barbed wire and dogs barking in the cold. If a prisoner lost a game of cards, upon release he had to kill on such and such date the tenth person he encounters on an evening walk. Or be killed. The Gulag's criminal network reached everywhere. Released prisoners lived in flotsam shanties or manholes and stole food from first-floor kitchens. If a prisoner escaped, the whole town would be on lockdown while soldiers hunted him down.

"Tea's ready," Sonya said. She tried to imagine barbed wire in her neighborhood.

"Pour for us, Sonya, and ask if your father wants some."

"He's sleeping." She poured the brew into two cups and added hot water. Her legs, from the knees down, were leaden. She parted the curtains again. Max's windows were still dark.

"Tell me about Makin. Nothing scary, please."

"Nothing scary, eh? When I arrived, the head of personnel talked to me, saw that I was Ukrainian—all the best petroleum engineers are Ukrainians—and decided not to send me to the mines . . . I will skip a few years. I became the director of the gas and petroleum depots in Magadan. I always preferred to be in the middle of the action, not in the office with the papers and the telephone. I traveled all over the region, and what situations I got into I can't begin to describe. Some near-deaths even, in the beautiful and cruel far north. I worked hard, I love working. Back then there was real enthusiasm among the young people. They didn't work just for the money. I've been lucky to meet many interesting people in my life, and I always stayed open-minded. People sense your interest and open up, Sonya. In Magadan, it wasn't just Makin. The whole Kolyma was a living museum of Soviet history."

Sonya yawned and sipped her tea while Deda Misha talked about all the people who were there in connection with the Kirov case. Whatever that was. Then he droned on about his coworkers—someone who used to be a senior engineer of some plant in Ukraine and was now a secretary, or someone with a German last name who used to be the director of the largest something in Leningrad and now shoveled coal. "I was twenty-six, but they never showed any bitterness or let me feel I didn't deserve my authority. They always tried to help me."

Sonya stared inside her teacup, where the tea leaves swirled like big, black snowflakes. "Deda, what about—"

"At the depot where I'd worked for twenty years, I had four hundred and forty people under me. New specialists who had just graduated from the universities on the continent, former camp guards and prisoners, and people who were still in the camps serving their sentences, and always I was proactive. Whenever I needed anything, a good-quality wall newspaper to celebrate the holidays or mark the progress of our headquarters, I went to the camps—a friend of mine was a behavioral counselor at one of them—and had my pick of the best artists and poets. I reconciled husbands and wives, rebuilt families, helped people quit smoking and vodka. I organized the construction of houses for my workers. I was a matchmaker to young people and arranged for them to move into studio apartments to have their privacy. And always I wanted to do more."

"You found Makin a bride?" Sonya interrupted. She was getting impatient. Maybe Deda Misha didn't know Makin that well after all? If they had been such great friends, wouldn't he have come to his birthday concert, even though Oleg and her mother were there?

"Makin? He almost got himself a bride." Deda Misha burst into such a fit of laughter that Sonya knocked over her cup of tea. She got up and found a rag to wipe the table.

"As I was saying, I built clubhouses, movie theaters, libraries, and gathered books to fill them. I required my workers to read, and then I held meetings to discuss the books. Who is the positive character? Who is the negative character? What is the author's message? Useful, isn't it? All the young people in town dreamed of working at my depot. It's very pleasant to remember. If someone showed up drunk, I cut their salary. They understood and corrected their behavior. I had half of my depot staffed with West Ukrainians—very hardworking people, don't drink, don't smoke. East Ukrainians, Russians, Tatars, they all like to drink and curse. Nothing in this life I hate more than cursing. I still get phone calls and letters from all over the country from people whom I helped in Magadan. *Da.*

"I worked for thirty years as the director of large projects, in Magadan and then in Ukraine, building a pipeline under the Dnieper, and I wasn't arrested once. I was very honest. I never used my connections to advance myself—I could've gotten in touch with Brezhnev if I wanted to, through relatives— but I didn't want any promotions or medals I didn't deserve. I never accepted bribes."

"Maybe you should have." Sonya's father was standing in the kitchen doorway.

"And if the bribes had been slipped secretly, I returned them," Deda Misha said. His face settled from surprise to babyish hurt. "Tolik, I'm sure you know that I would have gone to the camp for that, in our own backyard."

"What's three years? The curious thing is you usually get punished for small-time stuff. Steal billions and you'll probably get away with it. Become best friends with the president, drink vodka together, and listen to Gutman live at your dacha."

"That's a good lesson to be teaching your daughter."

"All right, Papa, tell us about Makin, like promised. Before your audience nosedives into the tea."

"I was just laying the groundwork. Do you want some tea, Tolik?"

"I'll make it. You get to your story." Sonya's tall father took up all the space in the tiny kitchen and cast shadows on the table as he moved.

"Tak." Deda Misha cleared his throat. "Makin lived in a *kommunalka* room upstairs from us, on Park Street. As part of his sentence, he had loss of civil rights and was not allowed to travel beyond a certain region after he was released from the camp, and, of course, travel or move to the capital and major cities. Many people, after they had been officially acquitted, stayed in Magadan because their personal circumstances had changed. Say, they once had a wife, and now she's dead or married to someone else. Or their family had rejected them. Many had found their second lives here."

"Papa, we know you are an engineer to your core but less technical details, please."

Sonya caught the spark in her father's eyes and felt united with him against Deda Misha. Her father fixed the tea and brought it out to the living room. He returned and poured himself a glass of vodka.

"You drink too much, Tolik," Deda Misha said.

"A little vodka keeps the spirit young and full of good ideas. A lot of vodka, on the other hand." He drank from his glass. "She's a grown-up, she made her own bed. She can sleep in his piss."

Heat rushed to Sonya's face when she realized he was talking about her mother and Oleg. She'd never actually seen Oleg drunk.

"My spirit is young, by natural method," Deda Misha said.

"I wish we were all like you," her father said.

"I am continuing. Tolik, please, no jokes."

"I will leave in a minute," Sonya's father said. He remained by the window, his back pulling down on the pear-patterned curtains.

"Papa, you'll snap the curtains," Sonya said. "Just sit down, please."

"I need to plan my great return, like the Count of Monte Cristo."

"To America?" If that was true, she was ready to forgive him all his teasing, and everything he'd ever said about her mother.

"China," her father said.

"China?"

"Sonya, what grade are you in?"

"Ninth."

"Exactly. Don't always believe the first thing you're told."

"Oh." So, America! She could barely contain her thrill.

"*Vot,* continuing," Deda Misha said loudly, like a teacher starting a lesson. "Makin was our upstairs neighbor, but once, he was the most famous tenor in the USSR."

"Like Pavarotti and Domingo," Sonya's father said.

"Really?" Sonya said.

"His mother and grandmother were gypsies and singers. That's where he got his singing genes. Gypsies have beautiful songs, almost as beautiful as Ukrainian songs. In the twenties and thirties, Makin sold out stadiums, and when a new record came out, the lines outside the record stores were so unruly that horse-mounted police were dispatched to maintain order."

"Like Beatlemania," Sonya said. Her father winked at her. They were fans of the Beatles together, and she was annoyed that Oleg also loved the Beatles. Sometimes, though, she wanted Oleg to like her; she couldn't explain it. Even when Oleg had said that her father was like the fool from "The Fool on the Hill." He'd intended it as a compliment, talking about the wise fool. Her mother had overheard and warned Oleg that for as long as he lived in their home and ate their food, he was forbidden to say a word about Sonya's father. But Sonya had understood what Oleg meant, and, in a way, she even agreed.

"He wrote his own songs or collaborated with a lyricist. And he had his own piano accompanist, his friend Mikhail Bondarenko. Another Ukrainian."

"I think Bondarenko was a Jew," Sonya's father said.

"Yes, Jews are good musicians. Like gypsies, but more educated in the classical tradition, not as soulful."

"As Ukrainians?"

"You are yourself an almost full-blooded Ukrainian, Tolik, you should be proud. *Tak,* next. The war. Makin sang at the blockaded Leningrad, the besieged Sevastopol, and for the sailors in Arctic Murmansk. By the way, because there was an ingredient in the plastic records that was necessary for some very important military production, people were called to bring in their broken or even new records for recycling. But Makin's records weren't accepted. He told me himself. On the contrary, his records were given out as a reward to the most active recyclers. He could hypnotize people with his voice. That's why he lasted as long as he did. The veterans say he made them want to not just survive, but to live. To return home and find love." Deda Misha got teary-eyed for a second, which made Sonya uncomfortable. She wondered whether any veterans had come to Makin's concert tonight.

"In '42, shortly before Stalin's birthday, Beria called Makin, the story goes, and asked why none of his songs were about Stalin. Have you studied Beria at school yet? He was the chief of secret police. At an earlier interview with the KGB Makin was asked—which means he was ordered—to write a song about Stalin. Makin replied that songs about Stalin did not suit a tenor voice. Can you imagine Beria getting such an answer? Beria! Who had personally signed thousands of execution orders. Who rode around Moscow in a black car, picking out women and girls on the street, then raped and murdered them. Stalin was like a jealous husband; he couldn't stand when someone might be more popular than him. Makin was sentenced to eight years in one of Magadan's camps. Not bad as Gulag sentences go, and he didn't have to do the real hard labor, where people died in the mines and from cold and starvation. He was part of the agitprop brigade with other singers, actors, poets, and dancers and performed at different camps. It was a part of the so-called cultural and reeducation program. The camp leadership always loved art, and of course wanted to use the talents of so many accomplished people who came their way. These brigades even received bonuses and extra pay, and they felt welcomed and needed wherever they went. Makin's talent saved him, but still it was devastating. He was cut down at the height of his career."

"Just for not singing about Stalin?" Sonya said.

"People were arrested for less. Tell a political joke and you just signed your arrest warrant. There was a rumor of another reason—actually, many conflicting rumors—but rumors were a dangerous thing. People kept their mouths shut."

"Love's a bitch and life's her lackey," Sonya's father said.

"Tolik, not for Sonya's ears."

"I'm sure she's heard worse, in their *kommunalka*." He poured himself more vodka. "The important question was not for what, Sonya, but for how long. With rights of correspondence, or without. If not, the family wouldn't even know where you were, whether you were dead or alive."

"Yes, it was like that. 'If there is a person, an Article will be found for him.'" Deda Misha sighed. "So, Makin. After all the years of my friendship with him, I can confidently say that like so many artists, he was not practical. He didn't know what was good for him. A tremendous shame, for someone of his stature."

"Get to the point, comrade general," Sonya's father said.

Deda Misha waved him away. "Makin's sentence was cut short, for good work and behavior. Afterward, he lived in Magadan with three cats. Everybody knew who he was, but many pretended not to. Even the walls have ears, that's what we said. Housemates behind our thin walls could've been working surveillance for the KGB. I'd seen Makin on the staircase of our building many times. He always looked so fashionable—in a long checkered coat and a silk scarf. His cologne lingered on the stairs long after he'd passed. He still had foreign friends and admirers, who closed their eyes to certain of his proclivities. Just like I later would. They couldn't help him move back to Moscow or restore his former glory, but they could procure for him an Italian scarf, a French beret.

"Every weekend, your baba Mila and I enjoyed music filtering down through the thin floor from his soirées. He played piano, his guests brought guitars, violins—and he sang, of course, he sang his long swan song. He was only in his midforties then and already starting to look old. His black gypsy eyes had sunk in and he was losing hair, but there was still an aura of nobility on his face, the way certain artists can look no matter how much they suffer. By the way, in '43, when he was still in the camp, he was flown into Yalta for several hours."

"Tehran," Sonya's father said.

"Yes, yes, Tehran. Yalta Conference was later. He was flown to Tehran under guard. It was Churchill's birthday, and all the famous singers in the world gathered to perform for him. Churchill's son had organized the concert and personally requested Makin. He, of course, had no idea that Makin was in the Gulag. As Makin was walking off the stage after his performance, he ran into Ida Shteynberg, a Yiddish singer he knew in his youth in St. Petersburg—she immigrated to Britain before the war. While everyone was applauding, she told him he must walk up to Roosevelt or Churchill, or even Churchill's son, and ask to be taken for political asylum. It was his only chance for a free life. She even taught him how to say it in English. Makin didn't do it."

"But why?"

"At that point he still thought he would be rehabilitated and continue to be a star in his homeland. In America or England, who would he be? Artists need their audience. Without it, they wilt like unwatered flowers. When you are open-minded and listen, it's not hard to figure people out."

"He told you all of this?" Sonya said.

"He didn't like talking about the past, Sonya. Understandable, with a past like his. Somebody else had told me."

"*Nu*, honest folk, I am off to the land of dreams and fools." Sonya's father kissed her on the top of her head. "Don't torture her for too long, Papa. Good night to all."

"Good night," Sonya said. She wanted to say something more—something comforting yet neutral—but couldn't think of it fast enough. She had this feeling ever since her father had returned from America, like she was constantly chasing a loose thread.

"Good night, Tolik. Don't worry, she'll see what a mistake she's made."

Her father shrugged his shoulders and winked at Sonya.

She watched him disappear into the darkness of the living room. He wore an old woolen sweater he'd left in Magadan when he went to America. It was too small for him then, and Oleg had worn it when he lived with Sonya and her mother.

Now it fit. For a whole year, Sonya had told her father on the phone what she wanted him to send with weekly flights: strawberry milk, sushi, cream-filled toaster strudels, yellow legal pads, highlighters. She had talked about school, complained about Faina Grigorievna and practicing piano, and described the ballroom dresses she wanted for the competitions. As if those were the most important things, the only things.

"I was never home in those years, that's how hard I worked, Sonya," Deda Misha continued. "Your father was just a baby, very fussy. Baba Mila noticed that in the evenings the singing from Makin's room soothed Tolik to sleep, so during the day she began to play the one Makin record we had over and over. It had all of my favorite songs: 'Friendship,' 'Autumn,' 'Goodbye, My Gypsy Camp.' You know, after Makin's first arrest, many of his records were pulled from stores, confiscated from people, and melted. He even burned his own records."

"Why?"

"I think because he was depressed, broken. One weekend, as I passed him on the stairs, I told him about his youngest fan in the person of our baby, Tolik. You should've seen the way his gloomy face lit up—balsam on my heart. If you'd like, he said, I'd be happy to sing a song for your son; nothing would give me more pleasure. He had a very pleasant voice up close, very aristocratic. It was surreal to me, a lad from a Ukrainian *hutor* and now talking to someone who had personally known Stalin and Mayakovsky. I thought about another point quickly: Was he saying this to be polite? Who might see him going into my room and what conclusions would they draw? Who would they report to? I decided to take the risk. A person is a person. A bird flies, a singer sings, and that's all there is to it. Never pass up an opportunity to do another person good, Sonya, even if it costs you a little extra. It will all be tallied up in the big book.

" 'Come in now, Comrade Makin, if you're not in a hurry,' I told him. 'My wife just made a wonderful *plov* with beef.'

"Baba Mila almost fainted when she saw Makin in our room. She rushed up to him and kissed his hand as if he were a king. She later told me she knew this was inappropriate, but, she said, she did it instinctively. She didn't know how else to express her heartbreak over Makin's situation. Whatever anybody decreed, she said, Makin was lonely in a way that only few could truly understand. At that point many people still remembered him—their youth was colored by his beautiful melodies—but it was they who benefited from this, in safety, not he. Such a kind and wise woman your grandmother was. She comes to my dreams almost every night." Deda Misha looked down at his lap, silent.

"I miss her, too," Sonya said, although the time she remembered most clearly was the summer of Baba Mila's death. Deda Misha had taken her out of the hospital and was administering natural therapy at home. Sonya remembered being scared of her grandmother's legs, which had become as thin as her own. And she was scared to ask Deda Misha whether it was true that he forbade anyone to tell Baba Mila that she had cancer, for fear of upsetting her. That's what Baba Olya had told her.

Was Baba Mila living a different life now, as a little girl? Maybe somewhere exotic and warm, like Brazil. And did she remember Sonya, her only granddaughter? Deda Misha now lived with another woman, whom he'd met in a village outside Kiev. She was nice, too.

"We sat with Makin, ate the *plov* and drank tea, and talked about the upcoming winter," Deda Misha went on. "He told us he was writing new songs he'd like to record. Of course, he was forbidden access to a recording studio. He didn't have to say it. Baba Mila got your father out of his crib. He'd just woken up and was preparing to start the siren. 'Look at those long eyelashes,' Makin said and shook Tolik's chubby hand. He sang one of the famous old Russian songs, '*Dance and sing, beautiful creature, and while you dance, I'll laugh. And while you laugh, I'll laugh with you, but inside I am burning.*' Makin's voice reached into my chest and wrung out my soul. By the time he finished, your father was rolling with laughter, and Baba Mila was crying. Makin himself was almost in tears. It is a love song, like most songs.

"Since that first tea performance, I began thinking nonstop about Makin's desire to record. We had a national treasure in our hutches, staring at the snow through his window, wasting away. We could help him resume work as a singer. That would be valuable both for him and for the people of Kolyma. You can't fight destiny, but you should always try to befriend it—that is my motto. I knew everyone in Magadan, from the regional head of education to the chief veterinarian at the poultry plant, and my engineer's mind began to work, calculate, draw connections, *tak tak tak tak*. At that point, Makin was employed at the library, typing up catalog cards and shelving books.

"Me, by the way, I understand music." Deda Misha crossed his arms on top of his hernia and nodded. "When I was at the Petroleum Institute back in Grozny, I sang in a men's a cappella group. I also played drums in a band. Musical accompaniments for banquets, weddings, funerals, ground-breaking for a new factory—for a small fee and a piece of kielbasa. You come from a very musical family, Sonya. Baba Mila sang, too, arias from *Prince Igor,* and played piano."

"As good as Mama?" Sonya said, on purpose.

Deda Misha pretended not to hear. "I decided to take Makin under my wing and invited him to sing at our Petroleum Workers' Club," Deda Misha carried on. "He agreed with pleasure. When I announced that we would have a special guest as a closing number in our musical evening in the person of Comrade Vadim Andreevich Makin, the same famous Makin, my otherwise respectable workers began to holler like monkeys, demanding Makin immediately and Makin all night. Those ensembles scheduled to perform before Makin, including my a cappella group, gladly stepped down. Maestro was in the house.

"Makin marched toward the piano in an impeccably ironed black suit. By the way—a curious detail for you—instead of sheet music, he clutched a small rubber cat to his chest."

"A cat!" Sonya exclaimed, about to tell Deda Misha that Oleg, too, had mentioned a toy cat at the party. She caught herself in time. She wanted to hear the end of the story, after all.

"Two hundred people held their breath as he began to sing. He sat at the piano half turned to the audience, emphasizing certain phrases with a pitch of his body or a movement of his hand. I remember the first song. '*When youth leaves, the nights seem longer . . . What could've been said before, cannot now be said. When youth leaves, one loves differently. When youth leaves, one loves even stronger.*' His voice was spellbinding. One forgot certain details of his biography as long as this voice poured and poured. Even now I remember with goose bumps. I felt like my soul was getting undressed in front of everyone." Deda Misha tugged at the skin of his Adam's apple. "A part of me even wanted him to stop. Such is the power of art—yes, a sudden, gripping power. It was too late to try to contain him. He had gone out of orbit . . . in more than one way.

"He sang until he was about to collapse—old favorite songs and new songs in front of an audience for the first time. There was so much cheering, so much 'Bravo!' and '*Bis!*' that the police showed up. They stared at Makin like at a tropical bird, but they enjoyed his singing, too. They didn't even ask to see anyone's papers, which was the bulk of their duties, you know." Deda Misha chuckled.

"I felt tremendous satisfaction in bringing Makin to the people. I developed the petroleum supply infrastructure that powered the extraction of valuable natural resources in Kolyma: gold, uranium, tin, fish, crab. In the arts sphere, Makin was our gold. I was building my family. Your aunt Angela would be born soon. The next fifteen years were the happiest and most fruitful time of my life."

Deda Misha took off his glasses and rubbed his eyes, smiling into the past.

"I organized a few more concerts for Makin at our Workers' Club and found him his own piano accompanist in the person of Galochka, one of our accountants. Remember this name, Sonya, for our story. Makin himself said that though she played too loudly, as if trying to outplay the racket of dishes in a restaurant, she had the soul of a real musician. Makin sang for free, of course, for the rehabilitation of his reputation."

"What do you mean, 'rehabilitation'? Like after an accident?"

"What are they teaching you in your English Lyceum? American slang? Rehabilitation is for those who were sent to the Gulag or executed without a good reason. Amnesty. The official restoration of civil rights and a good name."

"Oh, right." Sonya didn't remember studying that at school.

"I talked to Gumenyuk (a Ukrainian, by the way)—he was the head artistic producer at the Magadan Musical and Dramatic Theater—about organizing Makin concerts there. By the way, he told me that the imprisoned artists had performed at the theater. All the local party bosses and MVD apparatchiks sat in the front row with their wives, while the guards with machine guns sat in the wings and in the balcony and took the performers back to the camps before the applause died down. Makin performed, too. He was the biggest celebrity in Kolyma."

"This was at our theater?" Sonya said. "Are you sure?" She thought about all the portraits in the theater's hall; the biggest one was of Frenkel, the director, staring into middle distance. And the black-and-white photographs of old productions along the grand staircase with the red carpet held down by metal rods. The actors forever frozen in the heat of the fight or a love confession—were some of them prisoners? Would she be able to tell if she looked very carefully next time?

"Same theater, probably before I got to Magadan. I've never seen any armed guards at a concert. But now Makin would be returning as a free man. The theater was in a hole: intrigue backstage, boredom onstage. The socialist realism plays from the capital weren't popular with Magadan folk. We brought in Makin, and he sold out every performance, even the seats in the orchestra pit. He saved the theater. The following year he was hired full-time, though without any media fanfare or the northern coefficient. Makin didn't mind, he was happy to perform again. He also had a fan in the person of Konstantin Kazakov, the director of the regional guild of radio broadcasting, and this Kazakov began recording him secretly in Magadan's radio studio. I found this out only recently, through the grapevine of old acquaintances.

"It was brave of Kazakov. Makin was no longer a prisoner, and Stalin was dead, but there was still the unspoken ban on Makin. It was brave of me, too. If the KGB rang my doorbell at three at night and asked me why I was so interested in Makin's career, I would have told them it was for the benefit of the Soviet people. It was the truth. If they'd asked me if I, how to say, was of a similar persuasion as Makin, I'd have told them: I have a beautiful wife and healthy children. There isn't a single stain on my reputation."

Deda Misha licked the white corners of his dry lips as he talked. "I had noticed that our accountant-accompanist Galochka had taken an interest in Makin right away. At the first rehearsal for his debut at the Workers' Club, Galochka put her shawl around his shoulders—it might've been cold that evening. The next time, Makin brought her a casserole that, he said, he had cooked from a French recipe. We all had a taste after the rehearsal. Very exotic. After that, Makin and Galochka acted like they'd been best friends since diapers. About a year later, as Makin was gaining traction, Galochka was replaced by someone from the newly founded Magadan Philharmonic, but they remained inseparable." Deda Misha took long pauses between sentences. "I ran into her several times on the stairs of our apartment building. She was always bringing him food. A woman from the depot had told me in confidence that she'd heard Galochka boasting about the Italian silk stockings Makin had procured for her. Not my business, I said. Everyone gives what they can, and that's the only thing Makin could give a woman. Silk stockings. I almost asked him for a pair of tights for Baba Mila—after all, I was working hard on his behalf—but I didn't want to risk any rumors of foreign schemes. Commercial speculation was illegal. I was the director, you remember."

Sonya had fallen into the story's dreamy trance. Inexplicably, it felt like her life had somehow become intertwined with Makin's, years before her birth. Maybe she'd known him in her past life. She finally grasped what word Deda Misha didn't want to say out loud, as if the walls and teacups still had ears. That word and its female counterpart were popular insults at school this quarter, even though all girls who were best friends held hands.

"In a few years, through tireless negotiation with heads of this and that at the municipal and regional levels, Gumenyuk and I managed to arrange for Makin to go on a solo concert tour around Kolyma. He gave his all, at every performance, not the lip-synching that goes on with the pop singers these days.

"In the next few years he toured not only Kolyma but all of Siberia, Yakutia, Kamchatka, Chukotka, Sakhalin, and the Kuril Islands. He sang for the deer farmers, fishermen, petroleum workers, submarine sailors, geologists, scientists. He sang in small towns, too, and was more popular than any other touring shows. If people heard that Makin was in town, they would run over to his performance instead of attending concerts or plays from the capitals, full of award-winning artists. Can you imagine such a blow, when they sent telegrams to the Ministry of Culture in Moscow? He began receiving letters from his old fans. Many were surprised he was still alive. He told me himself. He even looked younger and healthier. His gypsy eyes burned with the fire of life again. He told me he was writing a new cycle of songs about Magadan and Kolyma, about its unique natural beauty, the rare kindness of its people. But I wasn't satisfied yet, silly me. I thought that the real comeback would be for him to return to Moscow with a solo concert. Gumenyuk and I continued to work on that. Our progress was slow: Makin was still blacklisted in central Russia. But we were able to convince some big artists we'd gotten in touch with in the process to add Magadan to their touring itineraries on the promise that they would get to meet the legendary Makin. And that was an unexpected benefit for everyone.

"Makin stayed involved with the music program at the

Workers' Club. Your baba Mila kept telling me to lighten his voluntary obligations, but a man, especially an artist, is only truly alive when he is working. Just as she herself had said before. You stop working, you start dying, and that's all there is to it. He had Galochka, but I'm sure he missed his friends and admirers at the petroleum depot, too. He was such an inspiration to our amateur musical ensembles.

"Listen carefully now, Sonya. There is nothing out that window. One day in the early sixties, Galochka came to my office for advice on a matter of the heart. I was used to fixing people's marital and personal problems, but this turned out to be a special case. She told me she'd been in love with Makin ever since that first rehearsal all those years ago, and she couldn't bear loving in secret any longer. I almost fell off my chair. Makin was teaching her to sing, Galochka rattled on, and explained to her the secrets of the old songs. He personally knew many of the authors who had written them and was apparently very upset about the vulgar interpretations of modern singers. One example she gave was about the way they announce on TV that 'Coachman, don't race the horses' is the national coachman's song. It irritated Makin because, according to him, it was written in his childhood home in St. Petersburg by some Baronessa von Ritter as an answer to another song—'Race, coachman, faster into the distance.' Such answers to songs were popular at the turn of the century, Galochka said."

Sonya liked this very much. Answer-songs. Baronessa von Ritter. Maybe that's who she was in her past life, a beautiful and wealthy baronessa. She went on sleigh rides hitched to a troika of white horses, warm under a bear blanket. Sonya looked out the window again. She really should start worrying about Max, but all she could think of was how great it would be to ride in a sleigh with her best friend, Sabrinka. She wouldn't have to wonder the whole time whether Max was waiting for a kiss.

"In Makin's cramped room, stuffed with books and old recordings, Galochka went on, the world was bigger and more interesting even than going to the Black Sea for vacation, with a two-day stopover in Moscow. He told her about growing up in St. Petersburg, listening to Mayakovsky recite his poetry in the parlor of his parents' house. His verses struck Makin's soul like whips. On her part, Galochka told Makin about her childhood in the suburbs of Moscow. Her great-grandfather had been a royal beekeeper.

"She loved him, she said, and was certain that he loved her. She didn't know why he hadn't made a move all these years. Maybe the age difference. Makin was in his mid-fifties by then, but she, too, had been on the edge of spinsterhood for some time. Should she ask him to marry her or should she continue waiting?"

Sonya scooted to the edge of her taboret, listening now in horror.

"Poor Galochka. She was a pleasant woman, femininely plump, big blue eyes, wavy black hair. Half a head taller than Comrade Makin, by the way. To me, she looked like a kindergarten teacher, someone who should be surrounded by children, not numbers. Her personnel file said 'never married'; I didn't pry. She'd always struck me as a bit 'not of this world,' as they say, but she was a hardworking accountant. That's what mattered to me most.

"So, Galochka and Makin. *Da*, I couldn't dream of this in my sleep. How could she not have known of his disease? How could she not see it? Granted, sometimes I felt that if I didn't know, I myself wouldn't be able to tell from just looking at him. But it is what a person chooses to do behind closed doors, seen only by his conscience, that defines his true character. I even wondered if he had played some kind of trick on her.

"'Galochka,' I said to her, 'I have to tell you something that, to be honest, I thought you knew.' She was blinking at me with those big blue eyes. 'Vadim Andreevich has been observed to, how to say, not fall in love with women. It is not your fault.'

"She smiled. 'Maybe he hasn't met the right one yet? For a special person like him it must be difficult.'

"'With any woman,' I said. How could I explain something I didn't myself fully understand?

"Galochka looked at me askance. I felt scrambled inside. I just couldn't bring myself to say it out loud. I was afraid, perhaps irrationally, that once I let the wild animal out of the cage, everything would fall into chaos. Our harmony at work. Our friendly, productive *kollektiv*. Of course, many knew, but it was all underwater. It wasn't an issue. At the same time, I realized that no matter what I said, it wouldn't change the truth."

"'His compass is broken,' I blurted out. 'Instead of women . . . it's the other way around. He likes men. It's a disease.'

"Galochka didn't fall into hysterics like I'd expected. She didn't even look very disappointed or betrayed. She asked me to please keep her confession in confidence. As you see, I'm only breaking my promise more than thirty years later.

"A few weeks after our conversation, Galochka came to my office again. She was pale and had even lost several kilos.

"'Mikhail Pavlovich, I decided,' she said dramatically, like the wife of a convicted Decembrist. Have you studied the Decembrist uprising at school yet, Sonya, when many wives had followed their husbands to exile in Siberia? 'I've thought hard,' Galochka said, 'I understand that with Makin I wouldn't get the kind of love women expect in a marriage. Besides, many husbands, normal husbands, beat their wives—'

"Here I lost my temper a bit. If my workers let their arms loose, I could call a disciplinary meeting and strip them of northern coefficient pay. She wasn't talking about my workers, she said. Her heart was telling her that she had to be Makin's companion, to love and serve him selflessly. Her life would be full, and they both would be happy. This was love between souls, bypassing the body, she said.

"I dismissed her. Told her that she'd been reading too much Turgenev.

"'A person always knows when someone loves him,' Galochka insisted. 'I will take care of him, and if one day he is able to return my love like a husband, to my joy there will be no end. If not, it won't change my feelings for him.'"

Sonya held her breath. The story was beginning to sound like one of Baba Olya's favorite soap operas—full of amnesia, misunderstanding, and love for the wrong people.

" 'Enough with the decorative language,' I said to her strictly." Deda Misha shook his finger. "To be honest, I thought she must be a little abnormal. Unwed and childless at thirty-five, living in her dream world of books and piano. Lost in her head. Of course, such marriages weren't unheard of. On the contrary, they were viewed positively, as a documented effort to change, to start a new life.

"I decided that Galochka needed to spend some time away from Makin, while I determined the feasibility of their union. My head began to work, *tik tik tik*. I surveyed my, so to speak, vast empire: there were gold mines all over Kolyma, and to each mine was attached a village, a camp, and an electrostation.

" 'I have a great idea, Galina Fyodorovna!' I told her. 'I can send you on a monthlong assignment to audit our accounting at the electrostations up north, and while you're gone, I'll talk to Makin. Don't send him letters or call. Let me sort this out and let him think.'

"Galochka liked my plan very much. She left my office with her beatific smile. But I had a heavy heart.

"I didn't know what I wanted to happen. On one hand, I hoped she would come to her senses and give up on Makin so he could live out his days in peace. I even considered keeping her up north indefinitely." Deda Misha smiled sadly. "Time cures everything, except, I guess, Makin's disease. On the other hand, this could be his only chance to rejoin Soviet society as a full member.

"The following month, Galochka began her work above the Arctic Circle, and I looked for the right time to talk to

Makin. I turned over and over in my head how I would present to him such a marriage proposal. I still hoped that he might get himself fully rehabilitated as a man. For that, Galochka wouldn't have been my first choice. . . . I lost hours of sleep thinking over this.

"Makin was not easy to catch in those days. Gumenyuk finally got the central arts committee to approve a solo tour outside his exile zone. Not Moscow or Leningrad, but Makin was moving inland, reconquering his former territories. He was rehearsing all the time. He had ordered a new tuxedo at the local atelier, which, by the way, was stolen from his room the night before he left on tour."

"How could someone do that?"

"Jealousy. Black-heartedness, small-heartedness. Makin returned home from the theater late, and I, let's not forget, had my own family to take care of. Galochka wrote to me every week asking about the progress of our scheme. We petroleum engineers know that we're always one mistake away from an explosion. I extended Galochka's assignment for another month.

"I decided to talk to Makin after he returned. I meant to stop by and wish him good luck, but there was an accident at the port."

"What happened?" Sonya said.

"An oil tanker was cleaning its pipes and flushed so much water—"

"No, Deda, with Makin. What happened with Makin?"

"What happened with Makin, what happened with Makin!" Deda Misha looked gratified. "It was equally shocking and predictable. His first stop was Sverdlovsk—now Yekaterinburg—a town east of the Urals. After a sold-out concert, he was caught red-handed at his old crime. In his hotel room, with a young man." Deda Misha ran his hand through his white mane. "Makin, so naive. The KGB had been watching his every move. He was returned to his old camp, and my decision was made for me: there would be no wedding."

"That is horrible. He should have been more careful. He should have known!"

"Yes. A tragedy for the country, to lose such a talented singer twice. He squandered the chance most other prisoners and former prisoners, millions and millions of them, never got—a second chance at life. To me, only one thing that could explain his behavior—madness. Perhaps he and Galochka weren't so different in the end.

"After this, a wave of gossip and paranoia rolled through Magadan. Those who had advocated for the relaunch of Makin's career got very nervous. People still remembered the years of repression, Stalin, Yezhov. Kazakov, the radio director, destroyed all the recordings of Makin's new songs. My own fears subsided a bit when Baba Mila was appointed official witness while the KGB inventoried Makin's property in his room, but you never knew whom they might play against whom."

"And you never saw him again?"

"I did. Once. A year after his second arrest. I was looking for the supervisor at a construction site for one of my depot workers' houses and instead found Makin. He sat at a desk in the corner of the room—well, you could hardly call it a room at that point, it was just a concrete box."

"Dedushka! What was he doing there?"

"He was the timekeeper. His job was to record the hours of the other inmates who worked toward shortening their sentences. My first impulse was to pretend not to recognize him, to save our dignities. He looked up at me and smiled like at an old friend. I smiled in return. Genuine smiles are contagious, Sonya. I instantly forgot everything.

" 'Vadim Andreevich, I'll try to do something to get you out sooner,' I said. 'Did you know how much Galochka loves you? She wants to marry you and take care of you as if you were her own child. We will restore you as the director of our musical ensemble at the Workers' Club. You will be rehabilitated.' I didn't have the power to do what I was promising. In fact, my rambling probably sounded crazy and foolish, too. I tell you, Sonya, he had a witching influence over me, just as he did over millions of Soviet people. One nod from him, and his welfare would've taken over my life again.

"Makin spared me that responsibility. 'Mikhail Pavlovich, please, don't worry about me. This time, I'll look out for myself,' he said with his gypsy smile. It was pride and shame speaking. Gypsies are a proud people. There was nothing more I could do. We soon acquired new upstairs neighbors—"

"Wait. Do you think he knew that it was you who sent Galochka away?"

Deda Misha looked surprised. "I don't know, I didn't tell him. It was beside the point. Makin hadn't changed at all, Galochka or no Galochka.

"I remember our new upstairs neighbors well because your father became best friends with the son, also named

Tolya. That Tolya's father was a police detective and his mother taught phys-culture at Baba Mila's school. Details, details. I'm glad to have such a greedy memory, to remember every day with my family and Baba Mila.

"Baba Mila and I moved back to Ukraine in the mid-seventies, after your father graduated from college. Just before leaving, I saw Makin on our local TV. It was the studio where they filmed all the concerts in Magadan, the one with the black-and-white four-leaf clover floor. '*All's ever, the same old guitar,*' he sang with his usual earnestness and accompanied himself on the piano. His perennial rubber cat perched on top of the piano. He was in that same familiar pose, turned toward the audience, emphasizing the words with his torso and hands. That same unmistakable timbre, though his voice was weaker now. Vocal cords are just muscles, and they get old whether you are a star or not a star. He seemed to be really enjoying himself. He sang the songs he'd written about Magadan: 'Snow Waltz' something, 'The Streets of Magadan.' I didn't like them as much as his old classic songs.

"Then, one of the listeners asked him about his early years as a singer, when he was worshipped by the whole USSR. Makin must've been almost seventy then, bald and chubby but still sprightly. He was finally free to leave Magadan. I don't remember much of the interview except that he said—in a friendly tone and smiling, that I remember—that he didn't regret anything. *Vot tak* . . . The end."

"The end? But what happened to Galochka?"

"Galochka? She returned to Magadan a few months after Makin's arrest and continued to work in our accounting department. Then she resigned and left for the continent. Some said she'd had a mental breakdown and went to a sanatorium on the Black Sea. I don't know for sure. I've never liked to get involved with the gossip. So you stayed till the end of the concert, eh?"

Sonya nodded. She was reeling from the story.

"Did they announce that he would finally receive the title of People's Artist of Russia?"

"I don't think so." She combed her mind. Could she have slept through it? The concert seemed like it had happened a century ago.

"I don't think Makin was ever officially rehabilitated. A pity, a pity, but what can you do."

"You don't have any connections anymore, to help him?"

He smiled. "No, Sonechka."

They sat in silence. Deda Misha stared into the empty teacup as if divining the tea leaves. Sonya rose and picked up the empty bowl and her cup.

"Leave it, Sonechka. I'll clean up," he said. "Go to bed."

She stood in front of the frosted window. "Deda," she whispered.

He grunted tiredly.

"Is it sometimes better to keep the animal locked up?"

"*Kak?* What animal?"

"The wild animal. Like with you, when you told Galochka about Makin. Sometimes, maybe it's better to keep it in the cage?"

"What are you talking about? The wild animal was just me saying . . . it's just a metaphor."

"I know it's a metaphor!" Sonya cried out. "I'm not totally dumb. I know it's a metaphor. I didn't open the stupid cage."

"Shhh!"

A hot wave of shame rose up through her chest and pushed on the top of her throat. "I didn't tell Papa about Oleg, not even when he moved in with us and ate the food Papa sent. I didn't want Papa to come back from America. I didn't stop them."

Deda Misha was silent for a long time. "Don't worry too much about that, Sonya. Your father knew. Magadan is a small town. He allowed it." His glance had a harsh, unfamiliar edge.

She grieved for her mother and her father—and for Makin.

"We didn't think that in the end she would be stupid enough to leave. Our side of the family doesn't give up easily, though."

She was suddenly disgusted with Deda Misha. For the last two years her mother had been both happier and more miserable. But what was she like before she met Oleg? Sonya could hardly remember.

"Too bad you're leaving tomorrow, Deda. We could've visited Makin," she said. He started at the mention of Makin. "I want to see that famous rubber cat. Maybe I'll go to his museum with Mama later, then stop by his apartment and ask him if he remembers you."

"The true tragedy is to have lived without a woman's love, Sonya, to not be able to love a woman. I don't regret sending Galochka away. Measure seven times, cut once, as they say."

Deda Misha stared at a space in front of him. "And he even denied it to the journalists, in the nineties. One of my old Magadan acquaintances had read in the newspaper and called me. I was shocked."

"Denied what?"

"He said he was only interested in those circles for the sake of art . . . he wanted to know how they lived, how everyone lives, to write better songs. And the incident in Sverdlovsk was pure provocation. Again."

"But if he wasn't, how. . ."

"A setup, he claimed. Because people were jealous of him, and certain people wanted revenge, but he didn't say who or for what. He had never been married but he had had an infant daughter, he said, and she died with her mother during the Leningrad blockade. For all the years I'd known him, he'd never mentioned any daughter. I don't believe that he was honest in the interviews. Or maybe he finally changed."

"Good night." Sonya walked out into the living room without kissing him. She had an unpleasant feeling in her stomach, like she'd eaten spoiled food.

She got to her room and realized that she'd forgotten all about Max. She switched off the lights and looked out: even through the curtain of snow she could see that his windows were still black. It was almost one in the morning. Everything would be better as soon as Max's windows lit up.

The old hysterical woman who had burst into Makin's museum opening, was that Galochka? Her fate was painful to imagine. She could have married, had children, and even grandchildren by now. Or she could have died years ago. Of a broken heart.

Sonya had to know now whether she loved Max or not. The ultimate test of true love was to give your life for your beloved. She thought of her homeroom at the English Lyceum, her favorite teacher, Lyudmila Abramovna, the scratched blackboard, the ficus plant on the windowsill, the portraits of the great Russian writers looking down sternly at the three rows of desks with chewed gum stuck to their undersides. Except Pushkin. He looked inspired and a little sad. Maybe because he had foreseen that he would die for love.

It was absurd to imagine yourself dying in such ordinary circumstances, in your familiar-familiar hometown, yet it shouldn't have to matter. Love was love. She imagined herself with a gunshot wound in her chest, bleeding into the sheets. She willed Max's windows to light up.

Glossary

~

apparatchik A functionary in a politico-bureaucratic organization; from the Russian word *apparat,* meaning a collective of people working in this type of organization.

dacha A summerhouse outside a city, usually with a vegetable plot. Dachas could be large and fancy or a simple wooden shed, depending on the person's status in the USSR and their financial situation afterward.

defitsit Lack or scarcity of most goods available for sale in stores.

grazhdanka Translated as "citizen" (female); a common officious form of address in the Soviet Union.

Great Patriotic War The portion of World War II fought in eastern Europe between the Soviet Union and Nazi Germany.

Gulag Originally an acronym for Main Camp Administration; later used to indicate the countrywide web of labor camps from 1930 to 1955.

izba A traditional Russian house, often made of logs.

khrushchyovka A type of five-story cement-panel building with one- or two-room apartments with private bathrooms and kitchens, mass-produced during the years of Khrushchev's leadership; they helped get millions of people out of cramped *kommunalkas.*

kolkhoz A collective farm owned by the State.

kolkhoznitsa A female member of a kolkhoz.

kollektiv A group of people, usually on friendly terms, working in the same company/organization, e.g., a teacher *kollektiv.*

Kolyma A region in the far northeast of Russia named after the Kolyma River, notorious for Gulag labor camps; Magadan is often called the capital of Kolyma.

kommunalka A communal apartment, where each family had a room and shared a kitchen and a bathroom. This was a solution to the housing shortage after people began to leave the countryside for the cities en masse in the early twentieth century. Older *kommunalkas* in the big cities were carved out of the big apartments and/or houses confiscated from the aristocracy and the rich during the revolutions of 1917; *kommunalkas* in other cities were designed as communal living spaces from the start.

Komsomol Youth division of the Communist Party of the Soviet Union.

Komsomolets A member of Komsomol.

Maslenitsa An Eastern Slavic holiday, with both Christian and pagan roots, celebrated the last week before Great Lent. *Bliny* (pancakes) are the traditional food of Maslenitsa.

medcarta A notebook where a patient's medical history is recorded.

New Russians A term used for newly rich businessmen and entrepreneurs who had most likely gained access to wealth and property through criminal means in the economic and legal chaos of early post-Soviet Russia.

polyclinika A clinic with doctors of various specialties under one roof.

Stakhanovites Laborers (in the former Soviet Union) who worked fanatically to surpass production quotas set by the State.

Yezhovshchina Named after Nikolai Yezhov, once the head of the Soviet secret police, the period of the most intense political repressions characterized by arbitrary imprisonment and executions (1937–1938).

Young Pioneers Members of the Young Pioneer Organization of the Soviet Union, a mass youth organization for children ten to fifteen years old, with communist undertones.

Acknowledgments

It would take another long short story to name every person who has helped or inspired me in some way over nearly ten years it took to write and publish this book. I remember and am eternally grateful for advice, encouragement, support, and critical insight to all of you, especially:

My amazing and generous teachers: Jennifer Vanderbes, John Reed, Darin Strauss, David Lipsky, Jonathan Lethem, E. L. Doctorow, Lawrence Weschler, Jonathan Safran Foer, as well as Deborah Landau and everyone at the NYU MFA program.

My smart and tireless early readers: Mariah Robbins, Amy Bonnaffons, Sativa January, Boris Fishman, Brock Tellier, Conor Robin Madigan, Sam Beebe, Axel Wilhite, Nitin Das

Rai, and everyone in the workshops and writing groups I've been a part of over the years.

My excellent agents, Simon Trewin and Dorian Karchmar, as well as Zoë Pagnamenta. My astute and patient editors: Sarah Bowlin, Olly Rowse, Clare Reihill, and everyone at Henry Holt in the United States and Fourth Estate in Britain. Also, thank you for early support to the editors who published my work in literary journals: Ollie Brock, John Freeman, Ellah Allfrey, Ted Hodgkinson, Ted Genoways, Michael Koch, and Natalie Young.

The biggest gratitude and низкий поклон—a deep bow—goes to my family. For their support and belief in me. For hours of conversations about the beauty and horror that is Russia. To my father, for bringing me to a country where I am free to write and publish anything I want, for helping me research, and for remembering the most minute details about life in the Soviet Union. To my mother, for sharing her sharp observations about people, love, literature, and art. To my grandfather, my aunt, and my late grandmother, for sharing memories of their youth. To my sister, Maria, my brilliant partner in crime, for keeping me on my toes. And to my husband, Ben, for everything.